PRAISE FOR CINDY SAMPLE

"Don't miss the Laurel McKay books. Like me, you'll be 'dying' to read the next one."
—*Brenda Novak, USA Today Bestselling Author*

"*Dying for a Diamond* is pure joy! The sixth entry into the Laurel McKay Mysteries is filled with laughs, memorable characters, interesting plot twists, and murderous intent, all served with a touch of romance. You'll be dying for more."
—*Heather Haven, IPPY Award-Winning Author*

"Sample's sleuth is an endearing character readers will adore."
—*RT Book Reviews*

"Quirky narrative peppered with quips. An intoxicating recipe for fun…*Dying for a Daiquiri* is a must read for the romantic mystery reader and contemporary romance reader!"
–*Connie Payne, Once upon a Romance Reviews*

"Cindy Sample's writing is positively fun, imaginative and all around tantalizing."
–*Romance Junkies*

"Cindy Sample knows how to weave a story that satisfies and excites. Time literally flew by as I turned the pages… simultaneously harrowing, exciting, tender, and uplifting, a true who-done-it combined with a romance that will warm the heart and sheets."
–*Long and Short Reviews*

Other Books in the Laurel McKay series

Dying for a Date (Vol. 1)
Dying for a Dance (Vol. 2)
Dying for a Daiquiri (Vol. 3)
Dying for a Dude (Vol. 4)
Dying for a Donut (Vol. 5)

To Jackie, enjoy the cruise!
Enjoy

DYING FOR A DIAMOND

A LAUREL MCKAY MYSTERY

Cindy Sample

CINDY SAMPLE

DYING FOR A DIAMOND
By Cindy Sample

Copyright 2017 by Cindy Sample

Cover Art by Karen Phillips

Visit us at http://www.cindysamplebooks.com

ISBN: 1542329515
ISBN: 978-1542329514

DEDICATION

This book is dedicated to my wonderfully supportive
children, Dawn and Jeff Sample.
How lucky and proud I am of both of you.

To my mother, Harriet Bergstrand, who taught us the
importance of laughter in our lives.

And to those readers from around the world,
whose emails make this journey so much fun.
Your kind remarks bring a smile to my face and magic
to my fingertips.

Some women spend years dreaming of their wedding day. They plan the ceremony and reception down to the tiniest and most intricate detail. Other women fantasize about their honeymoon, devoting their days and nights in search of the perfect romantic destination to spend with their new husband.

I, Laurel McKay, have very simple needs and make only one request for my upcoming nuptials and honeymoon.
No dead bodies.

Seriously. Is that too much to ask?

CHAPTER ONE

Many couples first meet over a cup of coffee or a glass of wine. Tom Hunter and I met over a dead body. As a homicide detective, investigating dead bodies fell under his job description. How I've managed to stumble into some of these situations remains a mystery to me.

Fortunately, my husband-to-be is not only a tall and ruggedly handsome man, he has the stamina to put up with me and my penchant for getting into trouble. Plus an excellent sense of humor, which I personally feel is the most important attribute in a man. Especially one who plans on marrying me.

When Tom proposed marriage, he received an affirmative response as well as a passionate kiss. We were in love and wanted to spend the rest of our lives together.

What I didn't realize was the complexity of choosing a date to exchange marital vows with a man who might be on assignment for days at a time. Tom was no longer chasing after criminals in our little county in the California Gold Country. Instead, in his new job with Homeland Security, he traveled from one coast to the other trying to keep our citizens safe from bad guys and terrorist plots hatched around the globe.

Coordinating the big event proved to be comparable to strategizing a military campaign. My weekends are normally filled with soccer games for my eight-year-old son, Ben. My daughter, Jenna, a high school senior, also has a full schedule with classes, a part-time job and her own social life.

I remained one determined bride, and I refused to let my wedding plans be trifled with by mere terrorists, or soccer coaches. Or teenage daughters, who can be the most terrifying of them all. We finally settled on the one day of the year when everyone in our combined families would be home in Placerville. The day after Christmas.

When I went to bed Christmas night, I was as excited as my eight-year-old son had been the night before. I knew the best gift of all would be waiting for me at the altar tomorrow.

Late the next afternoon, I stood in front of a full-length mirror and stared at the image of a woman on the verge of matrimony. The church bells chimed five times, signifying the beginning of the next phase of my life. Was I ready for my new journey? Had I forgotten anything important?

I mentally ran through my wedding checklist. Ivory cocktail-length satin and lace wedding dress. Check. Bouquet of white and red roses nestled among soft green juniper sprigs. Check.

Something old. My grandmother's antique pearl earrings. Something new. My incredibly uncomfortable Spanx undergarment. Something borrowed. My best friend Liz's satin evening bag.

Something blue. The lacy garter my hubby would remove at the reception. My eyes sparkled at the thought of other things he might take off me later tonight.

Numero Uno on my list—the unforgiving Spanx!

My makeup was complete and my coppery-brown hair professionally curled and highlighted with all hints of gray removed. Check.

I spun around as the door into the small church dressing room opened and Stan Winters entered. Stan was not only my friend and co-worker, he was the best personal shopper and wedding coordinator a girl could ask for.

"I guess I'm as ready as I'll ever be," I said to him. "Can you think of anything I'm missing?"

Stan lifted his arms and gave me a sheepish look.

"The groom?"

CHAPTER TWO

After I spent a few frenetic minutes trying to locate Tom's whereabouts, he finally texted me that he was on the way. His best man's SUV had broken down on a rural road in a no-cell service zone. My husband-to-be arrived at the church via a banana yellow AAA tow truck. Although Tom's ride wasn't as glamorous as the snazzy limo that brought me and my bridal party, it delivered the most crucial element.

With a sigh of relief, I stood in the church vestibule with my small but cherished wedding party. My daughter, Jenna, and my best friend, Liz Daley, wore knee-length emerald-green velvet bridesmaid gowns befitting a Christmas wedding. The dress flattered my tall, slender, auburn-haired daughter. But my British matron of honor's normally porcelain complexion had turned nearly the same shade as her dress.

"Liz, are you okay?" I asked my friend who suffered from a case of 24/7 morning sickness.

She looked down at her barely protruding belly and then at me. "You know I'd do anything for you, luv. But it might be prudent for the organist to speed up the Wedding March."

Everyone quickly lined up. My son, Ben, and his best friend, Kristy, soon to become his stepsister, held the official positions of ring bearer and flower girl. They led the procession, giggling the entire way. But it could have been worse. Their original plan was to sneak in a soccer ball and dribble it up the aisle.

Next came Jenna, followed by Liz, who by now was so green she could have passed for Shrek's sister. The last two family members included my mother, Barbara Bradford, and my grandmother. They would stand on either side of me as I walked down the aisle to meet the man I planned to spend the rest of my life with.

"Are you ready, toots?" asked my octogenarian grandmother. Gran was festively dressed in a gold lace mid-calf dress. I was grateful that she'd selected a curly gold wig today. She could have gone with her long black wig à la early Cher or her most recent addition—Katy Perry blue.

"Ready as I'll ever be," I replied.

"You got yourself a good man." Gran nudged me. "He certainly is a hunk. Bet he knows his way around a bedroom."

I blushed but Gran was right on all three counts.

"I'm so happy for you, honey," said my mother, who only last year had walked down the aisle with Robert Bradford, a recently retired homicide detective. Bradford, as I fondly referred to my stepfather, was Tom's former partner and one of his groomsmen.

Mother wore a pale gold dress that complemented her short blond hairstyle and tall, slender frame. She kissed my left cheek and enveloped me in a gentle maternal hug. We clung to one another for a minute before she released me and turned me over to my wedding planner.

Stan scrutinized me from head to toe. His gray eyes narrowed as they zeroed in on my ivory satin shoes.

"Lift your right foot, Laurel." Stan reached down and removed the tiny scrap of toilet paper that had attached itself to the heel during my last-minute pit stop.

He gave me a thumbs up and with a wide smile, waved at the organist to switch to "Pachelbel's Canon."

As our trio walked down the carpeted aisle, I smiled at all of the friends and co-workers joining us today. True friendship meant giving up post-Christmas sales to attend our wedding.

Gran waved to her roommate, Hank McKay, AKA my former husband and father of my two children. Ex-husbands aren't normally included on a bride and groom's guest list, but our family put the *fun* in dysfunctional. Hank grinned and gave me a thumbs-up. He'd gone through a few tough months recently, including an arrest for murder by none other than my future husband. Talk about awkward.

Once his innocence had been proven, Hank had fallen in love, only to have his heart broken. But his time would come. Mine certainly had. I reached the altar and stood beside the man to whom I'd given my heart.

Tom's chocolate-brown eyes glimmered with love and possibly a tear or two. My own baby blues were starting to tear up. The minister began to speak, but he could have been talking in Mandarin since it was impossible for me to concentrate on anything but the man next to me. A rumbling noise to my left woke me from my wedding day trance, and I turned to my matron of honor. Tom and his best man, Liz's husband, shifted their attention from the minister to Liz. She leaned forward and so did we.

"Kiss her quick," she advised Tom.

The minister shifted into high speed, and we exchanged vows so hastily that I wasn't certain whether I promised to love and cherish Tom, or do his laundry for perpetuity.

After an eventful year, we were finally married. And nothing, I repeat, nothing, could stand in our way now.

CHAPTER THREE

"Next," sang the gray-haired ticket taker behind the lengthy beige Formica counter. Tom and I moved forward, our lightweight carry-on suitcases rolling in tandem. When we reached the counter, we handed our passports to the Nordic American cruise line employee.

"Mr. Hunter and Ms. McKay, is it?" she asked.

"Technically, it's Mrs. Laurel Hunter," I explained. "We were married a week ago, but today is the official start of our honeymoon."

She smiled as she handed back our passports. "Congratulations." She grabbed a camera, snapped a photo of each of us, and logged them into the cruise line's tracking system. Then she handed over our key cards. "I'm sure you don't want to wait another minute to begin your honeymoon."

Tom wrapped his arm around my waist as he drew me closer. "We certainly do not."

She pointed to an escalator where a short line of passengers waited, and we strolled in that direction. I fanned my face with my left hand, my gold wedding band glowing in the artificial light. Although the Fort Lauderdale temperature was in the nineties, I didn't think all the heat could be blamed on the weather.

I stepped onto the UP escalator, and Tom moved behind me. As the escalator rose, I peeked over my shoulder. My new husband winked at me, and I smiled in return. The week between our wedding and the cruise had been hectic, leaving little playtime for us. It was long past time to get this honeymoon show on the road. Or, in our case, the high seas.

I stepped off the escalator and stopped short. My suitcase smashed into my calf. Tom nearly followed suit, managing to hop awkwardly around me.

My legs and feet froze in place as I stared in horror at the scene unfolding in front of me.

"Surprise!" The chirpy chorus assaulted my eyes and ears. My brow furrowed as I focused on the unwelcome welcoming committee.

"What are you doing here?" I asked my family in a clipped voice. The party of four, comprised of my mother and her husband, Robert Bradford, plus Gran and Stan beamed at us.

"We're coming on the cruise, too," Gran answered. "Stan got us a deal we just couldn't refuse."

They should have asked me. I would have had no problem refusing said deal for them. My brain still refused to believe that my family actually thought it was a good idea to intrude on our honeymoon.

Ever the diplomat, Tom cleared his throat and said, "How, um, nice that we can cruise with one of your best friends," he turned to me, "and every single adult member of your family."

Except one. My ex-husband. Now that would have been a honeymoon to write home about. Not!

"Who's watching the kids?" I asked Mother.

"Hank offered," she replied. "Said he would enjoy the extra bonding time."

Tom and I mutually sighed in relief that my ex wouldn't be popping by our stateroom. My perceptive mother noticed our dejected expressions. "We certainly aren't planning to spend every single day and night with you two."

"Definitely not the nights," my stepfather emphasized as he wrapped his arm around my mother and squeezed her tight. "As you may recall, Barbara and I never had the opportunity to take our own honeymoon last year."

"January is a slow month for selling real estate," Mother added, "so when Stan mentioned the ship wasn't full and they were offering last minute discounts, we jumped at the suggestion."

Stan proffered an apologetic smile.

"Remember what a great time we all had when we joined Liz and Brian for their honeymoon in Hawaii?" he asked. "Best vacation I ever took."

A dead body notwithstanding, our group did have a good time on the Big Island. While trying to prove that my big brother wasn't a murderer, I became a connoisseur of Kona coffee.

And of daiquiris.

"I won't get in your way, neither," Gran interjected quickly, reading my expression. "My friend Mabel will keep me out of your hair. Now where did that woman disappear to?" Gran snapped her head around so fast that her platinum pixie-cut wig toppled off. Stan snatched it before it landed and smoothed it back on Gran's head.

A stout woman with wispy carrot-orange hair, dressed in red plaid Bermuda shorts accessorized by support hose rolled to her knees, a white T-shirt, and a bra that did not cross her heart or provide any lift whatsoever, waddled to Gran's side.

She belched and sighed in relief. "That's better. That plane food went right through me. I never should have…"

Rather than listen to a lecture about the negative effects of airplane food on an elderly woman's digestive system, I gave in to the inevitable and put out my hand. "I'm Laurel, and this is my husband, Tom."

Mabel pumped my hand as if it were a slot machine lever before turning her scrutiny to Tom.

"He's a looker, isn't he?" she said to Gran as Tom's face reddened. "Maybe we can find ourselves some lookers on board this ship. I hear it's got over two thousand passengers. Gotta be a few available old coots for us."

Mabel lifted her paisley carryall and moved ahead, ready to board the ship and find herself a suitor.

I already had my own fellow so I grabbed my husband's hand and followed Mabel's plaid posterior up the gangplank. The rest of my family could do whatever they chose.

CHAPTER FOUR

Once Tom and I completed the mandatory safety drill on deck three, we decided to explore our cabin. We finished that in far less time than it took to explore the delights of each other.

I lolled on our surprisingly comfortable queen-size bed and read the information sheet about the *Celebration*. With a length of over 1,000 feet, twelve decks, nine restaurants, ten lounges, a casino and multiple pools, not to mention over twenty activities a day, plus five Caribbean island stops, there should be enough options to keep my family occupied. And out of our hair for the next nine days and eight nights.

The bed swayed and I realized that while we'd been otherwise engaged, our ship had left the dock. And here I thought Tom was responsible for all that rocking and rolling. Since I'd never taken a cruise before, I'd worried that I might be prone to seasickness. So far so good. In fact, our afternoon activity had left me with a healthy appetite for something other than my husband.

Since we'd signed up for open seating dining, we weren't locked into a set time or a specific table in the main dining room. For the first night on board, the ship recommended casual attire. I opened the stateroom door and discovered that our large suitcases had been placed in the hallway while we were otherwise occupied. Hopefully we hadn't provided any surround-sound entertainment for the cabin stewards or adjacent passengers.

I quickly unpacked my limited cruise wear and hung the items on the hangars provided. "I hope we'll have time for some shopping," I said. "There weren't a lot of summer clothing options available this time of year back home."

Tom's gaze shifted from his side of the closet to mine. "Yet you've still managed to take over three-quarters of the closet."

I stood on my tiptoes and kissed him. "Welcome to married life, sweetie."

After making only two wrong turns, we reached the main dining room located at the stern of the ship, the opposite end from our stateroom and four decks below. The glass-walled dining room took up two levels on decks two and three. We requested a table for two, but they were all currently occupied, so the maître d' led us to a table of ten with four open seats. Three couples were already seated and perusing the menu.

I sat across from a man who at first glance looked to be Al Roker from the *Today* show. Sitting beside him was a woman with short silver hair and a smooth café au lait complexion. She introduced herself and her husband, as Margaret and Fred Johnson from Daytona Beach, Florida. When I mentioned that we were on our honeymoon, she leaned forward and asked, "So that rosy glow isn't from sunbathing by the pool?"

I blushed, adding several shades of red to my post-coital glow. Tom chose to pick up his menu and hide behind it. I directed my attention to the woman next to me and asked whether she and her husband were celebrating any special events.

The brunette tucked her shoulder-length hair behind her left ear, displaying sparkling emerald earrings that matched her eyes. I doubted they were purchased on the shopping network. She patted her husband's knee and said, "Rick surprised me with this cruise for our twenty-fifth anniversary."

Her tanned, silver-haired husband leaned over to kiss her cheek. "Claire has put up with my horrible travel schedule for years. And with both our kids in college, it was time for a second honeymoon for the two of us.

The plumpish freckle-faced strawberry blonde seated to the right of Rick jumped into the conversation.

"We're the Abernathys. I can tell you that marriage takes work and a great attitude. And compromise." She jabbed a dimpled elbow at the man seated next to her. "Right, Darren?"

Her husband, a Mr. Clean look-alike sporting thick black glasses, nodded as he ran a hand over his shiny dome. "Lots and lots of compromise. Deborah is the most patient wife. We've had ten glorious years together, and I'm looking forward to another forty or fifty."

These three couples were so sweet to one another and excellent role models for newlyweds like us. I hoped my husband was taking notes.

Tom put down his menu. "This is the first cruise for both of us," he said. "Do you have any tips?"

Margaret replied immediately. "You've come to the right folks. Once Fred and I retired, we started taking advantage of last-minute deals. This is our twentieth cruise."

"Wow," I said. "You certainly must like cruising."

"You sure can't beat the price." Fred patted his well-fed paunch in affirmation. "All the food you can eat, non-stop activities and first-rate entertainment."

"We've taken a few cruises but never on this line," Deborah said. "I've heard their shows are fantastic."

"We're acquainted with the stage director," I replied, referring to Stan's boyfriend, Zac. "He's very talented so the productions should be terrific."

"As long as Stan stays off the stage," Tom muttered.

The white-jacketed waiter arrived to take our orders before I could object to Tom's comment. Actually there wasn't much to refute. He was completely right. Stan was convinced he was a late bloomer, and that someday soon Broadway would be calling him.

Much as I loved my friend, I wasn't ordering a congratulatory bottle of champagne just yet. Even Zac wasn't a miracle worker.

We enjoyed our five-course dinners with relish. As well as the bottle of chardonnay Tom and I split. Just as we polished off our desserts, another couple joined us. She wore a body-hugging red dress that emphasized every curve, while her long chestnut hair cascaded down her back. The white-haired man sitting in the wheelchair she pushed looked to be a half century older. Father? Grandfather?

Wrong on all counts. The beautiful young woman introduced herself as Danielle and her husband as Pierre. They looked forward to a warm break from their home in wintry Montreal. Although he was wheelchair-bound, Pierre regaled us with entertaining stories of their previous travels.

I was curious to learn how the couple met, but that would have to wait until another day. Tom and I had previously arranged to watch the evening show with members of my family. Since internet and cell phone service on board the ship cost almost as much as the cruise itself, our family was forced to handle communication the old-fashioned way, either via the phone in our stateroom or notes in the small mailbox holder outside our door. Gran had informed us that she and Mabel would save seats near the front so we could all enjoy the show together.

Tom and I arrived twenty minutes before the performance was scheduled to begin. Patrons packed the theater wall-to-wall. How would we find Gran and the rest of my family?

Silly me.

"Yoo-hoo, you honeymooners, over here," cried out my grandmother from near the front of the theater. For an elderly woman, her vocal cords are in amazingly good shape. We waved at her and scurried down the stairs.

I plunked down next to Gran and stared at the drinks she held in each hand. They were almost as big as she was. "I hope those are non-alcoholic," I said to her.

She handed one to me and one to Tom. "My treat for the lovebirds. Best piña colada you'll ever drink."

I sipped the fruity drink. She was right. Tom said he would pass, but Mabel was more than happy to down his cocktail. Based on the number of souvenir glasses under her seat, she would need an additional suitcase for her collection. Stan sat on Mabel's right, his face wreathed in a huge smile. I'd never seen my friend so happy.

Stan leaned over. "You'll love this opening act," he said. "It's like Cirque de Soleil meets Broadway. Zac said I can be the under-understudy for one of the chorus members."

Zac was truly a gem. And a wise stage director. The odds of Stan ending up on stage were lower than me losing weight on this trip.

The cruise director glided onto the stage. In her official Nordic American uniform, the tall stately blond commanded the audience's attention.

The same way she'd once commanded me to clean up my room.

What the heck was my cousin, Sierra Sullivan, doing on board the *Celebration*?

CHAPTER FIVE

I nudged Gran. "Did you know Sierra was the cruise director on this ship?"

Gran leaned forward, her chin nearly colliding with the person sitting in front of her. "Well, I'll be a monkey's aunt. How about that?" She lifted the hand not gripping her cocktail as if to wave to my cousin, but I yanked it back down.

Sierra peered into the audience, but I knew that up on stage the performers could barely see past the first couple of rows. It was highly unlikely she'd noticed her California relatives sitting in the audience. Yet. The last thing she needed was for us to disrupt the show, so I intended to make sure my grandmother remained silent for the next ninety minutes. I leaned back into my chair, took a swig of my drink and prepared to be entertained.

The show met all my expectations and then some. The two female lead singers were great, especially Nicole, the petite blond, who possessed a stellar voice and an engaging smile that made me feel like she was singing right to me.

Despite the rocking of the boat, the dancers, acrobats and trapeze artists kept the momentum going nonstop. I squeezed Tom's hand when Nicole was lifted far above the audience where she managed to belt out a song while rocking back and forth on a swing.

The show ended with a breathtaking acrobatic finale that literally took my breath away. Sierra briefly spoke into the microphone and invited everyone to attend the evening shows in the piano bar, the Queen's Lounge and the Downtown Disco. Then the heavy velvet curtain fell, and the lights came back on.

Mabel stood and stretched. "Good stuff. What's next on our agenda?"

"Let's hit the disco." Gran thrust out one bony hip then the other. "I've been practicing my Cupid Shuffle."

I turned to Tom. "Any preference where we go next?"

His dark eyes looked into mine. "I'll give you one guess."

Aw, he wanted to help me work off that chocolate cream pie I'd eaten for dessert. Although the disco might work it off even faster.

I beckoned him with my index finger. He leaned down and I whispered in his ear. "You do know that dancing is my favorite form of foreplay."

He grabbed my hand. "So what are we waiting for?"

Honeymoon lesson one: Don't let anyone tell you a drink doesn't have much alcohol in it.

Lesson two: Especially if that someone is your grandmother.

It turned out that Gran could pack away far more tropical booze than any senior should be able to. It made me wonder whether her weekly card games consisted of gin rummy or gin fizzes.

Her granddaughter, however, turned out to be a lightweight when it came to fruity concoctions. After three dances and two margaritas, or maybe it was two dances and three margaritas, it was all I could do to stumble alongside my husband as he guided me to our stateroom. Once inside, I stood on my tiptoes, wrapped my arms around his neck, told him I loved him, and plastered him with the biggest sloppy kiss ever.

Then I fell into our marital bed, face first. I woke in the middle of the night, the sheet tangled around my legs. The room felt sweltering, either due to my alcoholic consumption, perimenopausal state or hot hubby. Tom's internal furnace would provide much needed heat during winter nights in our communal bed back in Placerville. But right now, I needed to cool down.

Tom had removed my clothes leaving me in my lacy lingerie. I grabbed a short black silk kimono robe from the sofa where I'd tossed it earlier in the evening and wrapped the belt tight around my waist. Then I walked over to the desk and poured a giant glass of water from the bottle the ship provided its guests.

I glanced at the digital clock which read 3:30 a.m., a most inconvenient time to be awake. Maybe some fresh air would help. I unlatched the balcony door and pushed it outward. The gust of wind that assaulted me felt wonderful after the clammy heat of our cabin. I gently shut the door and settled into a chair on our balcony.

My head still felt groggy so I downed the entire glass of water, hoping to flush the alcohol out of my system. I leaned back against the cushion and closed my eyes. A sudden thump from above caused my eyelids to fly open.

Was someone moving furniture around this time of night? Maybe one of the occupants of the stateroom above us decided to rearrange the chairs on the balcony. Or maybe they also suffered from a splitting headache and hangover and were trying to find a way to deal with it.

I stared out at the mesmerizing sea. There was barely any moonlight, but I could still see the waves churning as the ship pushed its way under the velvety night sky. I rested my feet on the ottoman, wiggled my toes and relaxed into my chair. This was the only way to travel. It was so tranquil, so relaxing so…

A dark shadow suddenly invaded my musings. Then it disappeared. I leapt out of the chair and peered over the balcony railing. I'd heard about people hallucinating when they'd had too much to drink.

But I was fairly certain I wasn't hallucinating.

I was also fairly certain that a body had just flown past me.

CHAPTER SIX

I cautiously leaned over the mahogany railing, not wanting to become a shipboard casualty myself, and peered seven decks below. There was no sign of anyone frantically struggling in the sea. No cries for help from the water. Nor was there any shouting coming from the decks above ours.

I plopped back into the chair and wondered what to do. Had I imagined the entire thing? A combination of too much alcohol and a too vivid imagination?

Should I call our steward? Customer service? Who exactly do you call when you need to report someone going overboard?

Silly me. There was a detective sleeping in my bed. I flung open the glass door and tiptoed across the carpet. I slipped under the covers and nestled against Tom. It was wonderful to have someone you could lean on when times were tough. My own personal port for any future storms.

As I pondered whether to awaken him, I realized Tom was already wide awake. One vital part in particular appeared to be up and ready for action. He pulled me close and began to place soft kisses on my neck. Oh, my, but that felt good. I hated to interrupt our private party, but my priority wasn't my personal pleasure right now.

"Tom," I murmured in his ear.

"Mmm," he replied, as his lips moved lower and lower.

I yanked on his arm interrupting his progress. Such a shame since he had been progressing so nicely.

"I saw a body," I said.

"That's nice." He went back to what he was doing before. Gosh, that felt good. For a few seconds I lay there, pleasure short-circuiting thought. Suddenly he lifted his head. "What did you say?"

"I saw someone fall overboard. At least, I think I did."

Now I had his full attention. Tom sat up and leaned against the headboard.

"You're sure you weren't dreaming? You had a few drinks tonight. Alcohol can do strange things to your imagination."

"Have I ever imagined any dead bodies before?"

He winced and shook his head. "Unfortunately, no."

I explained what I'd seen, not that there was a whole lot of explaining to do.

"It's not that I doubt you, honey, but it's difficult to picture someone falling overboard without causing any commotion. You said there were no cries for help from the victim or anyone else."

"Correct."

"Unless someone decided to commit suicide that seems kind of far-fetched."

"How many of the murders you've solved initially seemed far-fetched to you?"

Tom sighed. "Too many." He stood and stretched. Clad only in his black boxers, he headed for the closet.

I admired the view for a minute before asking. "What's next?"

"We try to find the head of security."

Good. We had a plan.

"But there is something we need to take care of first," he said.

Men! Even with a potential dead body floating in the middle of the Atlantic Ocean, my new husband had just one thing on his mind.

I slipped back under the covers and waited for Tom to join me. When he continued to get dressed, I called out his name in my most sultry voice.

He turned and a puzzled expression crossed his face. "What are you doing back in bed?"

"You said we had to take care of something first."

Tom laughed. "I meant coffee."

We quickly dressed then set out on our mission. The cruise ship, unsurprisingly, was almost devoid of activity at four in the morning. We passed through the eerily quiet casino. A few stalwart gamblers claimed seats in front of the slot machines. The lack of smiles on their faces confirmed my opinion that gambling on board ship was akin to throwing dollar bills into the ocean.

I stared at the gambling night owls wondering if any of them might throw a person overboard as casually as they threw their money away.

One of the crew walked by, and Tom stopped him to ask the location of the Security Office. He told us to go down to deck two where someone would be able to assist us.

Tom pressed the elevator button, and the car arrived in mere seconds. We stepped in and I noticed that the beige carpet covering the elevator floor had Monday written across it in bold black letters. How clever. In case the passengers forgot what day of the week it was. With no pressing needs other than to wine, dine and play in the sunshine, I could see how the days could slip by while on vacation, one day blurring into another.

Except for today.

Did Monday stand for murder?

CHAPTER SEVEN

One would think that the possibility of a passenger falling overboard, whether intentional or not, would be a priority to the ship's staff.

Not so much.

Tom and I patiently waited in line behind a couple who had lost their keys, a woman who claimed her wallet was missing, and a short, portly man who had imbibed far too much and couldn't remember his stateroom number.

By the time it was our turn, I was so exhausted I could barely summon enough energy to share my story. The clerk was not impressed with my flat recital of passengers flying through the air. He suggested I go back to my room and sleep it off.

"But I'm positive I saw someone go overboard. Well, almost positive," I reluctantly admitted.

"Sometimes, when the moonlight shines on the ocean, it can play tricks on you," the clerk suggested. "Especially," he eyed me, "if you've been drinking."

"Yes, but…"

"We haven't received any other reports."

"Just because no one has reported a missing person doesn't mean it didn't happen," Tom said. "Maybe the person was alone when they fell over."

The clerk pointed to the tipsy passenger who was now arguing with another crew member. "And just because that gentleman claims he saw Mr. Spock lying on a chaise lounge on the pool deck, doesn't mean he did."

"There's a Star Trek convention on board?" asked a familiar voice.

I whirled around to see Gran and Mabel behind me.

"What are you two doing up so late?" I asked the women.

"We just closed down the disco." Gran waved a rubber chicken in my face. "I won the chicken dance competition."

I pushed the pathetic poultry aside. "Congratulations. So why are you down here instead of up in your room?"

Gran looked shamefaced. "My purse wandered off while I was dancing. They told me to report it, although someone could have taken it by mistake."

Since Gran's collection of pastel patent leather purses ranged in size from huge to gargantuan, it was highly unlikely anyone accidentally mistook it for one of their own.

"I hope you didn't have anything valuable in there."

"Her ship card and cash for the casino," Mabel said.

"And a five-dollar-off coupon for some special seaweed product they sell in the spa. Guaranteed to keep you regular," Gran added wistfully. Then she shifted her gaze to me. "So why the heck are you two down here? You're supposed to be doing the horizontal hula."

"Laurel thinks she saw something fly past our balcony," Tom explained to the women.

"Not something," I corrected him. "Someone."

Gran's faded blue eyes lit up. "You saw someone get pushed overboard? You mean there's a murderer on this ship?" she asked, her voice barely a few decibels lower than the *Celebration's* intercom.

Heads swiveled at Gran's remark. The drunk guy even stopped yelling and turned toward us.

"And now there's a serial killer running around," he proclaimed.

The couple behind us began arguing. "I told you we shouldn't have booked a Nordic American cruise, Henry. There are too many lowlifes on this ship," the woman said to her husband.

Gran spun around so fast her rubber chicken connected with the guy's I-love-a-buffet-sized belly.

"Ooph," he said bending over.

His wife glared at Gran and muttered, "See what I mean."

Gran immediately apologized. "Sorry about that. But don't worry about the serial killer. My granddaughter is a famous detective in California, and she'll ferret him out."

Tom cleared his throat.

Gran added. "And her hubby ain't no slouch either. They'll catch the murdererin' SOB."

"There is no serial killer on board," stated the clerk with clenched teeth. From behind him, a tall statuesque woman in her late forties intoned, "There is nothing for any of you to be concerned about. This is merely a misunderstanding with one passenger."

The tall blond met my eyes. "You're all grown up, but it looks like you're still creating mischief, Laurel."

"Hi, cuz. Nice to see you, too."

CHAPTER EIGHT

Five minutes later, Tom and I were seated in front of Chief Security Officer Sanjay Radhakrishnan. His office wasn't as plush or expansive as the executive offices at the bank where I work, but the cruise ship likely spent their pennies on guest amenities and not on employee offices. The officer brought in an extra chair for Sierra who chose to join us.

"You certainly don't get much sleep, do you?" I asked my cousin, noticing the dark circles under her eyes.

"There's always a multitude of things to attend to when we first set sail," she replied. "Plus we've kicked off a new show on this particular cruise, so there are lots of last minute details to be addressed." Sierra turned to Tom. "We haven't met but congratulations on your marriage. It's been quite a few years since Laurel and I've gotten together so we have some catching up to do."

The officer cleared his throat. "Perhaps you can postpone your family reunion until after we've resolved this situation. What did you wish to report?"

"I'm not sure how you plan on resolving this situation, as you refer to it. The ship has cruised far beyond where the person went overboard." I explained in great detail what I had seen. An explanation that took all of ten seconds.

The well-groomed officer splayed manicured hands on his desk. Not a strand of his jet-black hair was out of place. In his starched shirt and perfectly pressed uniform, he bore a commanding presence. "With no other reports, I'm not certain what you expect us to do. We can't turn the ship around based on what you think you might have seen. May I ask how much alcohol you consumed last night?"

I bristled at his suggestion that I was too intoxicated to know what I was seeing, although I'd lost count of the frothy drinks I'd imbibed in the disco. There was always the possibility he was right.

Tom leaned forward, mirroring the security chief's authoritative stance. "My wife does not make a habit of inventing scenarios like this. If she says she saw someone go overboard then she saw it."

"That's right, Mr. Radakra..." I fumbled with the correct pronunciation of his name.

"You can call me Sanjay," he said.

"Maybe you can check the twelfth-floor observation deck," said Sierra. "See if there's any sign of unusual activity. I'm sure it would reassure my cousin."

"Will that satisfy you?" he asked. His supercilious grin seemed to mock me and my good intentions.

I could tell by the tone of his voice that the officer did not expect to find anything, but it was better than nothing at all. I thanked him and the three of us left his office.

"I appreciate your help," I said to Sierra.

"Any time." She looked at her watch and yawned. "I can get in two whole hours of sleep before I begin today's activities. I suggest the two of you go back to your room and get a good night's rest, at least what's left of it."

We agreed to meet up later in the day. Sierra went off to her stateroom, and Tom and I headed for the elevator. I had an inkling how Tom wanted to occupy my time, but the sooner I took a much needed nap, the sooner we could engage in some creative stateroom activity.

If there were any missing persons to be found, I was leaving it up to the ship's staff to locate them.

The last thing I planned on adding to the daily list of activities was a murder investigation.

CHAPTER NINE

Tom and I woke with the sun shining in our eyes and someone pounding on the door. I reached for my robe, opened the door and peered into the narrow corridor.

"Hey, Stan," I said, pulling the door partially shut behind me. I tied my sash and ran my fingers through my unruly curls. "What's up?"

"Evidently not you." Stan's shoulders shook with laughter. "Are you going to sleep the cruise away? You've already missed bingo, the kitchen tour and the Champagne art auction."

Good. We hadn't missed anything important except maybe a phone call regarding the missing passenger.

"We had a late night," I explained.

Stan smirked. "I certainly hope so."

"It's not what you think. I saw a…" I stopped as a couple scooted past, the husband staring at my shorty robe. "Listen, why don't Tom and I meet you for lunch, and I'll update you then."

"How about on the pool deck? The Seaview Grille offer burgers and pizza made to order. And the steel band is playing for a couple hours."

This ship certainly didn't stint on entertainment. But some soothing Caribbean music might help dissipate the stress of the previous evening. I assured Stan we'd be there then slipped back into our stateroom.

The sound of the shower combined with off-key singing provided an excellent clue that Tom was getting ready. I decided to step out onto our balcony. Maybe if I stood there for a few minutes, I could recapture that terrifying moment of the previous night.

Or possibly confirm that I dreamt the whole thing after all.

I eased the heavy door open. The midday sun created warmth, but the balcony remained shaded from the noon rays. I grasped the railing with both hands and peered below.

My stomach plummeted as I gazed down at the white-crested waves. The crystalline blue waters that normally would have soothed my soul appeared almost frightening, as if a magnetic force tugged at me. Was I the last person to see someone's fatal fall into the sea?

The more important question—was there a next-to-last person and if so, why hadn't they reported the incident?

I jumped a foot when two muscular arms circled my waist and interrupted my reverie.

"Are you okay, hon?" Tom asked, his voice gentle and calming.

I nodded, comforted by his presence and the sense of security he gave me. "I can't help questioning what I saw and wondering if there was something I should have done."

"There is nothing you could have done, regardless, so don't let that bother your pretty..." Tom paused when I sent him a look, "...and very competent head." He gave me a long kiss that almost distracted me until our stomachs growled in unison.

First things first. Time to check out the poolside cuisine.

A few minutes later, Tom and I walked past the spa on our way to the outside café. A young woman, whose nametag read Andi from the Philippines, stood in the corridor passing out discount coupons for spa products, including a special seaweed digestive cleanser. I took one, knowing Gran would be thrilled to replace her missing five-dollar coupon.

We all wanted Gran to be "regular" for the duration of the trip.

Tom and I spotted Stan, Mother and my stepfather seated at a poolside table for six. We weren't the only ones to opt out of a formal lunch in the main dining room. The smell of burgers on the grill combined with the tangy salt air almost made me relax. I decided to lay off any alcoholic beverages for now and stick with diet cola. Life was almost perfect.

Almost. Unfortunately, my new Miracle swimsuit was creating a few problems. The salesclerk had assured me that I looked ten pounds thinner when I donned it for all of thirty seconds in a dressing room. What she didn't share was that after wearing the fat-sucking instrument of torture for more than a minute, I would barely be able to breathe, much less chow down on a half-pound burger.

"Your face is turning red," Mother said. "This tropical sun may be too strong for you."

"It's fine." I reached for a French fry then gasped as one of the built-in stays jabbed my rib. It might take a miracle for me to finish my lunch.

Bradford lifted a beer to his lips. "Tom told me about your commotion last night."

Stan raised both brows. "Time to dish, sweetie."

I shared what happened and waited for their reactions.

"Are you certain you saw a person?" Mother asked. "Maybe a large object fell overboard, like a chair cushion?"

"Inflatable doll?" Stan suggested. I rolled my eyes but shook my head.

"Crate of drugs," Bradford added.

All eyes turned to the retired detective. "Hey, it's happened several times on board cruise ships. A crew member obtains the drugs from one source, drops the package overboard at a pre-arranged place. The rest of the gang locates it by tracking the crate with their GPS."

Tom placed his palm over mine. "Does that make you feel better, hon?"

I shrugged. "I won't feel better until the head of security confirms that no one is missing. Until then, I'm keeping my eyes open for anything and anyone acting in a suspicious manner."

At that moment, I spotted Danielle, the significantly younger half of the Montreal couple we'd dined with the previous evening, engaged in conversation with a male companion, who looked to be in his late twenties. Once they reached the lounge chairs, he stripped off his polo shirt to reveal a muscled chest that would make a Calvin Klein model envious. When Danielle removed her cover-up, the rest of the men onboard turned to ogle her perfect figure.

Including my husband and stepfather. Good grief, even Stan. Men!

"Isn't that Danielle from Montreal?" Tom asked me.

"Yes," I said. "But that is definitely not her husband."

CHAPTER TEN

After a quick lunch, Tom and I returned to the stateroom. I was in a hurry to remove my uncomfortable bathing suit. Not surprisingly, Tom was equally anxious for me to do so. The flashing red voicemail light greeted us as we walked in.

Tom picked up the receiver and listened to the message. "The chief security officer would like us to come down to his office. He wants to update us."

I couldn't decide whether I was relieved that the head of security wanted to see us again or not. I quickly changed into a pair of comfort-waist capris and matching striped top, and we set off on our mission.

The majority of the ship's passengers seemed to be either going up or traveling down. We finally snagged a place on a downward elevator. When we stepped out of the car, I was surprised at the number of people milling around. The hospitality area seemed twice as busy as the previous evening.

"Should we wait for a clerk to tell Sanjay we're here?" I asked Tom. At the rate the lines were moving, it could take the entire afternoon.

We were saved from making a decision when the security officer's door opened. Sanjay ushered out a couple dressed in cruise-appropriate clothing, from the man's logo-trimmed shirt to her multi-colored floral sundress. As we approached him, we overheard his parting words.

"I'll report back to you as soon as I discover anything," he said to the couple.

Sanjay beckoned us into his office. With a grim look on his face, he closed the door and motioned for us to be seated.

"Are there more missing persons?" I asked, wondering if a serial killer had snuck on board.

He grimaced. "No, but there are several missing wallets as well as jewelry. The ship sailed less than twenty-four hours ago. Someone has been busy."

"And nimble-fingered," Tom added. "Have they left behind any evidence?"

Sanjay shook his head. "A couple of purses were found, emptied for the most part, devoid of any fingerprints."

"Can your stewards search the cabins and look for the missing items?" I asked.

"We guarantee privacy for all of our guests," Sanjay explained. "It would be completely unacceptable for the cabin stewards to rummage through their drawers and luggage. Unless the thief leaves a pile of jewels and wallets on his or her bed and then takes off to eat dinner, there's not much we can do other than warn the passengers."

"That won't go over well," Tom said.

"Not at all. But on to more pleasant news. You'll be happy to learn that all passengers with cabins above your deck are accounted for. We also found no sign of a struggle, blood or anything out of the ordinary on the observation deck."

"Which means...?" I asked.

"Which means no one fell overboard. So you have nothing to worry about." Sanjay stood and offered his hand to Tom and then to me. "It was a pleasure to meet both of you."

"But, but..." I sputtered. Before I could finish my sentence, he'd ushered us out the door and slammed it behind us. Tom guided me toward the elevator while I mulled over our conversation. The doors opened and we entered, alone for a change.

"Are you disappointed?' Tom asked. He slung his arm around my shoulders, and I slumped into him.

"I guess I am, although I should be relieved no one fell overboard." I gazed at my sandals, replaying the brief meeting in my head. The elevator stopped on the fourth floor, and two familiar faces stepped in.

"What have you lovebirds been up to?" Gran asked. I was about to explain when I noticed the pink purse that matched her pink plaid camp shirt.

"They found your purse," I said. "Did the thief take anything?"

"The scumbag took all her cash," Mabel said. "And her sunscreen."

"And my pretzels from the plane." Gran added. She reached into her voluminous handbag and pulled out a bright blue foil package. "Left the peanuts behind though. That could be a clue."

"So all we need to do is find a fair-skinned, nimble-fingered person who's allergic to peanuts," I summed up.

"Probably constipated, too," Gran added. "They kept my five-dollar-off coupon for the seaweed cleanser."

"We can't let this two-bit crook get away with it." Mabel nudged Gran. "Right, Ginny?"

"Yep. Looks like TWO GALS DETECTIVE AGENCY has another case." Gran eyed Tom and me. "You two want to join the firm? We could change the name to THREE GALS AND A HUNK."

The elevator pinged our floor before Tom and I could graciously refuse. We jumped out, not really caring what deck we landed on, and left Gran and Mabel hot on the trail of the thief.

"Do you think those two will get into trouble?" Tom asked, a worried expression on his face.

"Silly question," I said. "And the answer is yes."

CHAPTER ELEVEN

As I dressed for the first of two formal dining events on our nine-day cruise, I pondered our earlier conversation with the security officer. On the one hand, I felt relieved that no one had plunged to death in the churning sea, either accidentally, intentionally or murderously. Now I could concentrate on my honeymoon, not homicide.

On the other hand, why couldn't I erase that niggling suspicion?

I zipped up my new empire-waist turquoise evening gown, courtesy of Renfro's Bridal Shop back home. My zipper stopped two inches shy of the fastener so I swirled around to ask Tom for help.

Be still my heart. My husband could wear a black tuxedo like no other man. His Godiva-brown eyes twinkled as my mouth dropped open.

"What do you think?" he asked. "Shades of James Bond?"

"Daniel Craig, watch out." I gave him a lengthy kiss then turned around so he could finish dressing me.

We strode out of the room a few minutes later than planned. Tom couldn't seem to grasp the concept of pulling my zipper up, although he had mastered the opposite direction. We might have continued enjoying each other's company if my mother hadn't called our stateroom and interrupted us. Gran and Mabel were supposedly holding down a table for our entire group.

Honeymoon for eight. The story of my life.

When we arrived at the table, we found Bradford and Mother already seated, along with Stan, Gran, Mabel, and an older man with a thick thatch of white hair and matching moustache. He sported a double-breasted white dinner jacket with a yellow rose tucked in his buttonhole.

The elderly man, seated between Gran and Mabel, rose to shake our hands. "I'm Jimmy Bond," he introduced himself.

When I started, his lined face crinkled into a sweet smile. "No relation. I was born long before Ian Fleming dreamed up his famous spy."

"Are you as spry as that spy?" Gran asked with a mischievous expression.

He leaned over and in a stage whisper said, "In more ways than one." Gran giggled and Mabel snorted. Tom put his linen napkin over his mouth to hide his laughter.

Mother stared down her perfectly-shaped nose at the disorderly octogenarians. "How nice of you to join us, Jimmy," she said. "Where are you from?"

"I reside in London, but I enjoy cruising and do it as often as I can. It's the perfect escape from England's cold rainy winters."

"You must be loaded." Mabel blurted out what I was thinking.

"I'm comfortable," he replied. The wine steward arrived before Mabel could ask Jimmy for copies of his bank statements.

After settling on our wine selections, I directed my attention to Stan. "Is Zac tied up tonight?" I knew that Jimmy's seat originally was reserved for the stage director.

Stan nodded. "I had no idea that a stage director worked 24/7." He sipped from his water glass. "If it's not a technical glitch, then it's a personnel issue."

"Are there problems among the performers?" Mother asked.

"I really can't discuss it." Stan leaned forward and in a voice loud enough for the tables around us to overhear announced,

"Let's just say that one of the male singers has been, um, double-dipping with two of the female singers."

"So what's the big deal if he wants to get ice cream cones with two different gals?" asked Mabel, a confused look on her face.

Stan's mouth opened wide, but he was saved from answering by the arrival of the wine steward with our bottles of cabernet and chardonnay. I glanced over at our dinner companion, wondering what he thought of our dysfunctional group. Jimmy winked at me then raised his glass in a toast.

"To new friends," he said in a smooth baritone. "May our friendship last longer than this cruise."

The clinking of glasses was accompanied with strains of "I'll drink to that" and "cheers."

"So what's new with your floater?" Gran asked me.

I frowned. "According to the chief security officer, there is no floater. No one is missing."

"So you made it up?" Mabel asked.

"No. I didn't make anything up. I'm positive I saw someone fall overboard."

When Jimmy looked confused, Gran attempted to enlighten him. "My granddaughter sees dead people."

"Do you have a sixth sense?" Jimmy asked, his thick white eyebrows rising almost to his hairline.

"No, Laurel just has bad timing," Tom explained, but he placed his palm on my thigh and gave me an affectionate squeeze.

Our dinners arrived and the conversation turned to food. Mabel and Gran had toured the ship's kitchen earlier in the day, and they couldn't wait to share a few pertinent facts.

"You know, they cook 15,000 meals a day on board this ship," Mabel stated.

That was impressive, especially considering that every meal I'd tasted far surpassed my own cooking.

"And we chow down on over 28,000 shrimp on this cruise alone." Gran smacked her thin lips as she finished off the last piece of her garlic shrimp scampi.

"I wonder what they do with all the excess food." Mother pointed at the waiters clearing the tables, their heavy metal serving trays loaded with partially eaten entrees. "It seems like such a waste."

"They got that handled," Mabel said. "They grind it all up and feed it to the fish."

My appetite disappeared, and I placed my fork back on my plate. Mabel's comment made me ponder if the person I'd seen fall overboard had ended up as a snack for the local shark population.

My musings were interrupted when I spotted a familiar face. As the woman strolled by our table, I admired the silver lamé dress and matching jacket that looked terrific with her café au lait complexion.

"Hi, Margaret," I greeted our dining companion from the previous night. "Where's Fred?"

"He's laid up." She made a sad face.

"Seasick?" Mother asked.

"I'm not sure. I just hope he hasn't picked up a…" she looked to make sure the waiter wasn't listening, leaned in and murmured, "Norovirus, or he'll be confined to the stateroom for the rest of the trip."

"That seems kind of tough," Bradford said.

"It's the cruise line's policy. They don't want an outbreak on board ship or they'll have to turn back." The maître 'd beckoned to her. "Probably just something he ate for lunch. You all enjoy yourself." She scurried over to a table full of women travelers and settled into the one empty seat.

"Nasty thing, that norovirus," said Jimmy. "I've managed to escape it so far, but one of my ships suffered a horrible epidemic. Even the captain came down with a case."

Good grief. First I'd been overcome with worry about seeing someone fall overboard. Now I was fretting about one or all of us getting norovirus. What stressful shipboard event would come next?

"You're coming with us after dinner, aren't you, Laurel?" asked Gran.

"Sure," I said. "But where are we going?"

"Karaoke."

There was my answer.

CHAPTER TWELVE

Turquoise waters, a balmy breeze ruffling my unruly bob and a tropical drink in my hand. Now that's the way to spend a vacation. Our first island stop was Grand Turk, the largest of the many islands in the chain known as Turks & Caicos, and one of the premier diving spots on the planet due to its protected coral reef.

Bradford, Mother, Tom and I had signed up for a catamaran excursion that would take us to the Coral Gardens Reef, a shallow reef where we were guaranteed to see turtles and stingrays as well as a multitude of unique sea creatures. My mother preferred sailing to snorkeling so she remained on the boat while the three of us chased schools of brightly colored fish.

After forty-five minutes, I exchanged a wet smooch with my husband and told him and my stepfather to have fun exploring the mysteries of the ocean.

I relinquished my snorkel gear to an attendant then went looking for my mother. I located her on one of the bench seats chatting with a woman who also looked to be a member of the baby boomer set. I picked up one of the apricot drinks the bartender was pouring for the passengers. It tasted sweet but refreshing. I had no idea what the ingredients consisted of other than alcohol, something there seemed to be no shortage of on this trip.

I perched on the bench alongside my mother and sipped my cocktail. Between the warm sun and the cool drink, I felt completely at peace, so relaxed my eyelids slowly began to shut. Mother's next remark caused them to spring open.

"You saw someone go overboard?" she asked her companion.

Mother certainly knew how to get my attention. I leaned forward, anxious to hear the other woman's reply.

She ran a hand through her short salt-and-pepper hair. "Well, I didn't actually SEE anyone go overboard." Behind her thick bifocals, her hazel eyes looked worried as she glanced at us. "Until you mentioned your daughter's experience, I just thought someone accidentally dropped something heavy over the ship's railing. Never occurred to me it could be a body."

"What cabin are you in?" I asked, curious how close her stateroom was to ours.

"My husband Glenn and I are in 6070. I'm Lucille Blodgett. Nice to meet y'all."

I wiggled my hand in response. "Same here. Your stateroom is one floor below ours and only a couple of rooms over. Do you remember what time you heard the splash?"

The two indentations between Lucille's brows shifted closer together as I patiently waited to hear her reply.

Okay, not so patiently. But I remained silent, not wanting to lead my witness. Hmm. Maybe I'd been watching one too many crime shows lately.

"I know exactly when it occurred," she said. "I woke to go to the bathroom. My bladder don't hold my rum' n cokes like it used to." Lucille and Mother exchanged knowing looks. "Anyway, it was 3:33 a.m. On the dot. My husband was snoring away so I knew it would take me awhile to get back to sleep. I figured some sea air might make me drowsy. Just as I opened the door to the balcony, I heard a faint sound. Kinda like a splash. I peeked over the railing, but I didn't have my glasses on so all I saw was water. Lots and lots of it."

"We thought Laurel might have imagined it," Mother confided to Lucille. "She was a tad tipsy when she went to bed." She eyed my cocktail. "Those fruity drinks can pack quite a punch, dear. And pack on the calories."

Nothing like maternal dieting advice when you're on your honeymoon. I guess it doesn't matter how many times a woman gets married, she'll always be a daughter in her mother's eyes. As usual, her comment caused me to respond by doing just the opposite.

I thanked Lucille for her help then ambled to the bar for a refill. On the way over, I pondered our conversation. The fact that someone else heard a noise at the same time warranted a call to the chief security officer. Proof that I wasn't loopy and I did see someone go overboard.

But whom?

My eyes locked on a couple standing at the bow of the boat. Her long dark brown hair was wet and wavy, but it didn't detract from her model-perfect beauty. She pulled a multi-colored wrap from her Gucci tote bag. As she twisted to tie it around her waist, I realized the woman was Danielle, accompanied by the handsome young man we'd seen her with yesterday. Not that her wheelchair-bound husband could have managed a catamaran trip.

Being curious, or, as my beloved but blunt-speaking husband would state, nosy, I stepped over a few legs and beach bags and finally reached the bow.

I tapped Danielle on the shoulder. "Did you enjoy the snorkeling?"

I didn't need to be a detective to note the complete lack of recognition on her face.

"I'm Laurel," I explained. "We met briefly at dinner the first night on board the *Celebration*."

"*Oui. Excusez moi*. My English is not so perfect," she replied.

I tried to recall my high school French.

"*Ou est votre*," I stopped to search my memory for the correct word before giving up. "Hubby?"

She laughed. "The boat, she is too tricky for him. He prefer to play the game of bridge." She turned to her companion and introduced him to me. "This is Jacques, Pierre's *therapeute physique*."

I must have looked confused because Jacques lifted my hand and said, "*Enchanté*, Madame. I am Pierre's physical therapist. He is such a nice employer to give me the day off while he plays his cards."

They said goodbye and walked away, spouting French faster than the Paris Metro.

Was it odd that Danielle and her husband's physical therapist were enjoying the island without him? While her husband was playing cards, were they playing footsie with one another? If you asked me, it was somewhat suspicious.

But as usual, no one was asking me.

CHAPTER THIRTEEN

Tom and Bradford waited until the last second to return to the boat. Deep grooves from the dive mask encircled Tom's brown eyes, but he wore a big smile on his face. My stepfather's completely bald head glowed brighter than my tropical drink, but he seemed to have enjoyed the snorkeling excursion as well.

Tom grabbed beers for both of them, and they joined Mother and me. I was so excited about my sleuthing discovery that I plopped an exceptionally enthusiastic kiss on Tom's sun-chapped lips.

"Nice to know you missed me," he said, lifting an eyebrow at me.

"What, oh, yeah, of course," I replied, hoping the blush I could feel rising would be mistaken for sunburn. "I was counting the minutes until you returned."

He took a long sip of his beer and narrowed his eyes. "You're practically vibrating in your seat. What's going on?"

I gave both men a quick recap of my conversation with Lucille. "We need to tell Sanjay," I said.

"Just because this woman heard a noise doesn't confirm that someone fell overboard," Tom objected.

"Could have been a dolphin jumping in and out of the water," Bradford suggested. "We saw a herd, or whatever they're called, of dolphins while we were snorkeling."

"Fine. But what about Danielle hanging out with her husband's physical therapist."

"I don't believe that's a criminal offense. Plus her affairs aren't really any of your business," Tom added.

I stiffened, but Tom put his arm around me and drew me close. "How about you stop worrying about other people's romances and concentrate on us having a good time."

I relaxed against him. My husband was right. We were visiting one of the most beautiful places in the world. It was time to let loose and have fun.

After one more drink and some gentle persuasion from the crew, I agreed to enter the limbo contest. Two decades had passed since my last limbo contest, and it turned out I wasn't as limber in my body as I visualized in my mind.

Not to mention a few pounds and two cup sizes larger.

Despite landing flat on my back, the crew gave prizes to everyone who participated. They handed each of us a "buy two T-shirts get one free" coupon at Sam's Sand & Ocean Shoppe, one of the stores in the Grand Turk cruise port.

I decided to forego detecting for anything except discounts.

Once the catamaran docked, the passengers sped down the gangplank and scattered in all directions, trying to make the most of their remaining time on the island. We sauntered past the pastel-colored stores and thatched-roof open-air restaurants comprising the Grand Turk Cruise Center. Strains of lively reggae music combined with laughter from happy tourists filled the air.

We bumped into Gran and Mabel outside Sam's Shoppe. I asked where they were headed next and Gran replied, "We're off to Duchess Diamonds."

"I didn't know you were interested in buying jewelry," I said.

"I'm always looking for bargains, kiddo. Mabel and I went to the Port Shopping meeting this morning. We got the scoop on who has the best deals here." She squinted as she looked up at Tom. "You should join us. Doesn't my granddaughter deserve a diamond ring?"

Tom blinked, but his investigative training kicked in, and he maintained a stoic façade as he replied. "My wife prefers chocolate to diamonds. Right, Laurel?"

"Yeah, sure she does." Mabel said. She swatted Gran on her thin arm, almost knocking my grandmother into a palm tree. "Let's check out those chocolate diamonds Alisa mentioned in her sales spiel."

"Chocolate diamonds?" Bradford looked confused. "Do you wear them or eat them?"

Mother clasped her spouse's hand. "Let's find out." She winked at me from behind his back.

"Shall we go with them?" I asked Tom.

He frowned. "I'm kind of grimy from snorkeling, so I want to get cleaned up. Go ahead and I'll see you in the stateroom."

We exchanged kisses and I joined my family. Even if we couldn't afford to purchase diamonds, I could ogle them and try on some selections just for fun. While Tom's and my combined finances were sufficient to pay for our wedding and our honeymoon, with hefty college tuition expenses looming next year, it would be a long time before any diamond purchases were included in our budget.

I twirled my gold wedding band around my finger. The tiny diamond chips that ringed the band were perfectly sufficient for me. It wasn't the size of the diamond on your hand, but the measure of the man who put the ring on your finger.

And my husband measured up quite nicely. In all respects.

Once I entered Duchess Diamonds, I stood transfixed. Not being an expert on gems, I couldn't tell if the fiery sparkles were due to the outstanding quality of the stones or the best lighting diamond sales could buy. But the result was spectacular. Diamonds surrounded me on all sides, not to mention colorful stones ranging from fiery Australian opals to purplish tanzanite, lime green peridot to pale blue aquamarines. All shapes, sizes and price tags.

Cruise ship passengers swarmed the counters leaving me little room to maneuver. Lucille, the woman Mother and I met on the catamaran, and a man I assumed was her husband were checking out some watches. Danielle and Jacques, her husband's supposed therapist, were engaged in conversation with a salesman.

I spied my cousin standing in front of a dazzling display of gems. Next to her were two white-haired women, one of whom was trying on a diamond ring that looked large and bright enough to allow the ship to navigate at night.

We'd barely had an opportunity to chat on this cruise so I sidled up to her. "Cruise directors turn up in the most unlikely places," I said.

"You should read my job description," Sierra replied. "It's three pages long. Are you enjoying the trip so far?"

"Except for wondering whether I hallucinated a body going overboard, it's been great."

The more portly of the two elderly women shoved a ring adorned with an enormous light brown stone in Sierra's face. "What about this one? It's only $24,000. Do you think that's a good buy?"

"Yikes," I said, loud enough for most of the patrons to hear.

Sierra jabbed me with her elbow. If her intent was to silence me, it wasn't successful because I followed my previous cry with a very loud "Ouch."

"Are you all right?" asked the woman sporting the five-digit diamond.

I rubbed my elbow. "Yes, thanks. What a lovely ring. Is that one of those chocolate diamonds?"

She nodded. "If I buy three or more pieces they'll discount them twenty percent." She pointed to a glittering necklace and matching earrings sitting on the counter. "I'll save thousands," she crowed.

"A wonderful deal, Mrs. Peabody," Sierra replied. She muttered under her breath, "Nothing like spending thousands to save thousands."

I chuckled. Sierra must be used to this type of shopping behavior. Even I had to admit there was nothing I liked better than a "buy two get one free" deal, but in my case it was usually for chocolate bars, not chocolate diamonds.

"I'll take the set," announced Mrs. Peabody to the anxious sales clerk who'd been hovering inches from his wealthy customer. "But I'll need the ring resized to a seven. How long will that take?"

"About an hour, Madame. Possibly more."

"Oh, dear." She looked at her watch, which looked similar to mine. Except mine was a Target knockoff of the Cartier original. "I have a massage scheduled at the spa in forty-five minutes." She looked so forlorn, one would have thought she'd just lost her favorite pet.

"I can pick it up and deliver it for you," Sierra offered.

"Are you sure?" The older woman's lips might be questioning Sierra's generous offer, but her eyes said thank you.

"It would be my pleasure," my cousin said. "Go enjoy your spa activities. I'll drop the package off in your stateroom. You'll be able to wear your lovely new purchases to dinner tonight."

Mrs. Peabody paid for her purchases with a platinum AMEX card. How nice to whip out one piece of plastic to purchase $50,000 worth of jewelry. I'd have to take out a second mortgage on the house to make that kind of purchase.

Not that I was planning on it. Maybe when Tom and I celebrated our diamond anniversary, he'd give me a diamond solitaire. Although considering that sixty years from now we'd both be centenarians, I'd be better off with a diamond-studded walker.

Mother and Bradford interrupted my glittery reverie. "Look what my wonderful husband purchased for me." She held out her arm so I could admire the opal bracelet accessorizing her slender wrist.

"Beautiful," I said. "And the blue matches my eyes. Maybe your favorite daughter can borrow it sometime."

She chuckled. "We'll see. Now let's go find your grandmother and get back on the ship."

I swiveled my head left and right in search of my petite grandmother and her plus-sized friend. I recognized several passengers from the ship but no sign of Gran in the cluster of tourists. A cry from a sales clerk at the other end of the store pierced through the customer chatter.

"Stop. Thief," he yelled as he ran around the display counter.

All eyes, including mine, turned to see the culprits who were attempting to flee the store with their stolen goods.

Gran and Mabel?

CHAPTER FOURTEEN

The pudgy black-haired salesman yanked on the tail of Gran's plaid shirt, stopping her in her tracks. The momentum caused her to fly backward and land flat on her back, her skinny legs flailing in the air. Fortunately her fall was broken by the young man who'd tried to stop her. If not for his soft cushioning, who knows how many bones my osteoporotic granny could have broken?

Mother, Bradford and I rushed to Gran's side. We gently lifted her off "Ramon," as his name tag read and propped her against one of the jewelry counters. Ramon staggered to his feet and pointed at Gran.

"I'm calling the police," he declared as two other white-shirted employees joined him. All three glared at Gran. She lurched to her feet and gave them the stink-eye to end all stink-eyes.

"Keep your shirts on," she said, tucking her own shirt into her waistband. "Now what the heck are you talking about? I didn't steal anything."

Bradford's six-foot-five frame loomed over the employee trio. "You can get into a pile of trouble slandering someone like that. Not to mention assaulting this poor old woman."

Gran slumped against me, giving an excellent portrayal of an elderly woman unjustly accused of theft. Her wig listed off to the side. As I pulled it back over her ear, she winked at me.

My stepfather continued on in full-detective mode. "Now what proof do you have of this so-called theft?'

"These women," Ramon pointed at Gran and then at Mabel who hovered over my shoulder, "removed a ring from the counter while I was waiting on another customer."

"And you saw them do so?" grilled Bradford, who looked to be in his element. Once a cop, always a cop.

Ramon flipped his palms out. "Well, it disappeared after they looked at it, so they must have done it."

By now, Sierra had joined our little group. "C'mon, Ramon. Are you sure you didn't just put it back in the wrong slot? I can personally vouch for these women." She pointed to the clock on the wall. "And we need to get back on the boat, pronto."

Ramon started to protest, but the manager drew him aside. They spoke rapidly, and when they finished, Ramon looked chastened.

"We apologize for any harm we may have caused to you, Madame," the manager said to Gran. "But hopefully you can understand the concern of my employee when he discovered the ring was missing."

"No harm, no foul." Gran patted Ramon's hand. "You were just doing your job. But we need to mosey on. We got a boat to catch."

We said our goodbyes to the staff amid their fervent apologies. Sierra needed to wait while Mrs. Peabody's ring was being sized, so we thanked her for her intervention and headed to the ship.

"How do you manage to get into these situations?" Mother asked Gran.

"We were minding our own business," Mabel said defensively. "I don't know why he picked on us. We're just two innocent old ladies."

"Yeah," said Gran, "but there were some shifty looking characters in there." She pointed to a couple about twenty feet ahead of us.

"What's shifty about them?" I asked. From the back they looked like any normal couple, returning from an island shopping spree, loaded with bags.

"He has beady eyes," she mumbled. "And she kept smiling at me. Likely trying to throw me off my game while she stole that ring when the salesman wasn't looking. We need to keep them on our radar."

I rolled my own eyes, which hopefully did not qualify as beady in Gran's book, or she'd be keeping me on her radar.

And once I returned to the ship, I planned to be off everyone's radar.

Except Tom's.

After a lengthy wait trying to board the ship, along with two thousand cruisers who all postponed boarding until the last minute, my family finally reached the loading area. We slid our purchases through the ship's X-ray machine then joined the other passengers waiting for the three elevators to arrive.

Fifteen minutes later, I entered my stateroom prepared for a little afternoon delight with my husband, whom I found snoring soundly into his pillow. I decided to check in with the kids via email. With the internet priced at seventy-five cents a minute, our email exchange was short and sweet. All was well at home. I could take a worry-free nap alongside my hubby.

After a well-rested afternoon, we were both ready for a big night out. As Tom finished dressing, I sat on the hard-as-a-rock sofa in our stateroom and read from the daily cruise itinerary.

"They offer country line dancing, name that tune at the piano bar, blues in the blues bar, and the Island Magic show. Oh, they also offer a digital workshop in case you want to bone up on your iPad skills."

It was all I could do to keep a straight face when I mentioned that last activity. But Tom managed to one-up me when he replied, "I've always wanted to attend a couples' computer class."

He burst out laughing at the shocked look on my face. "Or not," he said. "Let's grab some dinner and then explore. The night is young and so are we."

Have I mentioned how much I love my husband?

CHAPTER FIFTEEN

Tom and I ran into Stan and Zac outside the main dining room. The maître d' seated the four of us at a partially filled table for ten. I was pleased to reconnect with folks we'd met the first night. Rick and Claire, who was once again decked out in expensive jewelry, was seated next to the plumpish Deborah, who was minus her Mr. Clean hubby tonight. Deborah's female companion resembled an older, taller and stouter Marilyn Monroe, down to the platinum curls, bright red lipstick and mole above her lip.

Deborah introduced us to her college friend, Sharon, and explained her husband, Darren, was gambling in the casino. "You know how men are," she said. "I was happy to run into Sharon this afternoon."

This must be what Deborah meant by being patient with your spouse. I hoped when Tom and I celebrated our tenth wedding anniversary, he wouldn't dump me for a blackjack table.

The maître d' walked past with a couple following behind him. The woman stopped and asked if they could dine with us.

"Of course," I said, delighted to see Lucille Blodgett again. "We'd love to have you join us."

Lucille introduced herself and her husband Glenn to the rest of the table. "We hail from Atlanta. How about the rest of y'all?"

We did the round of introductions again. When Lucille learned Zac was the stage director for some of the shows, she turned to him. "I always wondered how y'all produce a show on a moving stage. Is it hard?"

"Not yet," Zac replied. "But this is only my first week on board, and so far the weather has cooperated. A couple of staffing issues but that's show biz. Did you see the opening night production?"

"Lovely show," said Claire.

"Did you have any favorite acts?" Zac asked her.

"All the singers were fantastic." Claire turned to her husband. "Don't you agree, honey?"

"Of course, although I'm afraid we celebrated with a little too much champagne that evening," Rick said, his fingers lightly stroking his wife's shoulders.

Claire colored. "I don't usually drink more than a glass of wine, so that champagne knocked me out. I hate to admit it, but I was so hung over I slept until noon the next day."

"You're not the only one who overindulged." Stan pointed at me. "Laurel thought she saw a body go overboard."

"I didn't overindulge," I protested. "Much. But I am positive I saw someone, or a large something, go overboard. Lucille heard something splash into the ocean about the same time."

Lucille nodded. "We're one deck below Laurel and her husband."

"Did you report it?" Glenn asked me.

"Tom and I met with the chief security officer twice, but he claims no one has reported anyone missing."

"The case of the missing," Stan made air quotes with his fingers, "missing person."

"Omigosh. This is too exciting," Lucille said. "It reminds me of an Agatha Christie novel. So what's your next step? Do you need any help investigatin'? I've wanted to play detective since I read my first Nancy Drew book."

"Thank you for your offer, but no," Tom answered for me. "The investigation is in the chief security officer's capable hands." Tom reached for my hand and squeezed it. "We're going to enjoy our honeymoon and not get distracted, right, sweetheart?"

"Of course, sweetheart." I smiled at him.

Stan shook his head. "I'll believe it when I see it."

Tom sent him a dirty look, but I remained silent. After working together for five years, Stan knew me better than my new spouse.

Rick shifted the conversation back to the evening's performances. "Are you involved with the Island Magic steel band production, Zac?"

"No, thank goodness," Zac replied. "So I finally have a few hours to spend with Stan. The last few days and nights have been filled with technical issues and all sorts of minutia."

"Don't forget cast members' romances," Stan added.

"Now this sounds like some interesting gossip." Sharon leaned in. "Can you give us the scoop?" With her heavy makeup and elaborate hairstyle, I wondered if Sharon currently worked in the entertainment industry.

Zac frowned at Stan. "Nothing that can't be resolved. And nothing that should interrupt the production. As long as the performers show up," he muttered under his breath.

The waiter arrived with our drinks, and conversation moved on to other pressing concerns, such as what activities we'd each chosen for the following day when we visited St. Thomas.

"Lucille and I want to explore Blackbeard's Castle." Glenn stroked his own graying beard.

"Glenn wants to tour the castle," Lucille contradicted her husband. "I want to visit the jewelry shops."

"St. Thomas is supposed to be wall-to-wall jewelry stores," Claire said. "Your head will be spinning. I'm anxious to check them out myself."

"I've been working way too hard lately, so I promised my wife something special to celebrate our anniversary," Rick said. She patted his cheek with her left hand then turned to me. "Are you two hitting the shops, too?"

"We're taking an around-the-island tour," Tom answered.

I blinked my mascaraed eyes in surprise. "We are?"

"It's a surprise. Just you and me. Alone, except for the driver. No members of your family." He shot a look at Stan. "Or friends. For a change, we can pretend it's just the two of us on our honeymoon."

Hmmm. I squeezed his hand, but Tom's comment gave me pause. While initially I hadn't been thrilled to discover my family on board the ship, I hadn't really minded it too much. We're a close-knit bunch, and, despite an occasional tiff, enjoy spending time together. But considering how little time Tom and I normally can spend with one another, I realized he might be frustrated that our one and only honeymoon was continually interrupted by my family members. I would definitely make sure to keep my relatives at bay for the rest of our cruise.

"Hi, toots," said Gran, coming up behind me as if I'd conjured up her presence merely by thinking of her.

Mabel pulled out an empty chair from the table behind us and plopped into it. "Where are the two of you headed after dinner?"

"Wherever you're not," Tom muttered under his breath.

"I heard that, sonny." Gran pointed at her right ear. "Got my hearing aid set on high so I don't miss any of the ship's announcements. Hard to understand that captain fellow. He needs to e-nun-ci-ate so us old folks know what's going on."

"Speak for yourself, Ginny," Mabel said. "I still got bionic hearing. And more energy than half the folks on this ship. You want to join us for line dancing, Laurel?"

Line dancing sounded great. I was about to accept her invitation when I noticed the horrified look on Tom's face.

"Thanks, but Tom and I were planning on attending, um..." my mind went blank at the evening's activities I'd rattled off earlier in our stateroom. The only thing I could remember was, "the iPad computer class."

Stan snorted wine out his nose. Zac handed his napkin over to him, but I could see both their shoulders shake with laughter.

"That sounds like fun," Lucille said to her husband. "The line dancing, not the computer class. We can work off all the desserts I'm planning on sampling."

Stan dropped his napkin on the table and stood. "All I have to do is change my shirt and grab my hat. Laurel and Tom can meet us after their," he cleared his throat, "computer class."

"Don't be late," Gran said. "Sierra said there's a special surprise at the end of her dance lesson."

"Sierra is teaching line dancing?" I asked. My cousin seemed to be everywhere. But we still hadn't had time to catch up with one another. I batted my eyelashes at Tom. It took my detective hubby less than a second to catch my drift.

"Fine, we can go to the line dancing class," he said. "But you'll owe me."

"I can't wait to pay up."

He chuckled before adding, "Just remember my size thirteen feet may be landing on yours."

"That risk is well worth the reward. You may even enjoy it." I latched on to Tom's hand as our group, including Lucille and Glenn, took off. We said goodbye to Deborah and Sharon and Rick and Claire who turned down Gran's offer to join us on the dance floor.

A smart decision as it turned out.

For some reason I assumed that a man who once headed an entire homicide department would not find line dancing a challenge. All you have to do is follow the directions.

I was wrong. It turned out that not only did Tom have two left feet, he was also navigationally challenged on the dance floor.

When everyone else went to the right, Tom moved to the left, almost crashing into Gran in the process. Mabel wasn't much better. As in life, Mabel moved to her own beat. She wasn't going to let a little thing like rhythm stand in her way.

Stan and Zac, sporting matching turquoise satin shirts and black cowboy hats, danced in the front row on either side of Sierra. Show-offs! It was a good thing none of the *Dancing with the Stars* judges were on board. My husband would barely have eked out a four on Len Goodman's scorecard. On the other hand, Bruno Tonioli, the feisty Italian judge might have given him a six.

What Tom lacked in dance skills, he made up for in sex appeal.

After fifteen minutes, I grabbed Tom's hand and led him off the dance floor.

"What's the matter?" he asked, with an innocent expression on his face. I narrowed my eyes at him, wondering if his unskilled dance performance could actually be very skilled acting.

I decided that was an unkind thought and merely said that I was relinquishing him from his dance duties. We found two available comfy chairs in the lounge and ordered drinks from the waiter. It was almost as much fun watching the dancers as participating. Gran could easily have won *DWTS*—the octogenarian version. My mother performed a ladylike electric slide while Bradford proved to be surprisingly light on his feet for someone who bore a close resemblance to a grizzly bear, sans the hair.

Glenn and Lucille spent more time squabbling over the steps than dancing. When the music finally stopped, the dancers applauded, some of the more challenged participants in relief. Several couples stopped to thank Sierra for the lesson. We sipped on our drinks waiting for an opportunity to engage in conversation with my cousin.

A commotion caused me to turn my attention to the corridor outside the cocktail lounge. Sanjay Radhakrishnan, the chief security officer, entered the room accompanied by two elderly well-dressed women.

One of the white-haired women looked familiar although I couldn't place her. Not until she pointed a finger at Sierra.

"Arrest her," the woman shouted, her plump chin mere inches from my cousin's surprised visage. "She stole my diamonds!"

CHAPTER SIXTEEN

Shouts of "who" "what" and "are you crazy" followed her accusation. The security officer calmly moved in front of the woman to address the throng of dancers surrounding Sierra.

"I believe this lesson is over," he informed them. "Please check out the other excellent entertainment options aboard the ship."

Grumbling ensued although it was difficult to determine whether it comprised support for Sierra or annoyance that they couldn't stay to hear the details. Gran moved within an inch of the security officer and poked him in his chest. She might be barely five feet tall, but she knew how to get someone's attention.

"What the blazes is wrong with you?" she asked him. "Accusing my great niece of stealing. She's as honest as the day is long."

The female accuser glared at Gran. "Aren't you one of the women caught pinching jewelry from Duchess Diamonds today? I bet you two are in cahoots."

"Mrs. Peabody," said Sierra, "I have no idea what you're talking about." Sierra placed her palm on the irate woman's forearm who jerked it back as if a white-hot coal had touched it.

"See, officer," Mrs. Peabody said to Sanjay. "First she steals my jewelry. And now she's assaulting me."

Tom silently eased his way up to the security officer's side.

"It looks like there may simply be a misunderstanding here," he said in a soft but commanding tone. "Perhaps we should take this conversation someplace more private."

Mrs. Peabody looked reluctant, but the security officer persuaded her to join him and Sierra in his office. The rest of my family and the slender elderly woman who was Peabody's ever-present shadow followed behind. When we all entered the elevator, Sanjay directed his gaze at Gran and informed us our assistance would not be necessary.

"Well, someone needs to be in Sierra's corner," Gran protested.

"Do you mind if I sit in?" Tom asked Sanjay. The security officer looked relieved at the suggestion and agreed.

When the elevator reached the second floor deck, everyone piled out. My family plunked down on cushy leather chairs in the lounge area while I followed Tom into Sanjay's office.

"Why don't you join the rest of your family?" Sanjay suggested, glancing at Tom for his approval.

Tom looked around the small office. "Good idea. These quarters are tight with five of us in here."

Sierra placed her arm around my waist and drew me close to her side. I wasn't certain if she still felt the need to protect her little cousin or if it was my turn to provide support.

"Let Laurel stay." Sierra turned to Mrs. Peabody. "Can you please enlighten us? Why do you think I stole something of yours?"

Mrs. Peabody folded her arms and glowered at Sierra. "You promised to deliver the jewelry I purchased from Duchess Diamonds to my stateroom. But when I returned from the spa, there was nothing in my suite. I ransacked my closet and drawers thinking you might have hidden the items as a precaution, but I couldn't find them. My jewelry case is missing, too."

The color drained from Sierra's face. "Mrs. Peabody, I assure you that I delivered your purchases to your stateroom. I left them on the desk with a little note. I would never steal from a passenger or anyone else."

"Then where did they go?" Mrs. Peabody's face turned bright red. She looked like a volcano ready to explode.

"I...I don't know." Sierra's lower lip trembled and she dropped into one of the visitor chairs. "Did you speak to your stateroom attendant?"

Mrs. Peabody sank into the remaining chair. "Javier said he let you into the suite and then left."

"Sierra, did you make sure the door was closed when you left?" Sanjay asked.

"Of course I did," Sierra replied, although her voice lacked conviction.

"How many people have access to the passenger staterooms?" asked Tom.

"The cabin attendants, who are thoroughly vetted before they are hired," Sanjay assured him. "Also the hotel manager."

"What about other staff?" I asked. "Maintenance workers? Who makes up new keys if passengers lose them or they stop working?"

"Anyone at the guest relations desk, I guess," Sierra said. Sanjay nodded.

"This is all quite interesting," Mrs. Peabody stated, "except it isn't. And it's certainly not helping me recover my jewelry." She fixed the officer with a beady stare. "So what are you planning to do about it? I assume the ship will reimburse me if my jewelry isn't found."

Sierra and I gasped in unison. That wouldn't have been my assumption. I had a feeling it wasn't Nordic American's policy either.

"I assure you I will do my utmost to find your missing jewelry." Sanjay rose from his chair, indicating the meeting was over. "I'll accompany you to your suite right now, and you can show me where you stored your other jewelry. Do you have a receipt for the items you purchased at Duchess Diamonds?"

She pursed her lips. "It should be in my handbag. Unless she stole the receipt from me too."

A frustrated look crossed Sierra's pale face. "I apologize once again although I am not at fault." She peeked at her watch. "I need to run. I have to change before I introduce Island Magic. Their show begins in fifteen minutes." She turned to Tom and me. "Thanks for the support. I really appreciate it. Can we meet after the show?"

Before Tom could answer, I replied for the two of us. "We'd love to. Where?"

Sierra was halfway out the door. "The piano bar" was all we heard before the door slammed shut.

Sanjay ushered Tom and me out of his office. He locked it and left with Mrs. Peabody and her companion. We joined my family, all of whom were anxious to know if the situation had been favorably resolved.

"Sierra said she dropped off Mrs. Peabody's jewelry in her suite," I said in response to their questions. "She's upset by the accusation, but she had to dash off to introduce that Island Magic group. Tom and I are meeting her in the piano bar after the show."

"That's a relief," Mother said, releasing a deep sigh.

"Sure is," said Gran. "And it could be a lot worse."

"What do you mean?" I asked her.

"You could be meeting in the brig!"

CHAPTER SEVENTEEN

After hearing Mrs. Peabody's accusations, I didn't think I'd be able to enjoy the Island Magic show. My cousin managed to maintain her composure as she welcomed the act on stage. There was no hint the tall blond emcee with the sparkling blue eyes had been accused of stealing diamonds only a few minutes earlier. I could only imagine what Sierra was thinking as my own mind endeavored to come up with a reasonable solution to the missing jewels.

Tom leaned over and whispered in my ear. "I can hear your brain cells whirling from here. Try to relax and enjoy the show."

Years spent in law enforcement had given Tom the ability to separate work from his personal life. But it wasn't his cousin accused of a crime. Nevertheless, I attempted to concentrate on the performance for the next ninety minutes.

The steel drum group was fantastic. Eventually all thoughts of Sierra's predicament disappeared as the four male musicians plus the female singer performed classical and show tunes, utilizing only native Caribbean instruments. The audience bobbed their heads to the pulsating beat of the drums. The music offered a much needed temporary distraction for me.

At the end of the show, Sierra appeared on stage once more to lead the applause, which, based on the loud clapping and foot-stomping, didn't require much encouragement. Sierra mentioned additional late night activities in the disco and the Queen's Lounge. She also reminded everyone we would reach St. Thomas the next morning at eight.

We stood and slowly followed the audience members up the carpeted stairs. Tom assisted my climb by gently lifting my tush whenever I slowed. I had a feeling my husband was more interested in lovemaking than crime solving, but my cousin's dilemma remained first and foremost on my mind.

"Where is the piano bar?" Tom asked me as we stood off to the side to let the throng of pleasure-seekers walk past.

"I can only guarantee one direction." I pointed up. "Let's go find a map of the ship."

When the piano bar turned out to be only two levels above us, we chose the stairs over the elevator. A better bet than joining the thousand-plus passengers who'd attended the show. As we climbed the marble steps, I held on to the glossy brass railing for support before realizing it could be covered with norovirus bugs. I yanked my hand off the rail and rubbed my palm against the skirt of my sundress. Even though the ship posted gallons of antibacterial lotion at every entrance, it was worthless against the shipboard virus.

Cruising was fraught with potential perils! Germs, missing gems and possibly missing bodies. What was in store next?

The tuneful strains of "It Had to Be You" greeted us as we walked inside the piano bar. A large circular bar with every seat occupied surrounded a glossy ebony grand piano. I recognized two singers from the first night's show joining in as they hovered over the pianist's shoulder. I looked for the amazing blond singer, but she wasn't with the group.

Sierra sat tucked away at a corner table sipping a glass of white wine. She'd kicked off her high heels under the table. I joined her while Tom went to the bar to place our own cocktail orders with the female bartender.

"Cheers." Sierra took a large gulp of wine. "This is a heck of a way to conduct a family reunion."

"I'm trying to remember the last time we got together," I said.

Sierra cocked her head in thought. "Maybe Mel's high school graduation?"

"Could be. When was that? Three years ago?"

"Try six. My daughter's now a police officer, believe it or not. Married to another officer on the force."

"Congratulations," I said. "It seems like our entire family is attracted to law enforcement."

I updated Tom when he appeared with our drinks. "I just found out Sierra's only child, Melanie, is married and working for the police," I said. "So what brought you from the little town of Santa Lucia, California, to the high seas?"

"Stupidity." She drained her glass and smacked it down on the table. "I'd broken off an engagement with, of all people, the mayor of Santa Lucia. He didn't take it well."

"Break-ups can be difficult."

"I'm not sure whether he was more concerned about losing me, or losing votes in the next election, but it didn't end well. Not only were we engaged, but I managed his social and political calendar. I was at a loss about what to do next when a friend fairly high up the Nordic American food chain encouraged me to apply for this position. Since I'd worked as an assistant cruise director before Mel was born, I had enough experience to get the job. And they were desperate to fill the opening." Sierra flagged down the waiter and ordered another glass of wine. "So I'm stuck on this boat for another four months."

"There are worse places to be stuck," Tom said.

She laughed. "You would think so, wouldn't you? But most of the crew and staff are two to three decades younger than my forty-eight years. Even the captain is a couple of years younger than I am. Sometimes I feel like I'm a combination of Mom, nursemaid and Dr. Phil. These kids sign up for long gigs not realizing that they'll be ship-bound for eight months. They need an outlet and the only ones available are sex and alcohol. Life on board ship is far more like *The Days of our Lives* than *The Love Boat*."

"So you don't see this as a permanent gig?" I asked.

"Not really. I'm weighing my options."

Our conversation was interrupted by the arrival of Sanjay Radhakrishnan accompanied by an equally commanding man in dress whites and an official cap. The tinkling of the piano keys stopped, and the chatter at the bar dwindled to nothing.

It grew so quiet you could almost hear the ice melting in our glasses.

"Sierra, we'd like you to come with us," Sanjay said.

"I've already told you everything I know about Mrs. Peabody's jewelry." Sierra's voice rose and her cheeks flushed with indignation.

"Please don't make a scene," said the other officer. "This is difficult enough for us."

Tom stood. "Where are you taking her?"

"I'm afraid that is ship business," the official said. "And none of yours."

Sierra slipped her feet back into her shoes, hugged me and stood. Sandwiched between the two tall men, her five-foot-nine frame, even in three-inch heels, looked petite. The pianist struck a few chords and conversation struck up again.

"What do you think will happen to her?" I asked Tom.

"I don't know." He looked grim as he stared out the door. "But one thing is certain. Sierra's options aren't looking too good right now."

CHAPTER EIGHTEEN

I spent a sleepless night, and it wasn't due to any cavorting with my husband. I was too upset about Sierra's predicament to be in the mood for anything except the soothing massage Tom offered in hopes of getting me to relax.

The massage ended up soothing my masseur into a snore-filled bliss, while my head spun all night with varying scenarios concerning my cousin. None of them good.

Did the captain officially arrest Sierra for theft? Could he do that? I supposed if he could marry people on the ship, he could also jail them. Where would they have taken her? And why? Had Sanjay or someone else discovered new evidence?

At least my cousin was still alive as opposed to the person I'd seen fall overboard. Thinking of that evening made my head spin even faster. By the time I returned home, I would need a vacation to recover from my honeymoon.

In the middle of my meanderings, my stomach growled. I looked at the alarm clock. Almost seven. Tom remained blissfully asleep. I decided he could use the extra slumber time. His normal schedule rarely allowed him more than six hours a night.

I threw on a pair of shorts and a sleeveless top. As I recalled, the Lido Café buffet didn't open until 8:00 a.m. so the only place to get breakfast this early was the main dining room. My stomach applauded as I wrote a quick note for Tom telling him my destination. Some pancake magic might add some extra pep to my step.

Once I reached the dining room, I followed the host past a multitude of empty tables, wondering if any of my family was up and eating this early. I finally saw a familiar couple and asked to be seated with them.

Rick and Claire were deep in conversation with the chief security officer. Sanjay seemed perturbed that I'd interrupted them. Tough. He was just the person I wanted to see.

"May I join you?" I asked the couple. They graciously said yes.

"Did you have jewelry stolen, too?" I asked Claire.

"A bracelet disappeared," she said. "Sanjay told us they'd discovered the thief, but my bracelet wasn't in her stash."

Stash? My cousin had a stash?

I waved the server over and ordered an entire pot of coffee. I could already tell this day would require many cups of caffeinated fuel.

"Where is Sierra?" I asked Sanjay.

"She's confined to her quarters."

"For how long?"

"Until we've completed our investigation." Sanjay turned to the couple. "Thank you for the information, Mr. and Mrs. Nerwinski. I'll get back to you when I have an answer." He stood to leave, but I jiggled his arm before he could disappear on me.

"Can I visit my cousin?"

"I don't think that's wise."

"Are you afraid I'll sneak her off the ship?"

Oh. Good idea, Laurel. Or maybe not. Tom might not mind me being confined to our cabin for the duration of the trip, but that didn't tie in with my vacation plans. There were islands to see and souvenirs to purchase.

Sanjay sighed. "I'll take you to her stateroom. You can spend ten minutes with her. Not a second more. We'll be docking in St. Thomas in less than an hour, and I will have far more pressing things to deal with. Follow me."

I waved goodbye to Rick and Claire and also to my coffee. My java jumpstart would have to wait.

I'd previously heard that the crew's quarters were smaller than an office cubicle and normally located in the bowels of the ship. When it came to the entertainment staff, the ship ponied up.

Sanjay and I arrived at Sierra's stateroom on deck four just as a room service attendant walked out the door. It was a relief to know that my cousin would be well-fed while she was confined. My stomach smiled at the thought she might even share some of her breakfast. Even a day-old donut would be welcome at this point.

Sierra's initial scowl upon seeing Sanjay dissipated when she noticed me by his side. "Laurel, is everything okay?" she asked.

Sanjay graciously let me enter first before explaining. "Your cousin was concerned about your welfare. You can have a few minutes together while I attend to something." The door closed behind him leaving Sierra and me staring at one another.

Sierra indicated I should sit on the sofa while she sat on the firm chair across from me. She saw me eyeing the coffee pot and asked if I wanted a cup.

I almost jumped with gratitude, but I restrained myself and merely poured a cup then added cream and sugar.

"Sanjay isn't giving us much time to chat," I said. "Is there anything I can do for you? Can Tom help in any way? He is a skilled detective."

Sierra twirled a strand of her long hair, her expression a mix of fear and confusion. "I'm at a complete loss about what to do. The captain and Sanjay searched my room. They went through everything while I was hosting the show last night."

"What did they find that convinced them to lock you up?" I sipped my coffee, curious about her response.

"They found nothing in my drawers or cabinets. Then Sanjay searched inside my beach bag, the one I carry when I go ashore."

"And?" I asked, almost afraid of her answer.

"They found a small plastic bag from Sam's Sun & Sports Shoppe."

I crinkled my nose at her. "That doesn't sound so suspicious."

"It is when the bag contains a couple of the stolen items!"

CHAPTER NINETEEN

My hand shook and hot coffee sloshed onto the saucer. I set the cup down. "That's not good. Do you have any idea how the stolen goods wound up in your bag?"

Sierra slumped against her chair, her eyes closed. "I've wracked my brain trying to think who could have committed these thefts."

"And made the effort to implicate you," I added.

"I don't know what's more depressing," Sierra said, staring out the window. "Being imprisoned in my own stateroom or realizing someone hates me so much they're trying to frame me."

"Who had access to your tote?"

"I carry it whenever I leave the ship. Waiting for Mrs. Peabody's jewelry made me late to board. Plus it took me a few minutes to get in and out of her stateroom. I barely made it to bingo in the Queen's Lounge at three. The room was already packed so I just chucked my bag off to the side."

"So anyone could have placed those items in it?"

"Sure. I only carry my ship card, one credit card, and a few incidentals when I go ashore, so I never worry about theft." A wry look crossed her pale face. "Guess I'll be changing my attitude from now on. Once bingo ended, I came back here, dropped my bag on the coffee table, changed to my fringed shirt and cowgirl hat for the line dancing class and took off again."

"Who did the items belong to?"

"I'm clueless," Sierra said. "They took my bag to Sanjay's office. He has records of everyone who's filed a claim since we boarded the ship."

"What's next? Are you under arrest?"

"Not technically. Sanjay doesn't have the authority to arrest me since he's employed by the cruise line. I suppose he could turn me over to the local authorities if he wanted to."

I shivered at the thought of my poor cousin trapped in a dank jail cell. Someone had to do something, and it was beginning to look more and more like that someone was me. With Tom's help, of course.

We might even become desperate enough to bring in additional resources—like TWO OLD GALS DETECTIVE AGENCY.

A heavy hand pounded on the door so I gathered our time was up. Sierra opened the door, and Sanjay entered the room.

I picked up my purse and hugged my cousin. She clung to me like a drowning passenger clinging to a life raft.

I followed Sanjay out the door and asked, "What's in store for Sierra?"

Sanjay remained quiet for so long I worried he wouldn't respond. "Your cousin is well-respected by the staff and the cruise line. I admit I was very surprised when we discovered a few of the missing items in her bag."

"So you don't think she did it either?" I was so elated by his statement that I practically skipped along beside him.

"That is irrelevant. The evidence points to Sierra as the thief."

"Are you handing her over to the St. Thomas authorities?"

"Good grief, no. She deserves better than that. I will continue my investigation while she remains confined in her cabin."

"Tom and I would be more than happy to help you..." my voice trailed off as Sanjay stopped in his tracks.

"I appreciate your offer, but it will be easier for me to work alone. Without any outside interruptions. Why don't you enjoy your honeymoon and let me do my job?"

A most reasonable request.

Unless you were a multi-tasking mother. Besides, how could I enjoy my honeymoon when my cousin's freedom was at stake?

I was certain my husband would agree with me.

CHAPTER TWENTY

"Absolutely not," said Tom after I disclosed my plan to investigate the jewelry thefts.

"We can't let them throw Sierra in a foreign jail for a crime she didn't commit." Surely he realized that. "Besides, you're a brilliant detective. You're the perfect person to investigate these robberies."

Actually I wasn't half-bad myself although my approach was more Inspector Clouseau than Miss Marple.

A frustrated look crossed Tom's face. "You seem to have forgotten one important thing."

"I have?"

"We're supposed to be on our honeymoon."

Oh, yeah.

I plopped down on the bed and squeezed close to my hubby, whose chest remained damp from his morning shower. He bent over and landed one sizzling kiss on my receptive lips. His firm pectorals crushed against my breasts, and I almost forgot the subject of our discussion. Tom finally rose from the bed and walked over to the closet.

"I suggest a compromise," he said as he zipped up his khaki shorts, eliminating one thought-provoking view.

"What?" I asked, wary of Tom's ability to distract me from my investigative leanings. It certainly didn't take much to distract me. In fact, the less, the better.

"We have this tour planned for today. I paid upfront and arranged for us to see some of the island's most spectacular sites. Plus I have an additional surprise in store."

So far I'd encountered enough surprises on this ship, but I certainly wouldn't turn down a spousal surprise.

"It sounds wonderful."

Tom finished buttoning his shirt. He walked over and kissed me on the forehead. "I certainly hope you'll enjoy it. Then when we return, we'll attend to Sierra's situation. Deal?"

Deal.

Our outing proved to be a wonderful almost stress-free day. Peter, our driver of an older Mercedes, provided a delightful although sporadic narrative on the best that St. Thomas, the largest of the U.S. Virgin Islands, had to offer. Our journey would have been more enjoyable if Peter hadn't spent the majority of it arguing with his wife, driving around hairpin turns and mountainous crests, with one hand on the steering wheel, the other gripping his cell phone. On the wrong side of the road no less.

Technically, it was the correct side. In the U.S. Virgin Islands, everyone is supposed to drive their western-style cars in the left lane. In Peter's case, it was difficult to ascertain which lane he was in since he utilized both.

At one point, Tom commented on my green-tinted pallor, which matched beautifully with the lime-green shorts and top I'd chosen this morning. My original fashion statement did not involve my complexion matching my clothing. Just when I thought my stomach would rebel all over the car, Peter pulled into our first stop, the world famous Mountain Top restaurant and shopping center.

I practically leapt out of the car. In seconds, the fresh mountain air with its hints of jasmine and orange blossoms settled my stomach and invigorated me. The popular tourist venue claimed to be the birthplace of the banana daiquiri. Since my brother owned a daiquiri bar in Kona, I was no slouch when it came to assessing daiquiris. A few minutes later, with Tom holding on to one hand, and my other hand gripping an iced mango daiquiri, we walked over to the scenic overlook.

And I do mean SCENIC. The view far below was worth the twisty and tortuous drive up the mountain. The water in Magens Bay shimmered in so many shades of blue that it looked like the inside of my closet back home. We stayed for a few breathtaking minutes before Peter honked signaling it was time to move on. Our next stop was a stretch of sand with fewer bodies than most of the beaches we'd passed. We parked and Tom and Peter conferred while I visited the ladies room. Upon my return, I was whisked to a magical beachside picnic. Peter even played waiter, in between placating phone calls to his wife.

"This is lovely," I said as I popped a grape into my mouth. We'd dined on cheeses, salamis, nuts, bread, fruit, and some kind of rum-based drink that Peter provided in a thermos. "How did you arrange it?"

"Your cousin set it up for me." Tom's face reddened when he mentioned Sierra. "I guess I owe her one, don't I?"

"As the recipient of this lovely picnic, I'd say we both owe her." I twirled the straw in my libation before meeting Tom's eyes. "What on earth can we do to repay her?"

"Subtlety is not your forte, darling," he said, but he accompanied it with a full-wattage grin.

I blew him a kiss across the picnic table. "Where should we begin?"

"Let me discuss her situation with Sanjay. As long as I don't get in his way, he might appreciate some assistance from a professional. I can't imagine he has the manpower to conduct any type of decent investigation."

"I wonder if the culprit trolls the diamond stores checking out the ship passengers and their purchases."

"That's an excellent possibility," Tom said. "What do you suggest?"

"Maybe it's time you and I hit some shops. We might be able to lure the thief into our clutches."

Tom stood, his tall, broad-shouldered silhouette highlighted against the bright sun. He walked around the table then dropped down on the wooden bench. He placed the tips of his fingers under my chin and turned me around to face him.

"Once we successfully lure this thief into our clutches, I fully intend to lure you back into mine."

I could work with that.

CHAPTER TWENTY-ONE

Our return trip down the mountain proved equally hair-raising. I breathed a heavy sigh of relief when Peter dropped us off in downtown Charlotte Amalie. Although cruise brochures advertised the downtown area as a diamond mecca, it wasn't until I observed the wall-to-wall jewelry stores lining each side of the street that I realized diamonds truly are the St. Thomas merchants' best friend.

Passengers from multiple cruise ships crowded the narrow sidewalks. Sales staff stood outside their individual stores, loudly hawking their wares and urging tourists to venture inside to take advantage of their stupendous sales. Available today only, of course. Based on the activity inside, their sales approach seemed to be working.

The expression on Tom's face was priceless. He looked even more scared than when he'd faced down a killer not long ago.

I squeezed his hand as we maneuvered our way past throngs of tourists into one of the shops. "It's okay, honey. I promise not to buy out the store."

"I noticed a fudge shop down the street," he suggested. "Are you sure you wouldn't rather stop there?"

I shook my head. I was on a mission, and I wasn't about to let chocolate distract me from detecting.

For now.

I scanned the interior of the elegant jewelry store looking for passengers from our ship. Since Crown Diamonds was one of the three companies promoted by the cruise line, it seemed a likely prospect.

I recognized Mrs. Peabody and the crone with her. I meant crony. Was she replenishing her stolen jewels already? I latched on to Tom's hand and dragged him to the back of the store.

"Hello, Mrs. Peabody," I addressed the matron who was attired in an ivory linen pantsuit. Three strands of coral pearls adorned her fleshy neck with a matching bracelet on her wrist. "Do you remember me? Laurel McKay."

She frowned, causing her beak-shaped nose to look even more hawkish.

"You're the one who's related to that thieving cruise director."

"Uh, technically, yes," I sputtered. "But I'm hoping to catch the real thief soon. I would appreciate it if you would stop impugning Sierra's reputation."

"And I would appreciate you moving your pilfering hands away from the counter," she replied. "Watch out for this one," she warned the sales clerk. His dark eyes opened wide and he discreetly slid some of the diamond bracelets she'd been eyeing away from my "pilfering" hands.

Mrs. Peabody addressed the older man standing beside her. "What do you think of the quality of these stones, Jimmy?"

Jimmy Bond held the gems up to the light and replied. "Very nice quality, my dear. As you know, a diamond is forever." He winked at me as he laid the bracelet back in the jewelry tray.

Who knew Mr. Bond, Jimmy Bond that is, was a connoisseur of fine diamonds? Tom's hip bumped against mine. Were the pricey gems making him nervous? I waved goodbye to Jimmy, grabbed Tom's clammy hand and we walked out of the store. But not empty-handed. The sales clerk at the door made sure to give us a gift certificate for one hundred dollars off our purchase today.

That sounded like a great deal until I read the fine print. Minimum purchase of one thousand dollars required. I crinkled the coupon and shoved it in my purse.

"Back to the ship?" Tom sounded hopeful.

"Hey, shopping isn't popping into a single store." I rubbed my palm soothingly against his back. "Remember all those times I've tagged along while you wandered the aisles at Home Depot?"

"Yeah, but one of those tiny stones costs more than ten table saws."

I guess I could count diamonds out of my future if one short visit to a jewelry store made my spouse this uncomfortable.

"I have the feeling you're allergic to diamonds," I kidded him.

He shrugged. "Nah, these seaside stores are probably moldy or something."

My bet was on "or something."

"So I take it you'd prefer to skip the diamond detecting? I can continue by myself if you want to go back to the ship."

"And leave you alone?" Tom looked horrified. I couldn't tell if he was worried about the danger to me or to our budget if he left me alone in a virtual sea of gems.

I peeked at my watch. "There's less than two hours before the ship leaves."

He sighed. "I can suck it up while you check a few more stores. But let's make it quick. We'll concentrate on travelers who are throwing a lot of money around and anyone who's watching them."

In the next fifty minutes, Tom and I bopped in and out of so many jewelry shops on the main drag that the sales staff undoubtedly thought we were casing the joint. Or joints. Each time we entered an establishment, we would split up and take opposite sides of the store. Then we'd stroll around observing any unusual or over-the-top activity.

Nothing jumped out at either of us in the first eight or nine stores we entered. By the time we hit the tenth jewelry shop, I'd collected a large collection of discount coupons. Now if I could only raise ten thousand dollars, I could save one thousand on my combined purchases. Such a deal.

We finally saw some familiar faces in Venetian Diamonds, the largest diamond retail chain in the Caribbean, with stores on most of the islands. Rick and Claire conversed with a salesperson near the rear of the store. It was such a shame her bracelet was stolen on their twenty-fifth anniversary cruise. Maybe they could find a good deal in this store to make up for it. Closer to the entrance, Glenn looked over Lucille's shoulder while his wife pawed through trays of jewelry. A big smile lit her face. Her husband had the expression of a man about to undergo a colonoscopy.

I walked up to the couple from Atlanta. "Looks like you managed to get Glenn into a jewelry store after all," I commented.

Lucille looked up from the tanzanite necklaces she was contemplating. "I agreed to visit Blackbeard's Castle if Glenn would give me an hour to shop. I'm a speed shopper when it comes to jewelry," she said with a giggle.

"The woman takes fifteen minutes to decide between a tall, grande or venti mocha, but when it comes to this stuff," Glenn grumbled as he pointed at the shallow cases spread across the counter in front of them, "she can make a selection in seconds."

Lucille lightly punched her husband on his upper arm. "You old fart, you owe me something for putting up with you all these years."

Glenn rubbed his arm, but he chuckled. He turned to us. "Are you two honeymooners looking to buy some jewelry?"

The sales clerk's ears perked up, and he beamed an unctuous smile at us.

I shook my head and replied, "Nope, we're here looking to find a thief."

CHAPTER TWENTY-TWO

I should have phrased that last comment better. Upon hearing my remark, the salesman dropped the trays of diamond rings and earrings held in each hand. Gleaming jewels crashed onto the glass counter before bouncing across the floor. I didn't need to look behind me to know that heads were turning in our direction. Tom and I tried to assist the harried clerk by picking up some of the fallen gems, but his manager rushed over and shooed us away.

"Thank you, but we will attend to this ourselves," the manager said in a heavily accented voice. He directed the four of us to the back of the store.

Lucille nudged her husband. "You'll do anything to get out of buying me a new ring, won't you?"

Glenn pointed at me. "I didn't do it. She did." Glenn mouthed the word "thanks" to me before he continued. "You said you're looking for a thief. Didn't I hear someone mention you're a detective? Are you with Interpol?"

"You're close," I said to the couple. "Tom's with Homeland Security."

Tom frowned at me before clarifying. "This has nothing to do with my job since I'm on my honeymoon. Or, supposed to be on my honeymoon. My wife keeps coming up with mysteries for me to solve."

"Is this about that body you thought you saw go overboard?" Lucille asked me. "Did you figure out who's gone missing?"

"Right now the only disappearance I know about for certain is jewelry. Someone's been stealing valuables from passengers on our ship."

"Doesn't the chief security officer already have a suspect in custody?" asked Claire as she and Rick joined our small group. "I thought he mentioned that to us this morning."

How to answer that question? I wasn't certain how many of the passengers were aware that the cruise director was confined to her quarters. My plan did not include sullying my cousin's reputation any more than it already had been.

"Solving mysteries is sort of a hobby of mine," I said.

"Some people knit or crochet as a hobby," Tom elaborated. "My wife prefers to stick her nose where it doesn't belong."

The look that I lasered at my husband was sharp enough to cut through the Hope diamond. Tom threw his arm around my waist and pulled me close. "Just kidding. Laurel isn't half bad as a sleuth."

Talk about a half-assed compliment. I removed Tom's arm and shifted a few feet away from him.

"I think it's kinda exciting," Lucille said. "Laurel's mom told us all about you two. To think we have celebrity detectives on the boat. It's almost like being on a reality show. We could call it *Detectives in Paradise*," she said with a bright smile.

"More like the clueless detective," mumbled Tom under his breath.

"I heard that." I swatted his firm bicep, which hurt my hand more than it did his arm.

"This reminds me of the Pink Panther movies," Lucille said. "I bet the jewel thief is a suave Cary Grant look-alike, seducing elderly women and wooing them away from their diamonds."

"I haven't observed any Cary Grant look-alikes on board," her husband replied. Just then Jimmy Bond walked into the store, surrounded by his usual entourage of elderly women. A mini-entourage in this instance since the two women were Gran and Mabel.

A black felt hat decorated with a skull and crossbones perched rakishly on Gran's curly bewigged head. She could have passed as Captain Jack Sparrow's grandmother.

"Ahoy, matey," Gran greeted me. I brushed my cheek against hers and knocked her hat onto the floor. I bent over to retrieve it.

"Let me take a wild guess," I said. "You visited Blackbeard's Castle."

"Yep. Mabel and I had a grand time. We bumped into Jimmy here on the way back and rescued him from his captor."

"What?" I asked, totally confused.

"That Peabody witch," Gran explained. "The woman has more money than sense."

Jimmy laughed at her description. "She's no match for you, Ginny."

Gran ducked her head at his compliment, and her hat popped off again. I picked it up once more and returned it to her. "Thanks, dear," she said. "Now what have you two been up to?" She eyed my left hand. "Evidently not diamond shopping."

"We took an excursion all around the island," Tom said.

"We had a wonderful time," I added. "Sierra helped arrange it."

"How's my great niece doing?" Gran asked. "Everything copacetic with her and Peabody? Did they find her missing jewelry?"

"Some of it." I saw no need to share that they found one of the items in Sierra's tote bag.

"Evelyn Peabody isn't too pleased with the situation," Jimmy said, a solemn look on his face.

"I can understand her being upset about her missing jewels," I replied. "But she can't assume that Sierra took them. That's ridiculous."

"It might sound ludicrous," Jimmy stated, "but Evelyn told me if the cruise line doesn't hand your cousin over to the authorities, then tomorrow she's marching over to the San Juan police station herself."

CHAPTER TWENTY-THREE

As soon as Tom and I returned to the ship, we headed to the hospitality deck. I intended to tell the head of security that Lucille Blodgett heard a splash at the same time that I saw someone go overboard. Tom didn't think Lucille's information would light a fire under Sanjay, but at least it would keep him apprised.

The meeting also provided an excellent excuse to find out if the officer had discovered anything further about the jewelry thefts. All I'd learned was that one of the victims wanted to incarcerate my poor cousin in the first available jail.

The lobby area was devoid of passengers. Most were probably heading to their staterooms to prepare for dinner or any of the other dozen-plus evening activities. I hoped we wouldn't have to wait too long to speak to Sanjay. Tonight, Mother and Bradford were treating our family to dinner at the Chopsticks Restaurant, proclaimed to have the best sushi and lobster on this cruise line or any cruise line.

The door to Sanjay's office was closed. We stopped at the reception desk to check if he would be tied up long.

"I have not seen Sanjay for over an hour," said a young man named Vidal who spoke with a lilt. "He left his office and has not returned." The clerk tapped a young woman on the shoulder. "Do you know when Sanjay will be back?"

She shrugged a no and went back to her computer.

"Would you ask Sanjay to contact us when he returns," Tom said to Vidal. "We'll be in our stateroom 7066 and then dining at Chopsticks at 7:00 p.m."

He took down our information and we headed for the elevator.

"I'd like to check on Sierra," I said to Tom. "Just to see if there's any good news."

"Sure. I can jump in the shower first." A sly grin crossed his face. "Don't take too long. I may need some assistance."

The elevator stopped on deck four. I gave Tom a playful pat on the butt before exiting. A hunky husband with a sense of humor. How did I get so lucky?

I strolled down the corridor planning on a quick visit with my cousin. I hoped her cabin steward had kept her well-fed. Although by now, she might need something stronger. I should have stopped at one of the bars and stocked up.

Surprisingly, no one stood guard outside Sierra's stateroom. I knocked on her door. Nothing. I pounded my fist on the solid door and only succeeded in bruising my knuckle. Did the lack of a guard mean that the head of security had relocated her to more formal and more uncomfortable accommodations before he handed her off to island authorities?

The door flew open and Sierra greeted me, a staff phone pressed against her ear. She waved me inside while she continued a conversation consisting primarily of "uh huh" and "I'll take care of it."

Relieved, I plopped down on her sofa and waited for her to complete the call.

She finished with a clipped "I'll be there soon" and turned to me. "How was St. Thomas? Did you enjoy your picnic?"

"Wonderful. Thanks for helping Tom with the preparations."

She smiled at me. "It was the least I could do. You caught a good one. I'm really happy for you."

"I'm very lucky. The man has the patience of an ark full of saints. But what's new with you? Are you no longer under 'house arrest?'"

Sierra threw her hands in the air. "I've left several messages for Sanjay to see if I'm still restricted from going out, but I haven't heard back. I've spent most of today on the phone with Zac. He's ready to pull out all of his hair."

I pictured Zac's thick sun-bleached hair. "That would be a shame. What happened?"

"Nicole Robinson, one of the female singers in tonight's production, skipped her rehearsal. Zac hasn't heard from her, but he thinks she's still in a snit over an argument she had with the other lead singer. They couldn't come to an agreement on how to split their numbers."

"The perils of show biz."

"He asked if I could take her place." Sierra rolled her eyes. "I can't decide if I should be flattered or depressed."

"Why? You have a beautiful voice."

"He wants me to sing while I swing on that high trapeze. Not only have I not performed in ages, but I have a fear of heights."

"Sounds like he needs to find another solution."

Sierra walked over to her dresser and pulled her long hair into a topknot before securing it with two silver chopsticks. "I'm removing myself from house arrest and meeting Zac at the theater. If Sanjay has a problem with that, he can track me down and send me back to my room."

"Our family is eating at Chopsticks tonight," I said. "If you get a minute come join us."

She looked at her reflection in the mirror and giggled. "I guess I'm accessorized for it. If I can, I'll stop by for a few minutes."

Shortly after 7:00 p.m. our entire family was seated in the Chopsticks restaurant at an ocean-view table for eight. A black lacquer screen with an Asian motif provided a privacy barrier from the table next to us, a good thing since our group tended to be noisy.

Due to his production issues, Zac's chair remained empty. Stan sat on my right, attempting to maintain an upbeat attitude, but I could tell that his romance on the high seas was quickly turning into an unhappy reality show episode.

I patted Stan's hand. "Once Zac gets things squared away, he should be able to spend more time with you."

"I hope that's the only problem," Stan said with a hangdog expression. "Maybe he's bored with me. I doubt I'm as exciting as the performers surrounding him."

Images of Stan performing the Argentine tango, dancing the hula, and whooping it up during Placerville's annual Wagon Train Parade flitted through my mind.

"Trust me. You couldn't be boring if you tried."

Stan's frown morphed into a wide smile. "Sweetie, you are the absolute best cheerleader. Can I buy you another drink?"

I stared at the super-sized cocktail I held in my hand, wondering how many ounces of alcohol one coconut shell could hold.

"I'll pass for now," I replied. Our server, dressed in an elegant gold brocade jacket and black pants, came over and introduced herself as Mizuki. With her large almond eyes, a porcelain complexion, dainty figure, and graceful movements, she looked like she should be waited on, rather than waiting on us.

Mizuki informed us of the chef's specials, most of which included lobster in one form or another. An excellent culinary decision. She finished taking our order just as Sierra entered the restaurant. My cousin looked like she'd sprinted all the way from the theater. Her topknot was more of a bottom knot with one lone chopstick holding up her thick hair.

Sierra paused at our table, breathing hard. I motioned for her to sit in the empty seat between Stan and my mother. She slid into the chair with the grace of a former dancer.

"You look exhausted," Mother said to her. "Can we order you a drink?"

"I think you should order her a pitcher of something," Stan quipped. "Any news about the missing prima donna?"

"More missing folks?" Mabel asked in a low roar. "This is one dangerous cruise."

Mizuki, her arms laden with heavy dishes, narrowly missed dropping one of them on Gran's head when she heard that remark.

Sierra shook her head so vehemently that her pointed metal chopstick almost grazed mother's cheek. Mother leaned away as her niece removed the dangerous accessory and let her hair fall to her shoulders.

"No reports of anyone missing other than a spoiled entertainer who refuses to show up to rehearsals or return phone calls."

"Did you agree to fill in for her?" I knew that Sierra had been the lead in her high school musicals. I still remembered her crooning to me when she babysat several decades ago.

"Nope. Zac cut one of the numbers and gave the two remaining routines to Elizabeth Axelrod, the other lead. That should entice sulky Nicole into returning to the stage for the grand finale Sunday evening."

"I have a feeling Zac will be happy when his four-week stint is over," Stan said. "I certainly will be."

"I can relate," Sierra said. "I can't wait until my eight-month contract ends. Assuming I'm still employed when this cruise is over."

"Have you heard any updates from Sanjay?" Tom asked her.

"Not a word. I'm going with no news is good news." She looked at her watch. "I only stopped by to say hi to everyone. It's back to the theater for me. Let's try to spend some quality time together tomorrow."

Sierra made the rounds, hugging each of us before she left. Our food arrived and we dove in. For a while, the table remained silent with only the clicking of our silver chopsticks and an occasional "ooh," "yum," and "try this."

When my stomach reached maximum capacity, and I was too full to eat one more bite of the buttery shellfish, I laid my chopsticks on the table.

"I never thought I'd get my fill of lobster, but I can't eat another bite."

Tom whispered in my ear. "I'd be happy to help you work it off."

I smiled and squeezed his hand. My favorite form of exercise.

We decided to skip coffee or after-dinner drinks and head to the theater to ensure decent seats. As we walked out of the restaurant toward the elevator bank, Stan pointed to a set of glass doors leading to the area designated for passengers who are willing to pay extra moolah to rent their own private cabana.

"The rich and famous have their own playground," he said. "Want to take a peek?"

"You need a reservation to even walk through that door," I warned him.

He placed his finger on his lips. "If you don't tell, I won't. I'll just be a minute." He opened the glass door and slipped inside. The area appeared to be deserted so I gathered the rich and famous were off doing other rich and famous things. No one else cared enough to check out the private area so we waited patiently for his return.

Stan reappeared in under two minutes. Ashen-faced and eyes bulging, he babbled so fast I couldn't understand a word he was saying.

"What's wrong?" I asked him.

"I...I...found someone," he said, his teeth chattering.

"Uh, oh. I told you not to sneak in there. Did you catch them in the act?"

He shook his head. "Someone's been sk...sk..."

"C'mon, Stan, spit it out," Tom encouraged him.

Stan pointed toward the inner sanctum and shouted, "Skewered!"

CHAPTER TWENTY-FOUR

Tom and Bradford followed Stan back into the private sunbathing area. I followed, too, although I lagged behind, not certain I wanted to be privy to Stan's gruesome discovery. Whatever it was.

This area of deck eleven consisted of ten private cabanas plus some additional lounge chairs scattered about. Royal blue curtains could be left open to welcome the sun, or closed for complete privacy. While wandering around, Stan said he'd slipped on a wet spot on the wooden deck. To maintain his balance, he'd grasped the closed curtain to one of the cabanas.

With a handful of heavy canvas in his hands, Stan spied the victim sprawled across a chaise lounge, blood pooling under his body.

And a silver chopstick shoved through his ear.

Stan made a hasty exit, having no idea who the dead guy was, although since he wore a uniform, Stan assumed he belonged to the crew.

Since we had previously met the victim, Tom identified him immediately.

"This isn't good," he said to me.

I nodded in agreement. Someone had killed Chief Security Officer Sanjay Radhakrishnan. This was *so* not good. But now we knew the reason why he hadn't returned Sierra's phone calls.

My mind filled with a vision of Sierra, one lone silver chopstick dangling from her blond hair. Where had the other chopstick gone?

Bile rose in my esophagus at the thought that my cousin might have murdered the security officer. I took a few deep breaths and pushed those ugly thoughts far away. Anyone in the Asian fusion restaurant could have used the extremely sharp utensil for this deadly deed.

But why would they?

Tom and Bradford debated whether to use Sanjay's own staff phone but decided not to touch anything on his person. Bradford asked the restaurant hostess to contact security and send some people to secure the scene. At first she refused, but Tom managed to convince her of the necessity.

It certainly doesn't hurt for a detective to have oodles of sex appeal.

Tom waited by the elevator for official reinforcements from the security office while Bradford guarded the victim and the crime scene. I tried to console Stan who struggled to make the image of the dead man disappear.

"I think I'm gonna toss my dinner," Stan said.

I fanned his flushed face. "Don't think about it. Try to concentrate on something pleasant."

"Oh, you mean like a relaxing Caribbean cruise?" Stan asked sarcastically. "I'm beginning to think you're a magnet for murder."

"Hey, this has nothing to do with me or my family."

"Are you sure?"

Unfortunately, I wasn't.

A chorus of elevator bells announced the arrival of a variety of officials and crew including the captain, who could have walked straight out of a Hollywood casting call for ship captains. Tall and broad-shouldered, with the chiseled features of a Nordic God. I wondered if the cruise line required their captains to look the part as well as have the ability to steer a really big boat.

Tom and Bradford introduced themselves to the captain. The three men walked through the glass doors into the private area. The captain arranged for two crew members to be posted outside the doors to ensure no one would intrude on the crime scene.

I tried to gain entry but was turned away. Guess Tom forgot to include me on the guest list.

Mother, Stan and I debated what to do next. Gran and Mabel had already gone ahead to save us seats, so they missed Stan's announcement of his horrible discovery. I doubted the captain would have appreciated the two granny gumshoes giving him advice on how to conduct an investigation.

Inquisitive diners tried to grill the crew, but the two guards maintained their silence. The three of us received a few curious looks, but we kept mum. I wondered how long it would take before the passengers learned of the crime. Once they discovered how the murder occurred, Chopsticks would either be crammed with nosy cruisers or bereft of restaurant patrons.

The elevator pinged the arrival of the ship's doctor accompanied by a female nurse. I wondered if the physician had ever encountered a murder victim on board the ship. The odds of him running into death by chopstick were most likely zero.

They threw brief glances at our trio as they crossed the carpeted elevator foyer. The guards already had the doors open for the medical personnel.

"I wonder where they stuff their stiffs," Stan asked. "I hope it's not in the freezer next to the baked Alaska."

I wrinkled my nose. "Ew, gross."

Mother shivered. "How much longer do you think Robert and Tom will be tied up?"

"Who knows?" I replied. "The captain is lucky to have two former homicide detectives on board."

"There's no chance this is simply an accident, is there?" Mother looked hopeful.

"I guess there's always a possibility the chief security officer decided to clean his ear with a chopstick instead of a Q-tip, but..."

Mother held her palm up. "Enough said. What should the three of us do? Wait for Robert and Tom or head down to the theater?"

"I almost forgot about the show," I said. "I wonder if anyone told Sierra what happened."

The elevator pinged my answer.

CHAPTER TWENTY-FIVE

Sierra stepped out of the elevator car and stopped, her full skirt swirling around her knees. Her gaze first zoomed to the cabana area before it landed on our trio. The satiny fabric of her pale blue dress swished softly as she hurried over to us.

"What's going on? My assistant said there was some sort of emergency up here." Her frightened blue eyes scrutinized us. "Is anyone hurt?"

Stan answered her first. "Yes, definitely hurt. And definitely dead."

Her face paled. "Who is it?"

I tried to ease into an explanation. "You know all those messages you left for Sanjay this afternoon?"

"Yes." Sierra looked even more puzzled.

"Well, he won't be returning any calls today."

"Or ever," Stan mumbled.

Sierra turned whiter than her pearl earrings. She slid down the wall and landed in a sitting position with her legs splayed.

I jumped out of my chair and crouched by her side.

"Are you okay?"

A tear rolled down her cheek. "I'm better than Sanjay, obviously. Give me a hand." I helped pull her to a standing position.

"So what happened? How did Sanjay hurt himself?"

"It looks like he had help."

Sierra looked confused so I elaborated. "You know those chopsticks you were wearing in your hair earlier?"

She nodded.

"Someone shoved one of them into Sanjay's ear."

Sierra wobbled on her high heels and for a minute, I thought she was going down again. I was about to explain in more detail when several people walked out of the cabana area. Tom appeared to be arguing with Captain Andriessen. My husband held strong feelings about proper homicide protocol. I took a wild guess that the captain might not agree with some of Tom's suggestions.

"Thank you for your assistance," the captain said. "My men will handle it from here."

"I really think…" Tom began, but Andriessen cut him off.

"We have everything under control." The captain nodded in my direction. "Why don't you take your family to one of our bars?" He pulled a card out of his pocket and handed it over to Tom. "Drinks are on me."

Tom looked like he was about to say something else, but he merely thanked the captain and shoved the card in his pocket.

The captain beckoned to Sierra. "Ms. Sullivan. Please come with me." When she hesitated, he followed his request with a harsher command. "That's an order."

Sierra silently trailed behind the captain into the elevator. She lifted her hand to us before she was whisked away.

I placed my hand on Tom's forearm. "What were you and the captain arguing about?"

He blew out a breath. "We hold a difference of opinion on crime scene processing. Bradford and I offered to process the evidence to the best of our ability. We're not crime scene techs, but we know our stuff. The captain declined our offer."

"How does he plan to handle it?" I asked, surprised by the captain's refusal. Not often is a ship lucky enough to have a couple of homicide detectives on board when a murder actually occurs.

"His men have closed off that area. They'll be moving the body to the ship's morgue. When we dock tomorrow in San Juan, the FBI will take over the investigation."

"That sounds reasonable to me," I said, wondering why Tom differed with the captain.

"The FBI is the proper authority for this particular situation. I'm just worried that his inexperienced crew will destroy potential evidence. The doctor could easily miss an important clue. Timing is critical in a murder investigation."

"What should we do?" I asked him.

Tom pulled the coupon out of his pocket. "Get a drink? There's not much I can do without his permission. We certainly can't interview all two thousand plus passengers to find out who had a reason to kill Sanjay."

"Don't forget the crew," I added. "That's eight hundred more."

"From what I've read," Bradford chimed in, "it isn't that unusual for a shipboard assault to be brushed under the carpet, or in this case, the keel. The last thing the cruise line wants is for passengers to worry about a murderer on board."

"So you don't anticipate any announcements over the ship's intercom warning the passengers about chopstick-wielding serial killers?" asked Stan.

"I doubt this was the work of a serial killer," Tom said. "Using the chopstick as a weapon seems like a spur of the moment decision. It's possible the person might not have intended to murder Sanjay. It could have been an accident gone wrong."

"Maybe they just wanted to make a point," Stan said. I groaned at his puny pun, but his comment made me contemplate who might have had a beef with the security officer.

Unfortunately, I could only think of one person who had the means, the motive and the opportunity.

My cousin.

CHAPTER TWENTY-SIX

After one round of drinks in the Queen's Lounge, Mother and Robert decided their evening had been exciting enough. Stan left to go backstage and track down Zac.

I'd hoped to run into Sierra at one of the events she normally hosted, but her assistant appeared in her place. When asked about Sierra's whereabouts, she said my cousin was tied up on an official matter.

Tied up was one thing. Shackled in handcuffs would be a completely different scenario.

Tom and I walked silently down the corridor leading to our stateroom. Once inside, he said, "A dollar for your thoughts."

I smiled. "You've upped the purchase price."

He bent over and kissed the top of my head. "Knowing you, there are at least one hundred thoughts circling around."

I plopped onto the bed and picked up the cute animal our steward had left on the covers. Every night he turned a towel into some type of creature. Tonight I cradled an elephant in my arms. Or a dolphin. Marcel, our steward, was still interning in towel creation.

"Despite the captain's decision to keep Sierra in her stateroom, Sanjay didn't believe she was the thief. He told me he planned to continue investigating the jewelry and money thefts. Maybe he got too close to the thief, and he, or she, decided to get rid of him."

"You can't rule out Sanjay being killed in a moment of passion," Tom replied. "That's always a possibility."

I bounced off the bed. "That would open up an entirely new field of suspects."

"A baseball-sized field of suspects," Tom said. "And without the captain's permission, there isn't much we can do about it."

"Don't forget that I can be very enterprising."

"And so can I." Tom wrapped his arms around me and leaned in for one soul-searching kiss. "And there's someone I want to investigate right now."

Heck. You only get one honeymoon. The suspects could wait until morning.

After a nightmare-filled night dreaming about chopstick-wielding murderers, it was a relief to wake up in my stateroom next to my husband.

The clock read 7:15 a.m. so I slid out of bed, crossed the room and opened the heavy drapes covering the balcony windows. Our stateroom must have been facing east because the sun literally blinded me as I stepped out onto the balcony. I could see the sprawling buildings comprising the city of San Juan. Farther down the pier, another enormous ship approached the dock.

I wondered how the captain planned on conducting a murder investigation without the help of the chief security officer. Did they hand the poor victim off to the FBI, say *sayonara* and sail off into the sunset?

Would Sanjay's murder end up as front-page news or literally become buried at sea?

I had a feeling the captain would prefer to quash any notification to the public, but that didn't suit me at all. Especially if Sanjay's death was a result of him trying to prove that my cousin wasn't a thief.

Speaking of Sierra, I wondered if she was awake by now. Even though the ship had already docked, passengers were not allowed to disembark until eight. I dialed her stateroom, and she picked up immediately.

"How are you doing?" I spoke softly so I wouldn't wake Tom. "I was worried they'd accuse you of killing Sanjay."

She laughed, but her tone sounded more bitter than joyous. "If it were up to the captain, he would call Sanjay's death an accident, tell the crew to keep quiet, and get on with the cruise."

"Do you think he'll try to do that? And how does someone accidentally kill themselves with a chopstick?"

"What does Tom think?" she asked. "He and your stepfather spent a few minutes there before Captain Andriessen arrived. Did they retrieve any clues?"

I stared at my sleeping sleuth. "None that he disclosed to me. What are your plans for the day? Are you allowed off the ship?"

"I don't know. The captain didn't command me to stay on board so I suppose I am. Did you and Tom sign up for any of the excursions?"

"The rest of the family chose the jungle trip, but Tom and I wanted to see the forts so we signed up for the city tour. Although knowing Tom, he'll offer his services to the investigation, assuming the captain is interested in his help."

Tom's eyes blinked open at the sound of his name. He grabbed my hand, the one not holding the phone, and pulled me onto the bed. The warm kisses he planted on my neck turned my mind to mush.

"Sleeping Beauty is awake, Sierra. Let me call you back in a few minutes."

"I won't hold my breath." She chuckled and hung up.

Smart woman, my cousin.

A little over an hour later, Tom and I, our arms wrapped around one another, entered the elevator and pushed the button for deck eleven. Tom wanted to check if any law enforcement agencies had arrived yet.

We stepped out of the elevator to find most of the floor cordoned off with caution tape. Two men dressed in pristine white stopped us from going any further.

Tom explained that he had helped secure the scene the previous evening. He reached into his wallet and pulled out his Homeland Security credentials. The shorter of the two men took the card over to a tall, slender man dressed in a dark suit. He was directing a couple of guys wearing navy jackets. The trio looked completely out of place on the ship.

"Looks like the FBI is already on the scene," Tom said. "I'm impressed."

"Maybe they won't need your help." I couldn't decide whether I was relieved or disappointed that our assistance wouldn't be needed.

"That's fine with me. More time for exploring the islands and …" Tom's voice trailed off as the man in the suit approached us.

"Matt Patterson," he introduced himself. "I'm the agent in charge. The captain informed me that two homicide detectives were the first to arrive at the scene."

"Technically, our friend Stan Winters stumbled upon Sanjay first," I corrected the agent.

Patterson's pale silver eyes narrowed at my comment. "And why was your friend nosing around this area? I understand it closes at five every evening."

"Stan was curious where the more well-to-do passengers spend their time," Tom explained. "The door was unlocked so he wandered in and strolled around. He slipped on what we discovered was most likely the victim's blood and almost landed on top of the man."

"Was this friend of yours acquainted with the chief security officer?" the agent asked.

"No, but we were," I said. "We were helping him with other investigations."

The agent's eyes turned into slivers of gray as he pondered my comment. "Other investigations? Care to elaborate?"

We spent the next few minutes explaining the recent spate of thefts, although I neglected to mention Mrs. Peabody's accusation against Sierra. If the FBI agent was interested in the missing jewels, he could find out the details for himself.

"We also contacted Sanjay when I saw someone fall overboard," I added.

Now the agent really looked confused. "This is the first I've heard about someone going overboard. The captain didn't mention anything about it to me."

I started to respond, but Tom placed a palm on my forearm. "My wife thought she saw someone fall overboard our first night on the ship. No one has reported anyone missing nor did anyone else see someone fall into the sea. Sanjay assumed my wife had too much to drink that evening."

"I wasn't drunk," I protested. "Merely tipsy."

Tom and the agent exchanged looks. I knew no one believed me, and it was starting to tick me off.

"Maybe Sanjay's murder was tied to the missing person," I suggested.

"Right," said Patterson, his face devoid of expression. "I'll keep your theory in mind." He turned to Tom. "Would you care to go over your movements last night when you secured the scene?"

"I'd be happy to help," Tom said. The agent led Tom behind the caution tape. I tried to follow, but Patterson stopped me.

Tom must have noticed the steam coming out of my ears. "Why don't you have breakfast with your family while I help Agent Patterson?" he suggested.

Fine. I had my own investigatory methods. And they involved chatting with the first person on the scene.

Stan.

CHAPTER TWENTY-SEVEN

I dialed Stan the minute I returned to our stateroom. His voice sounded groggy as he mumbled a hello into the receiver.

"Wake up, sleepyhead. The FBI is on the scene," I told him. That statement worked better than an alarm clock.

"What? Do they want to speak with me? Am I under arrest?"

"You're not under arrest, but they may want to talk to you since you made the discovery. Tom's with them now. I offered to help, but they declined my offer."

"It's their loss, sweetie. Do you want to have a confab?"

"Yep. Let's meet at the Lido Café. I could use a waffle pick-me-up right now."

"Make that two, with strawberries and extra whipped cream on mine. I'll see you in ten minutes or less."

Stan's ten minutes turned into thirty, exactly the amount of time it took me to get to the front of the made-to-order waffle line. But it was worth it. One strawberry-topped waffle for Stan and an apple waffle with cinnamon whipped cream slathered across all four squares for me.

Good thing we booked that city tour of San Juan because my breakfast consisted of a full day's worth of calories.

In between bites, I updated Stan on what I knew. That took almost twenty seconds. Now it was my turn to grill him.

"Tom and Bradford secured the scene, and they certainly have more expertise than I do, but do you remember seeing anything unusual? Besides the body, that is."

Stan grimaced and pushed his plate away. "Thanks for ruining my appetite. I may never eat Moo Goo Gai Pan again. Who knew a chopstick could be so deadly?"

"Now that you mention it, you're right. It's not like a chopstick would be someone's first choice of a weapon."

"Or even in the top ten. So does that mean it wasn't a premeditated death? Who would have access to a silver chopstick other than the servers, cooks and diners at the restaurant last night?"

"Any woman who is too lazy to do her hair," my cousin explained as she slid into the empty chair beside me. My eyes opened wide as I turned to look at her. "I know I'm a suspect so I might as well admit it." She picked up the unused fork from the place setting next to mine and speared a bite of my waffle.

"Yum," she said. "The first thing I've eaten since lunch yesterday. Captain Andriessen does not serve hors d'oeuvres when he's cross-examining his staff."

"Does the captain seriously consider you a suspect?" I asked.

"I'm not sure, but he definitely suspects me of being a PITA," she replied.

I chuckled. "You were kind of a "pain in the ass" back in the days when you babysat me."

"Oh, and you were such a model child? Remember when you painted all over my history homework?"

"Hey, I was a budding Picasso," I defended myself. "At least you're not under house arrest any longer."

"For now. I guess the FBI took over the investigation of Sanjay's mur..." Sierra's eyes suddenly teared up. "I still can't believe Sanjay is gone. I wonder if he encountered the jewel thief. Maybe accused the person of the thefts, and the guy decided to get rid of his accuser. I sure hope the FBI can figure it out. I know this cruise line will do everything they can to delay the passengers from finding out what happened."

"Then they should have told the FBI to dress in flowered shirts and Bermuda shorts instead of pinstripes," I said. "The agent Tom and I met this morning might as well have had FBI tattooed across his forehead."

Sierra looked around. "Where is your hubby? You two are usually joined at the hip."

I blushed because that description would have been absolutely on target an hour earlier.

"The agent asked Tom to go over the crime scene with him." I frowned. "But they didn't ask me to help."

"I think this is one mystery you better stay far, far away from," Sierra said to me. "This person is dangerous. And not afraid to kill. I'd be devastated if anything happened to you."

I mouthed a thanks to her.

"I certainly won't be loitering in any 'private' areas for the remainder of the cruise," said Stan.

"Make sure you're with friends or family at all times," Sierra warned me.

"Aye, aye, Madame Cruise Director." Sierra giggled when I saluted her, although her giggles quickly morphed into choking. I passed my glass of water to her. She took a sip before she looked up and spoke to someone standing behind my chair.

"Hello, Captain Andriessen."

CHAPTER TWENTY-EIGHT

My husband accompanied the captain. I slid over so Tom could join me in the booth. Captain Andriessen chose to remain standing.

"Thank you for lending the services of your husband, Mrs. Hunter," the captain said to me.

"Any time," I replied. "My services are available as well."

The captain looked startled, so rather than have him contemplate what kind of services I was selling, I explained, "In our hometown, I'm also known for my investigating skills."

"Laurel is so famous she may open her own agency," Stan added, winking at me.

"Yeah, ONE GAL AND HER GRANNY detective agency," cracked a voice I knew too well. I greeted Gran and Mabel and invited them to join us.

"Well, aren't you a tall drink of water." Gran batted her few remaining lashes at the captain. "If I were a half century younger...."

The captain flushed then turned to Tom. "Please keep our discussion to yourself. We do not wish to alarm any of the passengers. I hope you all enjoy your visit to San Juan today." He politely ducked his head then strode off.

Mabel stared at the captain's retreating back before discreetly shouting, "What's he talking about? Alarm who?"

"He doesn't want us jabbering about that guy who lost his hearing," Gran said, "forever."

When Mabel continued to look confused, Gran illustrated by poking a finger in her ear. "That security guy—the one who got stabbed," Gran explained. "I think he wants us to keep mum about it."

Good luck with that, I thought, as heads turned in our direction. Luckily, most of the passengers were more interested in their breakfast than our conversation, although Lucille and Glenn, followed by Sharon and Deborah paused at our table.

"I saw the captain stop by," Lucille said. "Did y'all catch the jewel thief yet?"

"We're not investigating the thefts anymore," I replied. "Just trying to stay out of trouble."

"Hah!" said Mabel. "Trouble follows this family like a stealth missile."

"Nonsense," Gran said to her friend. "We just have a nose for murder."

"There's been a murder? On top of the jewel thefts?" Sharon asked, her mouth a big red-lipped "O." "Who? And why haven't we heard anything about it from the captain?"

Everyone started speaking at once. If I had a whistle, I would have blown it. Fortunately, an announcement came over the intercom telling the passengers they could now disembark from the boat and reminding everyone to return by six this evening.

Tom slid out of the booth and quietly explained to the group that a crew member had died unexpectedly and an official investigation was being conducted. There was no need for anyone to be upset.

"I still think the passengers should be warned. We could all be in danger," Deborah said. She glanced worriedly at her college friend, who was again filling in for her husband.

"What if there's a serial killer?" Glenn chimed in, his hands anxiously stroking his beard. "Another person could be attacked at any time."

"Don't forget that person Laurel saw pushed overboard," Lucille reminded her husband. "I swear this cruise is making me more nervous than a possum at a bloodhound convention."

"No one has fallen overboard that we know of, and I'm certain the crew member's death is an isolated incident." Tom tried to reassure everyone before switching to diversionary tactics, something he was a master of. "Do you have any excursions planned for today? My wife and I are looking forward to touring the city."

"We signed up for the El Yunque tour." Lucille sent an anxious glance at her husband. "Do you think it's safe to take the bus trip to the jungle? Someone could be waiting to hack us to pieces with a machete."

"You don't need to worry about any axe-wielding murderers," Stan informed them. "But if you run across someone holding a chopstick, you should definitely run in the opposite direction."

Lucille and Glenn, their faces pale, mumbled something about cancelling their jungle trip for something tamer. I slipped out of the booth. It didn't look like anyone would miss me so I was free to multitask.

No one can combine sleuthing and eating like I can.

The chef behind the made-to-order omelet station stood waiting for customers. I strolled over, picked up a plate and stared at the options available. If I chose everything they offered, my omelet would be almost as big as I am. The dark-haired chef smiled while I pondered.

Little did he know I was pondering something other than my breakfast selection.

I pointed to an assortment of veggies and cheddar cheese. While the chef grilled my veggies, I decided to grill him.

"Everyone seems to be talking about, you know…" I wasn't certain if the crew knew about Sanjay's murder, but this was one way to find out.

He dumped some egg mixture into the pan and turned the flame higher. I couldn't tell if he intentionally ignored me or if he was clueless about the crime that had occurred the previous evening.

I gave it one more shot. "Is the crew concerned about what happened last night?"

The chef indicated I should pass my plate to him. He scooped the omelet out of the pan, placed it on my dish and leaned forward.

"We have been told not to discuss certain matters," he said.

"Matters like…?" I still couldn't tell if we were on the same wavelength.

He pointed to his ear. That was enough for me.

"Does the crew have any idea who did it?"

He shrugged. "I did not know him well, but there are others who did."

An enigmatic statement if I ever heard one.

"Who?"

He picked up his carving knife and pointed at the next buffet station where a beautiful young Asian woman was dishing out Eggs Benedict.

"Her?" I asked, recognizing Mizuki, our server from Chopsticks.

He nodded.

What was it Hercule Poirot always used to say? When you're running out of suspects it may be time to *cherchez les femmes.*

CHAPTER TWENTY-NINE

My husband grabbed me by my arm and pulled me from the Benedict line before I could question Mizuki.

I protested but his stomach complained even louder. "I haven't eaten yet, and I can't handle any more questions," he said. "Would you share your omelet with me?"

"Only if you promise to share everything the FBI agent told you."

He hesitated and I waved the fragrant omelet under his nose. "You're on," he said.

I grabbed an extra set of utensils, and we walked out of the Lido Café to the adjoining outdoor deck. A couple of people relaxed in the bubbling spa, and a few others sat at the bar, but it appeared that most passengers were already exploring San Juan or were in their staterooms getting ready for a tour. We chose a table near the bow of the boat and away from any eavesdroppers.

Tom dug into the omelet with relish. I sat quietly, figuring it would be easier to quiz my spouse once his stomach was full.

"Good stuff." He pointed to the omelet with his fork. "Don't you want any?"

"Glad you approve of my selections. My sole reason for ordering the omelet was to find out if the chef and the crew were aware of Sanjay's demise."

"And?"

My husband never wasted words when he could get by with one.

"And the chef not only knew about the murder, he also indicated a woman who may have been involved with Sanjay."

Tom wiped his lips with his napkin. "Nice work," he said, placing his newly-tanned hand over mine. "Maybe we should open up our own agency."

I laughed. "What would Gran think of that idea?"

"She'd be the first to apply for a position with us. Let's keep that thought on the back burner for now."

"Nice try distracting me. Now what did you learn from the feds?"

"They won't know the exact cause of death until a medical examiner can do an autopsy, but there was a puncture to the carotid artery as well as other," Tom pointed to his right ear, "damage."

"Do they have any suspects yet?"

"After we discovered the victim, I looked around to see what type of camera coverage the ship maintained in that area. When we met with Sanjay Monday morning, he mentioned the lack of cameras on individual balconies, corridors and certain exclusive areas. I guessed that the cabana area would fall under that description and I was correct. There were no cameras in the immediate vicinity."

"Darn."

"But there are two cameras directed toward the elevators. The feds intend to scroll through all the footage on that deck, including anyone who entered or exited an elevator."

"That could entail hundreds of diners. Even us."

"That's how this job works most of the time. Staring at countless screens for lengthy periods, looking for that one eventful moment that can solve a crime."

"Was there any good news?" I asked him.

"Yes. One of the security guys the captain left behind noticed something sparkling under one of the lounge chairs in the open area."

"Sparkling like a diamond?" Now I was excited. My jewel-thief-turned-killer theory just got some traction.

"A small diamond stud. It could have belonged to the thief. Or the killer. Or anyone who frequented that area during this cruise. Male or female."

"So we still have an Olympic-sized pool of suspects."

Tom nodded.

"So what's our next step?" I asked.

He shoved his plate away and smiled.

"Touring the city of San Juan. Isn't that one of the reasons we came on this cruise?"

Well, yes. Visiting Caribbean islands was one of the reasons we chose a cruise for our honeymoon. And to enjoy eight glorious nights together. Uninterrupted by children, work and dead bodies.

I guess two out of three isn't bad.

CHAPTER THIRTY

The tour of San Juan proved enjoyable as well as enlightening. I learned that San Juan was the second oldest capital city in the Americas, founded by European explorers three hundred years before the Gold rush hit my part of the world. Amazing stuff.

Between the hills and cobblestone-lined streets, I was grateful I'd selected a good pair of walking shoes. Comfort before beauty was my motto.

So many people had signed up for this particular excursion that three busloads of cruise passengers were driven around the city, stopping at various historical sights. Whether the ship planned it or not, all three buses ultimately ended up at Castillo San Cristobal, one of the two San Juan forts, whose construction began in 1625 and was finally completed in 1783.

Although the rest of my family were off on a half-day trip exploring El Yunque, a tropical jungle located about forty miles from the city, I recognized several of the tourists strolling along the sidewalk headed toward the fort. Glenn and Lucille must have cancelled their jungle trip in favor of the city tour. They chatted with Sharon and Deborah. I wondered what Deborah's husband was doing today since as usual, he wasn't with his wife.

Maybe their key to a successful marriage was never spending time together.

I thought I saw Danielle pushing her husband's wheelchair up ahead. I shifted to the right for a better look and ended up stepping on someone's foot.

"I'm so sorry." When I found out whose foot I'd stomped on, I was even sorrier.

"You again." Evelyn Peabody threw a disgusted look at me before peering over my shoulder. "Where's the rest of your thieving family? Out shoplifting?"

"Are you always this disagreeable?" I asked her before I could stop myself.

Her companion covered her mouth with her right hand, but not before Mrs. Peabody and I both heard her muffled laughter.

"Well!" Mrs. Peabody replied. If I thought my comment would render her speechless, I was immediately proven wrong.

"This cruise line needs to be more aggressive in monitoring undesirable passengers," she said. "It looks like they'll let just about anybody aboard this ship."

We finally agreed on something. My suave hubby stepped in before I could alienate the woman even more. "Where are you two lovely ladies from?"

Mrs. Peabody's attention shifted to my handsome husband, and the old biddy's frozen demeanor thawed a few degrees.

"My sister and I live in Vancouver."

"A lovely city," he replied. "I've visited there several times. You must be enjoying a break from your cold winters." Tom continued to chat with the two women as they headed to the fort. I trudged along behind them, not interested in conversing with Mrs. Peabody any more than necessary.

Plus the view of my hubby's posterior was far preferable to looking at Mrs. Peabody's yapping mouth.

"He's like a young James Bond, isn't he?" said a strong baritone from a few feet behind me. I slowed down so the elderly man could catch up. "Reminds me of myself at that age."

The original James Bond winked at me. I imagined he must have been quite the charmer fifty years ago. Upon reflection, Jimmy was still a very personable man.

"If we walk faster, we can catch up to Mrs. Peabody," I said.

Jimmy reduced his speed to slightly faster than a snail's crawl. "There's no hurry, my dear. Those two ladies have received more than enough attention from me."

"I hope they're nicer to you than they have been to my cousin. Or anyone in my family, for that matter." I gazed at Tom's disappearing back. "Although my husband seems to be winning them over."

"Your Tom is quite the dashing dick."

I laughed. "And that's quite the compliment. Who told you Tom was a detective?"

Jimmy's bright blue eyes sparkled with humor. "I keep my ear to the deck, so to speak. Rumor has it the captain utilized the skills of two former policemen experienced in homicide investigation. I recalled a comment your grandmother made the other night at dinner and concluded that your husband must be one of the detectives."

"You're not a bad detective yourself," I said. "Are you a retired bobby? Or a spy, like your namesake, with one of those mysterious MI5 or MI6 departments?"

"No, no, nothing like that. I will admit to thirty years with Lloyds of London."

"Now that sounds glamorous."

"The words glamorous and insurance should never be used in the same sentence, my dear. It provided a comfortable living and a nice pension for me to enjoy the occasional holiday." He pointed to where Tom stood waiting for us to catch up. "Your husband awaits."

We sped up our pace and met Tom at the entrance to the national park.

"Hi," I panted, "honey." I desperately looked around for a water fountain since I'd forgotten to fill my own water bottle before we left the ship. "Do you have any water?" I croaked.

"What's mine is yours," Tom said. He reached into his backpack and pulled out his own bottle. I took him at his word and swallowed the majority of the refreshing liquid.

"Thanks, now I feel normal again."

"Honey, you'll never be normal to me."

I frowned at him, and he swung his arm around my waist. "And that's what I love about you." He turned to Jimmy. "What were you two gabbing about?"

"Just getting to know one another," I said. "Jimmy used to work for Lloyds of London."

The two men scrutinized each other. "Ever work on any diamond thefts?" Tom asked him.

"Primarily actuarial tables. Dreary stuff. Nothing that would interest a homicide detective." Jimmy smiled. "But tell me more about the ship's latest mystery. I understand you're consulting for the cruise line."

"That's news to me," Tom replied. "My former partner and I just happened to be among the first passengers on the scene. We did the best we could to maintain everything before the feds took over. I doubt there is anyone on the ship who hasn't heard the news by now."

"As a frequent cruiser, be forewarned that shipboard gossip travels faster than norovirus."

I made a face at Jimmy's comment. I was about to ask if he'd heard of any norovirus outbreaks on board the *Celebration* when Mrs. Peabody called out to him. "Yoo-hoo, Jimmy. We saved a spot for you."

Jimmy muttered "brilliant" under his breath although I gathered he meant just the opposite. He ambled down the path and joined the two women.

"Looks like I've been replaced," Tom said. "And by a senior citizen no less."

"I can explore the fort by myself if you'd rather spend time with your new fan club." I pointed at Mrs. Peabody and her sister.

"No, no, no. Kidding."

I plopped a kiss on his cheek. "Besides, no one can replace you."

"He's one smooth gent, though." Tom's gaze moved to Jimmy Bond and his companions. "I bet he's had a far more interesting past than he let on."

"I got that impression, too."

"Don't let his age or his charming facade deceive you," Tom warned me. "I believe your grandmother referred to Jimmy as one sharp cookie. I would watch out for him if I were you."

I promised to heed Tom's advice. If there is one thing I've learned in life, it's that cookies can be far more dangerous than you think.

CHAPTER THIRTY-ONE

With so many people converging at once, it took some time to pass through the entrance gate to Castillo San Cristobal. My Spanish consisted of only five words: hello, please, thank you, cat, and the most important of all, bathroom. I was pleased to see signs for both female and male *baños* near the entrance.

The bathroom was large and filled to capacity with women on a mission. Once I completed my own, I washed my hands. As I reached for a paper towel from the dispenser, my wet palm bumped into another one.

"I'm sorry," I said, before looking up and recognizing the cruise veteran. "Oh, hi, Margaret, I haven't seen you for a few days. Is Fred feeling better?"

"No," she pouted, "he's still laid up in our stateroom."

"What a shame. Have they officially diagnosed him with," I moved closer and lowered my voice, "Norovirus?"

She shook her head so vigorously that her sunglasses almost flipped off her silver hair and into the trash can. "I'm sure it's just food poisoning or something."

"Has the doctor looked at him?"

"Fred didn't want to bother the ship's doctor. He'll be fine. Nice to see you again, Laurel."

She threw her paper towel in the wastebasket and dashed out the door. Margaret certainly was in a hurry to tour the fort. She also seemed amazingly calm about her poor husband being laid up for the majority of the cruise.

Unbelievably calm. If Tom were sick and stuck in our stateroom, I'd be by his side, nursing him or trying to cheer him up. But Margaret blithely bounced from one cruise excursion to another.

One of the stall doors opened, and Danielle walked out.

"*Bonjour*, Laurel." She paused, possibly noting my confused expression. "You are okay?"

"Yes, just thinking about Margaret. Her husband has been sick, and I was curious how he was doing. But she doesn't seem worried about him. Are you and Pierre enjoying the excursion?"

"Yes, this fort is, what you say, handicap okay for persons needing wheelchair."

"Is Jacques also with you?" I asked for no reason other than being a nosy Nancy.

"No, he stayed on board. Just my sweet husband and I." She threw her towel in the wastebasket and said "*au revoir*."

I walked out of the restroom thinking about the difference between Danielle's thoughtfulness toward her elderly husband, as opposed to Margaret's indifferent attitude to her sick spouse. I was so deep in thought that I walked past my own husband.

Tom tapped me on the shoulder. "Missing anything? Or anyone?"

"Sorry, sweetie. I carried on a rather unusual conversation with Margaret. Remember the older Daytona Beach couple we ate dinner with the first night?"

"Sure. Nice folks. What's the problem?"

"Well, Margaret doesn't seem to think there is a problem. Her husband is sick, and he's been cooped up in their stateroom since the first night. They haven't called the doctor yet, and she doesn't seem to feel any compunction about gallivanting all over the place while he suffers in his cabin."

"Don't you think you're being a little melodramatic?" Tom asked. "Maybe she feels that since they've paid for the cruise, one of them should enjoy it."

"She acted oddly. Plus the minute I began to question her, she practically ran out of the restroom."

"Next time you decide to pry, try to find a more luxurious venue," he teased.

"Well, the next time you get sick, don't expect me to sit by your bedside spoon-feeding you chicken soup," I said in a huff.

Tom clasped my hand and we headed for the tunnel leading to the upper level. I remained silent, pondering whether I was overreacting to my conversation with Margaret or following my intuition. Sometimes my intuition is incredibly accurate. Other times, it has led me straight into the arms of a killer.

I hate when that happens!

The centuries-old tunnel wound up, down and around. We passed an ancient dungeon with beautifully carved graffiti on the stone walls. After what felt like a mile trek, we finally reached the main viewing area at the top of the fort. The bright sun blinded me, and I shaded my eyes while I took in my surroundings. Tom discovered a large detailed drawing of the Castillo hanging on a wall. The sketch even included the elevator that somehow had eluded my notice.

We walked along the perimeter and peeked into rooms depicting the living quarters when the fort was in use. Uniforms from 250 years ago as well as fully-set dining tables and bedchambers helped us to imagine a soldier's life at that time.

With the fort at 150 feet above sea level, a full harbor and city view spread out below us. We strolled over to the ramparts to check out the old cannons and ran into Rick and Claire.

"Have you tried lifting one of these cannon balls?" Tom asked Rick. "I read they're a mere two hundred pounds each."

Rick chuckled. "I work out as often as I can, but I think I'll skip the cannonball toss today."

"You better," Claire scolded her husband. "We don't want you to strain your back again."

"I threw mine out two months ago merely by sneezing during …" I paused trying to come up with something other than the actual answer—sex.

"Backs can be fragile." Tom rescued me from any additional faux pas. "And we don't want to spoil the cruise."

"This cruise has already been ruined for me," said Deborah who had come up behind us. "I feel like I'm looking over my shoulder all the time, wondering when a killer will strike next." The plump worry-wart peered over her shoulder to reinforce her point.

"You have nothing to worry about," Tom reassured her. "It's far more likely that the motive for the officer's death was a personal one."

"Love, money or revenge," I said emphatically. "Isn't that what you always tell me, honey?"

Tom shook his head. "Uh, no."

"Oh, maybe that's what they always say on *Law and Order*. You have to admit those are the primary reasons behind most murders."

"Except when it's a sociopath," Deborah added.

"There is that," Tom agreed. "But please don't let this isolated incident ruin the cruise for you."

Claire shivered. "I feel like a ghost just walked over my grave."

I thought about the men who had lived and died within these castle walls. Did their spirits wander through the tunnels late at night?

Ghosts I could deal with.

It was the live killers who worried me more.

CHAPTER THIRTY-TWO

On that somber note, our group split up and went various directions. Tom wanted to check out the lookout towers located at the corners of the outer walls. A sign pointed to the *Garita del Diablo,* the Sentry Box of the Devil. Legend said that guards on duty in that particular *garita* would suddenly disappear, as if they were spirited away by the devil.

Or maybe the soldiers found a discreet way to go AWOL. Tom walked off to ask a question of one of the docents. I decided to take some photos of the magnificent view with my new camera. I snapped some wide-angle shots of the old buildings painted in vivid shades of pink, yellow, blue and green, and gardens equally brilliant in color.

I zoomed in on one shot of a colorful café decorated in a parrot motif. Two men conversed at a small table. When the dark-haired one looked up, I recognized Jacques, the physical therapist. I waved at him, but apparently he didn't recognize the crazy woman flapping her arms at him from the top of the fort

Now where was my husband? I scanned the area and found Tom still conversing with a docent. I crossed the enormous expanse to the opposite side to snap shots of the harbor and the dry moats that comprised the defensive network. Margaret was also taking photos, so I stopped to chat with her.

Or grill her. It all depends on your interpretation.

"Hi, Margaret," I said. She must not have heard me come up behind her because she almost dropped her camera over the parapet at my greeting.

"Sorry, I didn't mean to startle you. This is such a great vista point for taking photos of the city and harbor, isn't it?"

"Yes." She turned to leave. I stepped in her path and tried to think of an approach that would get me some answers without scaring her away.

"I feel awful about Fred missing out on everything. I'd like to drop off a get well card to perk him up. Maybe a bottle of rum for when he's recovered. What's your stateroom number?"

"Oh, that's lovely, dear. What a kind thought." She slowly backed away from me. "But you needn't bother. I must be off. Don't want to miss the bus." Before I could protest, Margaret zipped away and stopped to talk to Glenn and Lucille.

"What did you do to scare the lovely Margaret off?" asked Jimmy who'd magically appeared at my side. The man was as light-footed as a cat.

I turned to face him. "I merely professed my concern for her sick husband, and she got all weird on me."

"Some people are more reserved than others," Jimmy suggested.

"Meaning I'm not?" I grinned as I said it. Jimmy was probably right. "I guess I need to work on my investigative, I mean, my conversational skills."

"It can take decades of practice," he replied. "So what have you learned so far? Any thoughts as to the killer? Or the jewel thief?"

"I'm only an amateur sleuth. My primary goal is to make sure my cousin isn't charged with any crime."

"Be careful, my dear. Sleuthing can occasionally lead to a deadly result." The quiet was suddenly shattered by Mrs. Peabody's foghorn voice. She and her sister scurried to his side.

"Jimmy, we've been looking all over for you," she bleated.

"Ah, of course you were." He threw out his elbow and she

tucked her arm in his. "Lovely chatting with you, Laurel." He winked as the threesome walked away.

I peeked at my watch. Our tour group still had half an hour before we needed to reconvene. I swiveled my head left and right but couldn't spot my husband anywhere in the viewing area. Now where had he gone off to?

Then I remembered he wanted to check out the devil's parapet. I could snap unobstructed photos of the harbor from that angle. I headed for the turret closest to the sea, expecting to find my missing husband when I arrived.

The ancient turret was empty. As I gazed at the harbor far below, an ominous gray cloud suddenly blocked the sun, leaving the narrow tower in complete shadow. I'm only five-feet-four inches tall but long-legged. The sentries from years gone by must have been on the short side because the wall around the tower barely seemed high enough to provide a sufficient barrier to keep someone from falling through the large opening.

And it was a very long fall to the ground.

I couldn't resist snapping shots of the panoramic scenery below me. The wind whistled through the turret, and a thick strand of hair fell into my eyes, temporarily stabbing my cornea. I closed my eyelid and gently rubbed my eye, trying to get my contact lens settled. Normally I would remove it and put it in my case, but with such a strong wind, it might blow out of my hand and over the parapet. And I'd become accustomed to seeing out of both eyes.

A firm hand pressed against my back. Tom had finally arrived. Maybe he could block the wind while I got my contact lens settled. I relaxed, expecting him to begin nuzzling my neck.

Suddenly I was shoved against the short barrier wall. I cried out as my camera flew out the open window. What was Tom thinking? This wasn't like him at all. If he didn't stop pushing me, I would be following my camera over the wall, falling 150 feet to my certain death. A low voice whispered in my ear, "*la curiosidad mato al gato*."

"What?" I said before a searing pain shattered all conscious thought.

Then everything went black.

CHAPTER THIRTY-THREE

I woke with my head cradled in my husband's lap, his anxious brown eyes peering down at me. I could tell from the pain pinballing through every nerve in my head that I was still alive.

"What happened?" I asked.

"That's what we all want to know," he said. "Did you trip and hit your head? Do you remember anything?"

I shook my head, which turned out to be a very bad idea.

"Maybe we should save the questions for when she's back on the boat," said a familiar voice.

"Sierra?" This time I braved the pain and forced myself into a sitting position, my head resting against a hard surface. I glanced down at my shirt. Rust-colored blobs dotted it like a Jackson Pollock painting. My bangs felt glued to my forehead. When I attempted to brush them aside, a sticky substance covered my fingers.

A wave of nausea engulfed me, and I fought hard to keep from fainting. What exactly had happened to me? When I glanced down, I noticed my purse beside me with some of its contents scattered around. I gathered everything up before remembering. "My camera is gone. It fell over the parapet."

"Oh, my goodness. She's been mugged," said Sharon. "And in broad daylight. They warned us to be careful."

"Do you think you can walk," Sierra asked me. "Or would you rather go to the hospital?"

"She should certainly see a physician. How's your noggin, dear?"

This time I slowly lifted my head to answer my British friend. "Just tip-top, Jimmy."

He chuckled. "She still has her sense of humor."

"Honey, what do you want to do?" asked Tom. "We can have them call an ambulance and take you to a hospital. You could have a concussion or other injuries."

The long drawn out peal of a cruise ship about to depart made my decision for me. I looked at my watch. "Do we have time to make the ship?"

"If we hurry," Sierra said.

I took a deep breath. "Then let's move it, fellas."

Ninety minutes later, I sat propped against the plump pillows of our stateroom bed, surrounded by my family who seemed intent on smothering me with love. And chicken soup. I personally would have preferred a margarita.

"We never should have let you go on an expedition without us," grumbled Gran. "I could have taken out that mugger."

"Were you going to beat them off with your rubber chicken?" Mother testily asked Gran. "Laurel has a husband to protect her." She directed a frown at Tom. "Supposedly."

Tom's face turned as red as the burgundy sofa in our stateroom. "I'll never forgive myself for not being there."

I pushed myself up and clasped his hand. "It is nobody's fault. I still don't know why the mugger attacked me. Neither my clothes nor my clearance sale purse shout 'wealthy American.'"

"You didn't hear anyone come up behind you?" Bradford asked.

I started to shake my head then switched to a verbal negative. "Whoever the person was, they were as quiet as a cat."

Cat. Wait a minute. A tiny twenty-watt light bulb clicked on in my foggy brain.

"I just remembered. The mugger said something before he or she clobbered me. Something in Spanish that ended in *gato*."

Mabel and Gran looked confused. "Gotta what?"

"*Gato* means cat in Spanish," Tom said. "Why would someone talk to you about a cat and then clobber you and steal your things?"

"I don't know. I'm grateful I only had my ship's card and a little cash in my purse."

"Who else did you talk to today?" asked Stan.

"Lots of people. Three busloads of cruise passengers converged on the fort at the same time."

"I bet it was one big pink *gato*," Mabel said excitedly. "You know from that Pink Panther ring of jewel thieves. I read those guys have stolen half a billion dollars in jewels from all their heists."

"But why would they pick on me?"

"Maybe you got in their way somehow," Mabel suggested.

"Was that old biddy Peabody there?" Gran asked. "She might have bonked you just out of spite."

"Tom did an excellent job of entertaining her and her sister while Jimmy and I chatted."

Gran licked her lips. "That Jimmy is a stud muffin if I ever seen one."

"Hey," Mabel squawked. "I got dibs on Jimmy. He likes his women tall and…" she looked down at her plus-size frame "… sturdy."

"I already claimed him," Gran protested. Mother interrupted the two women. "Stop bickering. You're going to give Laurel an even bigger headache. She needs to rest."

Mother shooed everyone out of the room. The quiet sounded odd after the clamor of the past hour and a half. Tom and Jimmy had helped me walk down the long drive from the fort to the street. Since the hired buses had already returned to the ship, the men flagged down a taxi. Sierra had gone ahead to plead with the captain to wait an extra ten minutes for our arrival. He acceded, whether in sympathy for my injury, or because he needed Tom's skillset for the ongoing homicide investigation.

I closed my eyes, hoping that if I concentrated, I could remember additional details of the incident. Tom remained quiet, his fingers gently kneading my palm. Despite my painful headache, I could feel my body responding to his touch.

"So do you want to…? You know," I said to him.

"No," he said, although he grinned. "One of us has a headache, and she needs some rest."

"It could be a good distraction." I smiled then winced. Even that small movement hurt.

"I think you've had enough distractions for one day." A light tapping on the door indicated another distraction had arrived. Tom walked to the door and let Sierra in. She rushed to my side.

"Oh, Laurel, you look so pale," she said, smoothing my hair. "Maybe you should have gone to the hospital in San Juan."

"Dr. Cartwright, the ship's doctor, checked me out. He said it was a mild concussion. I only needed two stitches. And some bed rest."

"Are you certain you were mugged?" she asked. "Could this have anything to do with Sanjay's murder?"

"Why would you think that?" Tom asked Sierra. Then he turned to me. "What were you doing while the docent gave me a short tour?"

"Merely chit-chatting. You know. A little chit here and a little chat there. All very discreet."

He leveled a look at me.

"Mostly discreet," I added.

Sierra wrinkled her brow. "You might have asked the wrong person a question and set things in motion. Tom, we need to keep an eye on her from now on."

"If I know my wife, one knock on her noggin will not deter her."

"You have to admit, there's been some weird stuff happening on board this ship," I replied. "A dead security officer. A missing body. Stolen jewelry. Plus there are two husbands I haven't seen since our first night on board–Darren Abernathy and Fred Johnson."

"Good grief," Sierra said. "What happened to them?"

"That's what I've been trying to find out. We don't want another murder to occur."

"No, we don't," my husband said, his face more serious than I had ever seen it before. "And that's why you're not leaving my sight for the rest of the cruise."

I could live with that. Too bad it was easier said than done.

CHAPTER THIRTY-FOUR

When I woke the next morning, my head felt like the Island Magic band had moved their steel drums inside and taken up residency. I was grateful the ship would not be stopping at any ports today so I could rest and recuperate from my injury.

The room seemed oddly quiet. No husband singing off-key in the shower. I gazed out the window to our balcony. No sign of Tom there either.

Good grief. Not another missing husband.

The door into our stateroom opened. I froze before realizing it was Tom.

"I didn't think you'd be up so early," he said. He walked over and plopped a gentle kiss on my lips and a cup of coffee in my grateful hands. "How are you feeling?"

"You don't want to know." I gulped down half the coffee. "But this shot of caffeine should help. Did you run into anyone else?"

"I met with Captain Andriessen."

"And?"

"He contacted his main office in Los Angeles and told them about my position with Homeland Security. They authorized him to share any evidence with me. Matt Patterson, the FBI agent, also concurred, figuring the more assistance the better. Although the FBI crime scene team combed the area for evidence, they didn't come up with any suspects. And not much in the way of clues other than that one diamond stud."

"So they want you to wander around examining everyone's ears?" I chuckled at the thought of such a monumental task.

"Their own security team is handling that task via some subtle inquiries, although conceivably the earring could have remained hidden during multiple cruises. I doubt the cleaning crew scans the area like crime scene techs do. The captain asked me if I would review the video footage near the elevators that day. The FBI team had to leave on an urgent matter and didn't have time to do it."

I pouted. "So I'm on my own today?"

"Not if I can help it," Tom replied. "One of your family members will be with you at all times. I can't believe I'm saying this, but I'm grateful they all came on board."

I held mixed feelings about Tom's arranging a full-time babysitting service for me. Then he shot me a look filled with concern and love, and I realized his only thought was to keep me safe from harm.

With a vision of Gran and Mabel dressed in Rangeman black, each armed with a rubber assault chicken, I agreed to his terms.

An hour later, dressed in a knee-length cover-up with a swimsuit underneath, I accompanied Tom to Mother and Bradford's floor. Their room was almost directly above ours, although two decks higher and a couple of staterooms over. As we walked down the corridor, hand in hand, a door opened ahead. Sharon and Deborah stepped out of the room and closed the door behind them. Deborah blended into the hallway décor in her usual neutral beige, but Sharon was dressed to the hilt in gilt. It was a good thing the ship was at sea today because her hot pink sequin-studded top would set off the metal detectors.

"Hello, you two," Deborah said. "Are you feeling better, Laurel?"

"A tad. Where are you off to?" I asked.

"We're going to check out the art auction," Sharon replied. "We love collecting art. Toodles."

The two women were lucky they'd run into each other on this trip, even though it was weird that Darren never accompanied them. But then weird was becoming the new "normal" on this cruise.

Tom knocked on my mother and stepfather's door, only two down from Deborah's stateroom. Or was it Sharon's?

Bradford opened the door and we entered. Their room was identical to ours, although less messy. Mother wore a yellow shift that made me crave lemonade. She'd even managed to find a matching sunhat.

"You look better than you did yesterday," she said. "How are you feeling?"

"Hungry," I replied. "And ready for a relaxing day by the pool." I looked at Bradford. "Are you also guarding me?"

He shook his head. "Tom asked me to come along and review the video footage with him."

"Be my guest. By the way, there's a woman from a stateroom two doors down from you. I haven't seen her husband since our first night on board. She seems to spend all of her time with a girlfriend of hers. I'm wondering how come no one has seen her spouse in a while."

"Maybe he's off doing guy stuff," Bradford said.

"I suppose."

Or maybe she pushed him overboard.

Not a bad working theory. Not a good one either, but certainly something to ponder while we explored all the breakfast buffet options the ship offered.

Two hours later, feeling like a beached whale from my sumptuous repast, I lolled on a chaise lounge fronting the main swimming pool. With my Kindle in hand, I attempted to read the latest mystery by one of my favorite authors. After thirty minutes, my e-reader showed I'd progressed from twenty percent all the way to a whopping twenty-two percent of the story.

I laid the device on the table between our lounges. Mother looked up from her paperback. "Are you enjoying your book?"

I shrugged. "I can't seem to get into it. I don't know whether it's due to my concussion, or if I'm distracted by the crime wave on this ship. It makes the mystery I'm reading pale in comparison."

She pushed her designer sunglasses on top her head and peered at me. "You do remember you're on your honeymoon, right?"

I sent her a scathing look. "And my husband is spending our honeymoon hanging out with your husband reviewing video footage."

"Touché. Once a detective, always a detective, I suppose."

"I guess. Was it difficult for you when you and Bradford first married? When he was still on the force?"

"Worrying about Robert's safety was one problem." She swiveled around until she was facing me. "Don't forget I'd been a widow for thirty years and living alone once you left for college. There are a lot of adjustments when you cohabit with someone."

"C is for compromise?"

"Definitely. I still don't understand why a retired detective, responsible for solving multiple homicides, can't remember to put the cap back on the toothpaste tube."

I chuckled at her comment. Married life meant a huge transition for Tom and me, but I was definitely ready for the adventure. "I wonder if the two of them discovered anything important this morning."

Mother pointed toward the automatic door. "Here they come. We'll soon find out."

The men joined us and Bradford pulled up a chair by Mother's chaise, while Tom squeezed in beside me on my own lounge.

"You fellows look very pleased with yourselves," Mother remarked.

"Haven't lost my touch or my eyesight yet," Bradford replied. He removed the Giants baseball cap that kept his bald scalp from burning, reached over and kissed my mother.

"Old Eagle Eye spotted someone heading to the cabana area about five minutes after Sanjay arrived," Tom explained.

"What time was that?" I asked.

"Around 5:10 p.m. according to the footage."

"And why are you so intrigued by this person?"

"She's a female server at Chopsticks. We think there might have been something going on between them that was beyond professional."

"You could be right. One of the chefs mentioned her the other morning. Mizuki is her name, right?" I high-fived my husband. "So why are you wasting time here instead of grilling her?"

"What if I said I missed you?" Tom said to me.

"What if I said you're checking on me?"

He threw back his head and laughed. "Okay, that too."

"So what exactly is your plan for the rest of the day?" I asked, snuggling closer to him.

"The woman is working at the Lido Café during the lunch rush. The captain will arrange a meeting with her around two when her shift is over."

"Did you run across any other suspicious characters when you reviewed the footage?" I asked.

"We're not finished yet. A few people went into that area earlier in the day. The security staff will try to contact as many as they can, but I doubt if they'll come up with anything new."

I was about to ask Tom another question when I was distracted by Margaret walking on the opposite side of the pool deck from us. Once again, she was alone. Did she ever spend time with her poor sick husband?

"Did the captain give you access to all the ship's footage?" I asked, my gaze fixed on the single woman's retreating figure.

"I assume he would if we asked for something in particular. It's a big ship. There are literally miles of video footage to wade through." He sent me a worried glance. "It could take the rest of the trip to scroll through it all."

"Don't worry. I'm not that ambitious. I wondered if you could check the footage from our first night when I saw that person go overboard. It occurred around 3:30 a.m. so it's a narrow window of time. And location. Remember, Sanjay said he would look at it. But he never got back to us with the results."

Tom sighed. "You have a different definition of how to spend a honeymoon than I do."

"I'd be far more relaxed if we could learn more about that evening." I kissed him lightly on his lips. "You won't regret it."

Tom fiddled with his left ear lobe. "If I promise to review the footage from the first night, will you agree to let it go? No more worrying about someone being thrown overboard? No more detecting?"

That was an easy decision. After yesterday's disastrous outing, I was more than ready to give up my investigation.

At least for the day.

CHAPTER THIRTY-FIVE

The changing of my bodyguard occurred at lunchtime. Mother wanted Bradford to accompany her to the art auction so they grabbed a quick sandwich and disappeared. One of the security staff stopped by our table with a request from the captain for Tom's immediate presence.

I was given the choice of watching a shuffleboard competition with Gran and Mabel or getting an advance peek at the final stage production, compliments of Zac. I could hardly turn down the opportunity to watch the dress rehearsal of one of my favorite musicals—*Grease*.

Stan and I chose seats in the center section, about eight rows up from the stage. I would never have thought to pack a leather jacket for a cruise, but Stan could have passed for one of the male members of the production. He'd even slicked back his thinning hair.

I jerked my head toward the stage. "Are you planning on joining them? You're certainly dressed for the part."

"You never know. Nicole Robinson, that lead singer who was a no-show at rehearsals, finally emailed Zac yesterday. She decided to leave the ship when we were at port and flew home to be with her boyfriend." He whispered in my ear. "Her married boyfriend."

"How did you learn that?" I asked.

Stan flapped his hand at me. "Oh, you know me. It doesn't take long before I become everyone's GBFF. The stuff I could tell you would make your jaw drop to the floor. I decided it wouldn't hurt to understudy the understudy, in case one of the male dancers disappears, or breaks a leg."

"So that's what you've been up to. I've barely seen you on this cruise."

"It's not quite the lark I thought it would be. I've learned a lot about stage directing, though."

"Will Zac be relieved when his one month contract is up?"

"I don't know." Stan chewed on his lower lip. "I certainly will be. I used to think that working in the entertainment industry would be glamorous. But Zac spends his days and nights babysitting the talent and worrying about a multitude of details: lighting, sound, props, and the music. It makes banking look like a kindergarten class in comparison."

"I'm shocked. After getting a taste of live theater up close and personal, I half expected you to quit Hangtown Bank and follow Zac around the country."

"Yeah, well, it's not exactly the romantic vacation I envisioned when Zac first suggested it." Stan squeezed my hand. "What about you? No surprise that your honeymoon has turned into a murder investigation."

"As Sue Grafton would say, H is for Honeymoon has been retitled H is for Homicide."

"Do you have any idea who thumped you on your very hard head?"

"I've been wondering that, too," said a newcomer, who patted my shoulder. I twisted around to discover Sierra slipping into the row behind us.

"Thanks for helping delay the ship's departure yesterday," I said to her. "I don't think I could have handled waving *bon voyage* to the *Celebration* from the pier."

"I wish I could have seen the culprit," she said. "Better yet, surprised him and stopped the attack."

"That makes two of us. By the way, how did you happen to end up at the fort in time to help your concussed cuz?"

"I did a little shopping in old town and had time to kill before returning to the ship. I remembered you and Tom had signed up for the city tour, so I decided to trek up to the fort. Wish I'd arrived sooner."

"I guess I'll never be too old to need a babysitter," I pouted. "By the way, have you heard any updates about the jewel thief? Any more reported thefts?"

"Not that I've been told. So I'm attempting to do my job while maintaining a low profile. I wanted to see how the production was coming along."

I was about to ask Sierra another question when the lights dimmed and the music began. I settled into my seat and looked forward to a preview of the show.

The performance opened with the full cast singing the title song. Elizabeth Axelrod had taken over the lead role of Sandy that originally belonged to flighty Nicole. Elizabeth and the guy playing Danny Zuko were every bit as good as Olivia Newton John and John Travolta had been in the movie version.

My feet kept time to the music, and it was all I could do to stay seated. Every now and then Stan would rise in his seat, and I would push him back down. The last thing his boyfriend needed was for us to interrupt what looked to be an excellent dress rehearsal.

Until Gina, the woman playing the part of Rizzo, the leader of the Pink Ladies, stuck her remarkable breasts against Danny Zuko's muscled chest. She followed that with a kiss that seemed to last for a full minute and only ended when sweet, demure shirtwaist-wearing Sandy stomped on Rizzo's foot.

"What do you think you're doing?" The new lead yelled at the other singer.

"Acting," Gina sneered. "Something you wouldn't be acquainted with."

Even from eight rows back, I could see beads of perspiration forming on the male lead's forehead as he stepped between the two women. He held out his palms in a supplicating manner, but the women weren't in an accommodating mood.

Elizabeth's right-handed punch landed on his left cheekbone at the same time Gina's left fist crashed into his full-lipped mouth.

Before you could say "Greased Lightning" one hot young stud went down for the count.

CHAPTER THIRTY-SIX

The stage erupted into a cacophony of sound and movement. One of the Pink Ladies shoved Elizabeth into the wings. A guy wearing a leather jacket and cuffed jeans attempted to lead Gina off the stage. She pushed him away and rushed to Danny's side. With the mikes still on, we could hear every word she said.

"Oh, baby doll, I never meant to hurt you. I was aiming for that witch." She crouched by his side and held his hand while he lay prone on the stage. Zac raced up the stairs with Sierra not far behind him. I remembered her chasing me as a kid. Those long legs could still move.

"Should we leave?" I asked Stan.

"Are you kidding? This scene has more drama than the actual show."

Elizabeth returned to the stage. She dropped down on one knee, opposite Gina, and held Danny's other hand. The poor guy remained flat on his back. I'd be afraid to get up, too.

We could hear Sierra requesting that both female performers move away so Zac could assess Danny's injuries.

The girls exchanged angry looks, but they exited the stage and headed to opposite wings. As soon as they left, Danny sat up, his hand holding his jaw. With the assistance of another male performer, Zac helped the actor to his feet. A trail of blood

141

dripped across the stage as Zac led Danny down the stairs and up our aisle.

Zac stopped for a minute to talk to Stan. "We're going to the doctor's office." Then in a lower voice he muttered, "Although we really need a dentist."

I smiled at the singer and he smiled back, probably by reflex. He certainly wouldn't be smiling if he'd known that his two front teeth were nowhere to be seen.

I could feel myself wanting to rub my own teeth just to make sure they were still in place. Danny would wise up soon enough. And when he did, his screams would carry from the bow of the ship to the stern.

"Do you want to come along?" Zac asked Stan who then turned to me. "Is it safe to leave you alone?" he asked.

"Don't be silly. Zac can use your support. I'll be fine."

Stan followed Zac and Danny up the aisle. I glanced at the stage. The actors stood in a forlorn group as Sierra addressed them. I knew almost nothing about show business, but I had an inkling that the male star usually needed a full set of teeth. Unless he could pick up two new incisors in St. Martin tomorrow, he was basically screwed.

I hoped the show's understudy was prepared to go on in the current Danny's place. But who would replace the understudy?

Not my problem. I debated whether to wait for Sierra, but it looked like she might be tied up for a while. After four months on board the ship, she would be familiar with what it took to put on the weekly shows, even though the production of *Grease* was new for this cruise. Perhaps the dress rehearsal would go on after all.

I picked up my tote bag and debated how to entertain myself. My stomach remained full from lunch, and I'd basked in the sun a sufficient amount of time this morning. I briefly thought about going to the gym but quickly talked myself out of it. My body needed to be pampered not exercised.

Pampering. What an excellent idea. I checked the map and discovered the ship's spa located five decks up from my current location. The elevator whisked me to the spa faster than you could say lava rock massage.

With a decor in soft cream and taupe, the music of Enya playing softly in the background, and a light tropical scent perfuming the air, the spa offered a soothing sanctuary. Even if there were no appointments available, I might just lie down on the plush sofa in the reception area and nap.

Due to a recent cancellation, one of their estheticians had an opening for a fifty-minute facial. I could relax under her skillful hands and depart with a glowing complexion. The receptionist gave me a soft white robe emblazoned with the ship's logo.

I entered the small changing room, quickly disrobed and then re-robed. I stuffed my clothing, key card and watch in the small locker, locked it and stuffed the key in the pocket of my robe. Then I waited for them to call my name.

Thirty minutes later, I lay blissfully cocooned under a lightweight blanket, my parched-from-the-sun skin revitalizing with layers of magical lotions and potions containing lots of natural products. Including a special ingredient—chocolate.

Chocolate—the wonder product. Also my favorite antioxidant.

I felt so relaxed that I began to wish I'd signed up for a three-hour facial. My eyelids closed and my mind drifted into dreamland.

The door to our room burst open with a thud as it slammed into the wall. A strident voice shouted, "I've been robbed!"

Not again.

CHAPTER THIRTY-SEVEN

I sprang up and the woman standing on the threshold screamed. I must have looked like the Bride of Frankenstein after a tour through Willy Wonka's chocolate factory.

"Hello, Evelyn," I said to the stocky woman who wore a robe similar to mine although several sizes larger.

Evelyn Peabody chose to ignore me and instead concentrated on berating my esthetician.

"Did you take my Patek Phillipe?"

My Filipino esthetician shook her head. Her dark frightened eyes resembled those of a fawn about to be mowed down by a bulldozer. A fairly apt description for the Peabody woman.

"Who is Patek whatchamacallit?" I asked her, wondering if she was traveling with someone besides her sister. "And why would Andi want him?"

Her dark penciled-in eyebrows knitted together in disgust. "Patek Phillipe produces the finest watches in the world. And mine has gone missing."

"When did you last see it?"

She shoved both hands in her pockets. "I didn't feel comfortable leaving it in the locker. It's worth…" she paused, "a lot. So I put it in my robe pocket. I've had three treatments today and this," she pointed at Andi, "person did two of them. I bet she swiped it out of my robe while I dozed on the table."

144

Andi continued to proclaim her innocence. "I take nothing." She turned to me and pleaded. "Please. You help me?"

Now why was it that every time Mrs. Peabody confronted a purported thief that I became involved? Maybe I shouldn't have mentioned earlier in the conversation that I was the cruise director's cousin. I thought a little nepotistic name-dropping might encourage Andi to slather me with everything on the menu. Instead I was back to playing amateur sleuth.

So much for a break from my chaotic life.

Several staff members and one robed client clustered around Mrs. Peabody. I briefly wondered if there was a Mr. Peabody or if he'd escaped with his sanity intact.

"I'm calling the chief security officer," Mrs. Peabody forcefully announced. "He'll get things straightened out."

Good luck with that. Evidently the cruise ship gossip line hadn't reached her ears yet. I wondered if the overworked security staff could handle this new development. Or would they call in reinforcements?

Which at the rate this cruise was going would be my husband and my stepfather.

Talk about Honeymoon Hell.

My vertical position was causing the chocolate to drip on the sheets, the floor and my cleavage. I laid back down hoping to stop the brown deluge.

"What do you think you're doing?" Mrs. Peabody screeched as she stomped into the room, her flip-flops flapping on the tile floor. She stared down at my mottled chocolate-dotted cheeks.

"Um, finishing my facial. If that meets with your approval." Geesh. The nerve of this woman. Who did she think she was?

"I thought you were some type of hotshot Nancy Drew." She poked her finger against my bare collarbone. "You need to figure out who did this to me."

Or else what?

Andi added more encouragement. "Yes. Please, for me, or I could lose job. Find person who do this bad thing to the huge lady."

Mrs. Peabody snorted, but she added a "please" as well.

A small woman attired in a soft beige suit, whom I presumed was the spa manager, stalked past the cluster of uniformed spa staff and into my room. Her shiny dark pageboy swung around her face as she turned to look at each of us. "What is happening here?" she asked.

Mrs. Peabody employed her usual tactful method of conversing by shoving her finger in the woman's face.

"Your gang of crooks here took my watch. I'll have the whole bunch of you fired."

The manager straightened but her action only added a half-inch to her petite stature. "I do not understand what you are saying. Please follow me to my office." She gestured to Mrs. Peabody and Andi. I sat on my bed, dripping chocolate left and right. "You, too," she pointed at me and then clarified. "Andi, please clean her up first."

Mrs. Peabody followed the manager out of the room. Andi motioned for the other therapists to leave before she closed the door. She then proceeded to remove the chocolate mess from my face before finishing my procedure with some soothing moisturizer that smelled faintly of peppermint.

We left the room together and headed for the manager's office. I continued to reassure Andi that I would help resolve the situation, but I wasn't certain how well she understood English. Her responses alternated between pleading with me and thanking me.

We crossed paths with Mrs. Peabody and her sister, both changed and now decked out in pastel tops and slacks. "Find my watch," Mrs. Peabody snarled at me as we walked past the two women. I felt like saluting her and almost said, "Aye, aye, Ma'am." Her sister, as usual, remained silent, merely smiling at me. It must be difficult to have such a dominating sibling always present in your life.

Once seated in the spa manager's office, Andi rattled on in what I guessed to be Tagalog to the boss whose name was Ramona. Hands flew as they chattered back and forth in triple speed. I crossed my legs then pulled my robe tighter to keep my thighs covered, wishing I had changed back into my clothes before this impromptu meeting.

Andi abruptly stood, and with a quick bow of her head in my direction, left the office.

I began to rise, unsure what my role was in this situation.

"No, please stay," said Ramona. "This is most distressing. The Peabody woman is a platinum member of Nordic American. She has much weight to pull."

Not the most flattering way to put it, but I got the gist of her comment. Mrs. Peabody was an influential guest on this cruise line.

"I would be upset, too, if an expensive watch disappeared, although she could be less abrasive about it," I replied. "Have other spa patrons suffered any thefts while they were in the treatment rooms this past week?"

"One woman lost her wallet a few days ago, but she didn't remember if she lost it here or not. And another woman complained about her watch going missing. I can vouch for my girls. They would not do such a thing. Their employment is very important to them. Some of the girls are the sole support of their families. They can't afford to lose this job."

I rubbed my finger over my chin. It felt silky smooth although I still smelled like a Peppermint Patty.

"I suppose one of the other guests could be responsible," I ventured.

Ramona's eyes lit up. "Of course. That must be it. A passenger took her watch."

"Do you have a list of all the guests here this afternoon? I gather Mrs. Peabody was in the spa for several hours."

"I can check," she said. "I do not know whether I can share that information with you. I must talk to security first."

"My husband has an 'in' with security." Unfortunately. "We're in room 7066, so call me when it's available and I'll come down."

"Thank you. I am very appreciative of your involvement."

I wasn't certain how appreciative my husband would be, but the ship had been keeping him plenty involved. I left Ramona's office amid a multitude of thanks and headed for the locker room.

My hair and chest felt grimy from my chocolate downpour, so I decided to shower before I went back to our room. I hung my robe on the hook near the opening of the shower stall and stepped in. The same giant bottles of shampoo, conditioner and shower gel that were located in our staterooms were attached to the walls of these showers. The sound of water streaming in the shower stall next to mine made me realize how accessible the spa patrons' robes were to anyone walking by, whether customer or employee.

I quickly finished my shower, grabbed one of the fluffy bath towels and dried myself off. My locker key was still tucked in the pocket of my robe. But how easy it would be for a thief to snatch a key, steal something from the appropriate locker, and return the key, all before the owner finished an off-key rendition of "I am Woman, Hear me Roar."

I walked into the changing area and bumped into another robe-clad woman.

"Lucille," I said to the Atlanta resident. "Fancy meeting you here."

Lucille's short graying hair was pasted to her skull, evidence of a recent massage or facial. "I always take advantage of the spa on days at sea. The perfect way to relax." She sniffed. "You smell good. Did you enjoy your treatment?"

"Until that Peabody woman accused my esthetician of stealing her expensive watch."

"Darn. I missed the fireworks. Did they find it?"

"Not yet. Evidently I've been assigned the case."

Lucille giggled. "You always seem to end up in the thick of things. Now don't forget, I'm happy to help. I can be your sidekick. The Watson to your Sherlock Holmes."

I threw her a look. My would-be baby boomer sidekick giggled.

"Well then, how about the Lula to your Stephanie Plum?"

Sidekick to a bumbling amateur sleuth. Sounded about right to me.

CHAPTER THIRTY-EIGHT

I left the spa promising to keep Lucille, my new sleuthing buddy, in the loop. With all the goings on in the spa, I'd lost track of the time. I pulled my watch out of my small tote bag and winced.

Time certainly flies when you are working on a case. It was already past five. I race-walked to the elevator, not an easy task when wearing flip flops. The ship's intercom blasted an announcement. I normally avoided their annoying hourly broadcasts about shipboard activities, but it's difficult to ignore them when the announcer bellows your name.

"Would Laurel Hunter please return to her stateroom? Immediately."

Wow. My first thought was how cool it was to hear my new married name over a loudspeaker. My second thought was—*huh*?

Illogically, I pressed the elevator button over and over wondering what was going on. At this point, I didn't think I could handle one more catastrophe. The elevator finally arrived and I jumped in, almost knocking over one of the elderly women inside. She jabbed her cane at my foot and narrowly missed my instep.

Danger in every corner of this ship.

All the deck buttons were lit up, and I impatiently waited until the door swooshed open to my floor. I sidestepped the cane-whacking senior and gracefully exited the elevator before running down the corridor to my stateroom.

From a distance, the door to our room appeared to be open. Maybe Marcel was cleaning it, although he normally finished earlier in the day. That gave us time to mess it all up getting ready for the evening meal so he could clean it once again while we dined.

I slowed down. On this cruise you couldn't be too careful.

As I drew closer, I recognized familiar voices emanating from the stateroom. I crossed the threshold to be greeted by Mabel, my family and my husband.

"Where the hell have you been?" Tom asked, the expression on his face a combination of relief and really pissed off.

"We've been so worried about you," Mother said, enfolding me in her arms.

"I was at the spa," I replied, wondering what the big deal was. Then it dawned on me that once Stan left with Zac, no one actually knew where I'd been the last few hours. "I only booked a one-hour facial, but then Mrs. Peabody's watch disappeared from her robe pocket. She accused my esthetician of stealing it, and the next thing I knew, I was deep into another investigation."

I mouthed a sorry to Tom who looked torn between berating me and hugging me.

Wary of my head injury, he went with a gentle hug and light kiss.

"I guess you imagined the worst," I said with a chuckle.

"Only because that's your usual M.O.," replied Bradford.

"That Peabody woman is a thorn in everyone's rear end," grumbled Gran.

"She was really upset. I guess her watch was extremely valuable. A Pitty Pat or something like that."

"Oh, my," said Mother. "A Patek Phillippe? Those are so expensive. I can see why she'd be distraught. Did she ask you to help?"

"She did. Then I ran into Lucille, you know that nice woman from Atlanta, and told her about the supposed theft." I laughed. "She offered to be my sidekick."

"Hey, what about us?" Mabel said. "I thought your grandmother and I were your sidekicks."

Gran elbowed Mabel. "No, we're the CEO and CDO of TWO GALS DETECTIVE AGENCY."

"I'm almost afraid to ask," Bradford said. "CDO?"

"Chief detecting officer," Gran said proudly. She tapped an arthritic finger against her chin. "You know, maybe this Lucille person could open up a branch for us in Atlanta. It would be nice to have an operative in the south. We could start franchisin' our offices."

"You mean TWO GALS?" asked Mabel.

"We might need a better name," Gran said. "If we're going global."

Bradford butted in. "Like the crazy old ladies agency?"

Gran whacked my stepfather on his thigh with her jumbo patent leather purse. "Behave yourself, sonny. Or I'll take you out of my will."

"I feel like I'm watching an old Abbott and Costello routine," Tom murmured in my ear.

Yep. Business as usual.

"I appreciate everyone's concern, but Tom and I have to get ready for tonight."

"I almost forgot. Formal night." Mother tucked her arm under Bradford's elbow. "Come along, dear. It's time for you to show off your new tux."

Tuxes come in Grizzly Bear sizes?

The four of them left our stateroom leaving Tom and me alone. I flopped on the bed and Tom joined me.

"Is it just me," he said as he traced a finger from my neck down to my cleavage. "Or is this one strange honeymoon?"

I gulped at the touch of his finger. "When we exchanged wedding vows we promised to love and cherish one another. I don't think living a normal life was included in our vows."

"I guess this is the new normal," he said. "For us."

"I hope the new normal doesn't equate to no sex."

He gave me that cockeyed half grin I love so much. "Never."

CHAPTER THIRTY-NINE

Wandering through half the dining room in search of my family let us look at how the other passengers interpreted "formal." We walked past tables where the women were covered head to toe in beads, sequins and occasionally, feathers. While a few men wore tuxes, the majority were dressed like Tom in a dark business suit. He claimed his cummerbund had vanished, but I had a feeling it was misplaced in one of the bureau drawers.

Tonight I wore a short red cocktail dress I'd borrowed from Liz. With six months of pregnancy left, she wouldn't be needing it any time soon. I rarely wore red and felt very Mata Hari-ish.

The waiter pulled out my chair. My red silk-clad derriere was still a few inches from landing when he shoved the chair forward. I dropped into the seat with a thud.

"We've been wondering where you two were," Gran said. "Out detecting?"

If my grandmother referred to Tom's expert detection of my erogenous zones, she was a hundred percent right.

My cheeks colored to the same shade as my dress. Tom rescued me by placing the wine list in my hand.

While my eyes scrutinized the lengthy wine menu, my ears tuned in to the conversation at our table.

"So you don't think his girlfriend stabbed him?" Mother asked Tom.

"Are you talking about Sanjay?" With the conversation in the dining room set at maximum volume, I raised my voice so they could hear my question.

Mother placed a finger over her lips. "Ssh. Robert and Tom met with her this afternoon."

I turned to my husband. "You didn't tell me that."

"It's difficult to keep you apprised of my investigation when I don't know where the heck you are," Tom responded.

Point taken.

I nestled against my husband's arm while he discussed his interview with Mizuki.

"She seemed quite distressed about Sanjay's death. Since the Chopsticks restaurant is located by the cabana area, the staff found out about the murder fairly quickly, although we asked them to keep it to themselves."

"Did she admit to an affair with him?"

"Eventually. High-ranking officers are not supposed to dally with the rest of the crew, but in reality, it's not that uncommon. Especially when you're basically confined to the ship for an eight-month stretch. I guess he broke up with her that very evening."

"So how did the two of them first hook up?" Gran asked, as intent as an investigative reporter about to get a front-page story.

Mother rolled her eyes, but she still leaned in to hear Tom's response.

"This is a murder investigation, not *Inside Edition*," I replied since I was far more interested in why Sanjay dumped Mizuki than how they got together.

"Hell hath no fury…" Mother began with Gran finishing her version of the famous quote. "Like a woman royally ticked off." Gran waved her steak knife over her head. "So you think she stabbed him with that silver chopstick?"

Tom shrugged. "Mizuki is used to carrying trays loaded down with dinner entrees so she's strong enough. It was difficult to get a read on her. She's very self-contained."

"You should have Laurel give it a try." Gran pointed her sharp knife at me. "She's good at worming stuff out of folks."

Thanks, Gran. I could now add "excellent worming skills" to my resume.

"Mizuki contributed one helpful possibility," Tom added. "Whether it proves useful to the investigation or not is something else. According to her, Sanjay was blackmailing two members of the crew."

"Whoa, who knew?" I said.

"That's what we need to find out. Mizuki only knew that one of the blackmail victims was a female bartender."

"Which one?" I asked.

"She didn't know, but fortunately, it's a shorter list than the male bartenders. We have our work cut out for us."

"What's next?" I asked the two men. "Do you get to enjoy the rest of your vacation? We dock in Sint Maarten tomorrow. Or should I say St. Martin?"

"Yeah, what's the deal with that?" asked Mabel. "Two countries on the same island. How did that come about?"

"That's an interesting story," Mother replied. "Supposedly the French and the Dutch, who both occupied the island, decided to hold a contest. The Dutch men started walking west while the French went the opposite direction. They decided where they eventually met up would be the dividing line across the island. The Dutch fellows filled up with gin then stopped along the way to sleep. You know that old saying," Mother said with a wicked grin. "If you booze, then snooze, you lose. The French ended up with a larger share of the island."

"Great story," Bradford said, "whether it's true or not."

"I hear there's a famous beach on the French side," Gran said, "where all the naturalists go."

"Mother, you wouldn't dare," said my own mother to Gran.

"Just watch me," Gran replied with a wink to me. "It's supposed to be mighty popular with the senior set. Wanna come along with us, Laurel?"

Eew. "No, thank you," I said, trying to erase the vision of Gran frolicking with a bunch of nude octogenarians.

I called our waiter over. I would need a stiff drink or two to eliminate that picture from my mind.

We finished dinner in stages. Mother and Bradford wanted to catch the comedian's late show. Gran and Mabel decided to cruise the lounges. I had no idea what or who they were cruising for and didn't intend to find out.

Tom and I decided to skip the big show and catch an act in one of the smaller more intimate lounges. We settled on the Queen's Lounge where a jazz band provided a less hectic atmosphere. Perfect for cuddling and conversing.

Tom ordered a glass of merlot, and I went with the drink of the day, a Caribbean Sunrise. We snuggled together, Tom's left arm resting on my shoulder, as we sipped our drinks and listened to the music. Life was perfect.

Or so I thought.

Tom shifted in his seat. He placed his glass on the table in front of us and removed his arm. "We need to discuss something," he said to me.

My hand froze in mid-air. I couldn't move or speak. Tom lifted my glass from my hand and set it down. Then he clasped my palm in his. "Now, don't freak out."

I, of course, immediately freaked out. I removed my hand from his, picked up my drink and downed half of it.

"My opening line needs work," Tom said.

"Why don't we skip the opening and get to the point."

He took a deep breath. "I'm not sure I want to stay with Homeland Security."

I sat there, dumbfounded. "What? Why? And why now?"

"You wouldn't think the combination of a murder and my honeymoon would make me contemplate a career change, but a couple of things have led to this decision."

"I'm listening."

"First, despite the fact we're dealing with a gruesome murder, Bradford and I have enjoyed working together, trying to follow the limited trail of clues the killer left behind."

I nodded. "I can see that. You're a fantastic detective."

"On top of that, I spoke to my boss at Homeland Security. Once we return home, I'm off on a task force with another agency that will take me to Eastern Europe. And he didn't know for how long."

I've read descriptions of a person's face falling upon receiving bad news. Mine just plummeted into my cocktail.

"But, but, what about us? And Kristy?" Our families had been officially merged for only one chaotic week before we left on our honeymoon. I loved Tom's daughter, but how would she feel about her father disappearing for what could conceivably be months at a time.

"That's why I'm considering giving notice. As they say, life is too short. Something I've learned during my career and as you know, personally experienced." As a widower, Tom knew all about loss. As did I.

He reached for my hand again. "Now that I've found you, I don't want my career to keep us apart."

I bent over and kissed him. "I couldn't agree more. So what's your next step?"

"My next step is finishing what we started before dinner."

CHAPTER FORTY

Before Tom and I could return to our stateroom to "enjoy" one another's company, we were joined by Sierra, Stan and Zac.

"I'm so glad we found you," said Stan, squeezing in beside me.

Tom and I exchanged glances. Lucky us.

Zac and Sierra dropped into the two chairs across from us. While the two of them shared a "gloomy Gus" countenance, Stan beamed at us.

"What's going on?" I asked the trio.

"We've been rehearsing the new Danny for the final show," Zac said.

"So the understudy is playing the part?" I asked. Zac and Sierra nodded glumly.

"And guess who is now starring on stage?" Stan burst out.

To Stan's disappointment, we turned blank faces to him.

"Me," he trilled, pointing both thumbs at his chest. Just in case we missed his point.

My mouth gaped open while Tom cleared his throat.

"One of the male dancers, Seth, is the Danny understudy. Zac was short one dancer so I'm filling in." Stan's smile was almost as wide as the table.

Tom cleared his throat again. "Well, this calls for a celebration. How about a round of drinks?"

Zac and Sierra looked like they would prefer a pitcher of drinks—one for each of them. The server came over and we placed our order.

"That's so exciting," I said to Stan. "How can you learn your part so quickly?"

"Piece of cake, sweetie," he said. "You know I'm a natural."

Zac gulped and smiled at me. Or was that a grimace? Hard to tell.

"How is the original Danny doing?" I asked.

"Not well," Sierra replied, as she thanked the server for her cocktail. "He lost two front teeth, and his face looks like he had a run-in with both Batman and Superman."

"It's his own fault," Zac said. "Screwing both women. What was he thinking?"

He wasn't, obviously.

"Do you think the production will be ready in time?" I asked Zac.

"I sure hope so. First we lose our female lead singer and now the male lead. I don't think I can take much more of this, but as long as there's no more drama on the stage other than the show itself, we should be good to go." He threw a look at Stan. "Provided our new chorus member learns all of his moves."

"*No problemo*," Stan said.

"I hope there will be no more *problemos* on this cruise," Sierra said. "I can't handle much more."

"Do you get any time off to visit the island tomorrow?" I asked her.

"Our *cuisine du jour* tour guide called in sick, so I got volunteered to lead the gastronomy tour on the island."

"Astronomy tour?" asked Tom.

"Gastronomy," she replied, patting her flat stomach. "Eats all over the island. St. Martin is considered the culinary capital of the West Indies."

"That sounds great," I said. "Not that there is any shortage of food on the ship, but it would be fun to sample some French cuisine. Tom, what do you think?"

"I am as anxious as you are to get off the ship. I'll check with the captain first thing in the morning to make sure he doesn't need me."

"That sounds like so much fun," Stan said. "Sign me up."

"Not so fast," Zac replied. "We're rehearsing tomorrow, remember? You are officially part of the cast."

"Shoot."

I leaned closer to Stan. "I'll bring back some snacks for you. How do you feel about leftover snails?"

The expression on his face gave me my answer.

Tom rose early the next morning in an attempt to finish reviewing the footage before the around-the-island eating tour. Being a simple meat and potatoes kind of guy, Bradford declined the island foray saying he preferred watching boring video to dining on nouvelle cuisine.

Mother joined Tom and me for the tour. Gran and Mabel also signed up for the trip, which surprised me since my grandmother is more of a Campbell's soup casserole kind of chef. Maybe she wanted to spend more time with the family and with Sierra.

Or more time with that dapper Jimmy Bond, who showed up as we were boarding the tour bus. We walked down the aisle in search of available seats. Gran shoved Mabel in the empty seat next to Mother leaving a pair of seats for herself and Jimmy. Tom and I scooched in behind them.

Jimmy turned around to greet us. "Good to see you again, Laurel. You seem to have recovered quite nicely from your attack yesterday."

"Just a couple of scabs on my hard head," I replied. "What have you been up to lately? Anything exciting?"

"He's been trying to avoid that Peabody woman," Gran butted in. "She clings to Jimmy like nylons on a hot summer day."

Jimmy gave us a gentle smile. "Evelyn seems to think I'm her own personal bodyguard and escort."

"Not to mention 'boy toy'," added Gran.

"Why, thank you, my dear," Jimmy said to Gran. "At my age, I take that as a compliment."

"Does Mrs. Peabody think she's in danger?" asked my ever vigilant husband.

"The woman has encountered a string of bad luck as far as her jewelry is concerned," Jimmy admitted. "So she's concerned about her own safety as well as her diamonds."

"She shoulda' left her gee gaws at home," Mabel interrupted him. "Instead of lording it over everyone."

"Oh, crapola," said Gran staring ahead. Evelyn Peabody lumbered onto the bus followed by her sister. The abrasive woman abruptly stopped in the middle of the narrow aisle. Her sister's curly white head clunked into her broad back.

"Jimmy, where are you?" she bellowed.

"Bloody hell," Jimmy muttered under his breath as he ducked down in his seat.

With the intensity of a missile, Evelyn's gaze zoomed in on Jimmy and Gran. She waddled down the aisle to greet him.

"I thought you were taking the boat tour," Evelyn said to Jimmy. "Good thing I found out you switched to this one. Did you forget to tell me?"

"Something like that," Jimmy replied.

"Trade seats with me," she ordered Gran.

"Not a chance, sister." Gran pointed to the rear of the bus. "Lots of empty seats back there."

Evelyn grumbled but with a line of people waiting behind her, she forged on. Her sister followed, apologizing in Mrs. Peabody's wake as she moved down the aisle whacking people right and left with her large Louis Vuitton tote.

I checked my watch. Five more minutes before take-off. I leaned across Tom to peek out the window and saw Sierra collecting a few tickets from the late stragglers. Sharon and Deborah climbed aboard, followed by Rick and Claire. We exchanged hellos as they made their way to the few remaining seats in the rear of the bus.

Sierra was the last to board. She stood next to the driver and greeted everyone with a *Bonjour*.

"Thank you all for joining us today. In case you don't know, I'm Sierra Sullivan, the Cruise Director. I'm filling in for Claude, the regular tour guide. We're going to have a fantastic time today. Or as they say in St. Martin, *"Tres formidable."*

"That means terrific in English," I translated for Tom.

Suddenly a voice boomed. "Just keep your wallets zipped up and your eyes open," said Mrs. Peabody. "There's some thieving scum on this bus."

The passengers began to babble, swiveling their heads left and right, wondering what and who she was talking about.

Sierra grasped the mike, but for some reason decided to remain silent, only murmuring to the driver. He started the engine, and she dropped into the single tour guide seat.

Now why did I get a feeling this tour wouldn't be as *formidable* as promised?

CHAPTER FORTY-ONE

Although the tour got off to a rough start, Sierra quickly turned it around by demonstrating her impressive knowledge of the unique dual-citizenship island. As we drove past the colonial-style buildings in Phillipsburg, Sint Maarten, she pointed out cultural as well as popular attractions. The Dutch side drew visitors from all over the world to their numerous casinos.

Once out of town, we encountered a unique species of lizard. According to Sierra, legend had it that a male and a female orange iguana each escaped from a ship that docked on the island. And you know how those lizards are. Within a very short time, the original Adam and Eve managed to create a population numbering in the thousands. I snapped photos of groves of trees teeming with the orange reptiles.

Simultaneously captivating and creepy.

Gleaming white stucco villas surrounded by fuchsia bougainvillea perched on green hills overlooking the turquoise sea. We drove past the Simpson Bay marina where huge luxury yachts docked, including a three-hundred-foot yacht owned by an internet billionaire. What was that saying? The bigger the boat the smaller the—

We also passed by a couple of ramshackle boats and houses devastated over twenty years earlier when Luis, a category four hurricane hit the Caribbean. With winds of 132 miles per hour, it destroyed more than sixty percent of the island. In the Caribbean, there is always the possibility of another storm just around the corner.

Sort of like my life.

Our first restaurant, a French bistro in Marigot, would be serving a variety of hors d'oeuvres. The restaurant offered intimate tables for two and banquet-size tables for bigger groups. We quickly commandeered a large table for the six of us, leaving room for two more. Since Rick and Claire had been seated in the back of the bus, they were one of the last couples to enter the restaurant. Claire looked somewhat lost, so I waved them over to our table. Unfortunately, Mrs. Peabody and her sister arrived first.

"These seats are taken," I said to her.

"Yes, they are." She plunked her hefty posterior in the empty seat by Jimmy. Her sister thanked us as she sat down.

I mouthed an embarrassed "sorry" to Rick and Claire. They chuckled and headed off to an empty table in the rear of the restaurant.

"So what's new with your investigation?" Evelyn grabbed a slice of French bread and slathered it with half the butter sitting on a silver dish. "You find my watch yet?" She turned to Jimmy and informed him that she'd hired me to find out who stole her Patek Phillipe.

Hired? Did that mean I was getting paid to be bossed around?

"Laurel, I didn't realize you were also a detective." Jimmy's lips quivered as he tried not to laugh. "How lucky that Mrs. Peabody found you."

The piece of bread I'd swallowed stuck in my throat as I gagged a response. "Yep, lucky me."

"Her husband is a detective, too," Gran added. "Same as me and Mabel here. Although we don't have an official badge like him." She turned to her friend. "We got to get those business cards printed up. You never know when someone will want to hire us."

"So you're a family of detectives?" asked Mrs. Peabody's sister.

Tom quirked an eyebrow at me. "Evidently."

"My husband is the only official detective," I explained to the two women. "He was formerly a homicide detective and now he's with Homeland Security, so he's helping with the investigation into Sanjay's mur…, I mean passing."

Evelyn Peabody made a sound somewhere between a snort and a harrumph. "Whatever. Just find out whose sticky hands took my watch." She motioned with her own sticky hands to get the waiter's attention. "*Garcon*, over here. We can use a bread refill."

Our *garcon* tilted his Gallic nose in disapproval, but he brought another basket of crusty rolls and bread for our table. Maybe he thought Mrs. Peabody would be less disruptive if she stuffed her mouth with an endless supply of gluten.

Mrs. Peabody's sister, whose name I finally learned was Vera, chatted quietly with my mother. As an accomplished real estate agent, my mother could draw the shyest person out of their self-imposed shell.

Evelyn Peabody tried to be helpful by giving me a list of possible thieves. She kindly excluded my grandmother and Mabel, now that she knew they were detectives. She seemed particularly interested in my husband's career.

"So that security guy who croaked, you working on that case?" she asked Tom.

He blinked. "I'm helping somewhat."

"Well, maybe you can lend your wife a hand. We only have two more days until this ship docks. I want my watch back."

"A watch as valuable as that must be insured. Isn't it?" Mother asked.

Evelyn chomped on her escargot before reaching in, removing it from her mouth and dropping it on her dish.

Ick. Escargot doesn't look all that appealing even before someone masticates it to death. Mrs. Peabody could use a few table manner tips from Emily Post.

"It's insured, but that's not the issue." Her eyes suddenly teared up, surprising me. "That watch was the last gift my husband gave to me. It's very special."

Jimmy patted her hand. "I'm sure the lovely Laurel will track it down for you."

I shot Jimmy a look. Lovely Laurel was beginning to wish she and her hubby had skipped their honeymoon. Tom's cell suddenly rang, causing conversation in the bistro to come to a halt. With international roaming calls running five dollars per minute, most passengers used their phones only for snapping photos.

Tom answered the phone, replied "yes" three times then hung up.

"Who was that?" I asked him.

"Bradford," he replied.

"Is anything wrong?" Mother half rose in her chair.

"He's fine but something came up he wants to show me as soon as possible."

"I bet it's a big clue," Gran said, gleefully rubbing her hands together. "Tell us what he discovered. Inquiring minds want to know."

"Sorry, no can do." Tom looked at the original James Bond and said, "As the saying goes, it's for my eyes only."

CHAPTER FORTY-TWO

One would think that if you're sharing a marital bed, there would be no secrets between you and your husband. Including details of a murder investigation he's involved in. But when Tom said "for his eyes only" he meant it.

Although the captain had requested my husband's immediate presence, Tom still asked for my consent before hiring a taxi to take him back to the pier. I agreed that finding a murderer always trumped sightseeing. I offered to accompany him, but he insisted I stay on the tour and stick close to Sierra. Whether he was being considerate or just trying to keep me out of his hair, I agreed to his request.

Before he left, he shared one tidbit of information. Bradford had unearthed something while reviewing the video footage. And it might be the killer.

We boarded the bus and I sat next to my mother, confiding that her husband had discovered an important clue.

"I'm glad it was worth Robert staying behind then," she said before sighing. "My husband has yet to get the hang of retirement. I hoped a cruise would entertain him, but I think he's been having more fun since they found that dead body."

"I know Robert loves you very much," I replied, "but you have to remember that he's still an active man."

"He certainly is," replied my mother with a wide smile and a wink.

Oh boy, we were so not going there.

"I just think he needs additional mental stimulation. Besides your wonderful companionship," I added.

"I suppose," she conceded. "If it takes a murder to make my husband a happy cruiser, so be it. But you're on your honeymoon, Laurel. You shouldn't have to share your husband with the captain."

"Not a problem. I have you and Gran to entertain me." A cackle followed by a bray could be heard from across the aisle. "And Mabel."

Our bus made a sharp ninety-degree right turn onto a gravel-strewn lane. My teeth clanged together as we bounced in and out of a pothole bigger than my bathtub. Our destination proved to be a smallish pale blue stucco building with a large veranda stretched across the front. Empty white wrought-iron tables and chairs awaited our arrival. What yummy delicacies were we about to sample?

A half hour later, I dropped my fork onto my plate, satiated from multiple dessert and port tastings.

"I can't believe I'm saying this," I announced to my family, "But I couldn't eat one more bite of chocolate. Even if you paid me."

"Hah," said Gran. "That leaves more for us." She speared another light-as-a-feather bite-sized treat from the colorful petits fours stacked on a three-tier silver tray. Sierra, who had been chatting with the restaurant owner, joined us.

"Did you enjoy your dessert tasting?" she asked.

"Scrumptious," I replied. "Did you get a chance to taste his goodies?"

"I sampled a couple of them. He normally makes a delicious chocolate peanut butter cheesecake, but Mrs. Peabody and Darren Abernathy both have peanut allergies. We didn't want to take any chances in the kitchen today."

Gran nodded. "Yep, cause if Peabody died, she woulda' found a way to blame you for it."

Well, technically, that was impossible, but knowing Evelyn Peabody's quarrelsome personality, she might have managed it. I was just glad that I didn't have a peanut allergy. PB&J sandwiches were a staple in our family cuisine.

Sierra began rounding up everyone for our last stop back on the Dutch side of the island. We lined up behind Sharon and Deborah and Rick and Claire.

"I swear I've died and gone to chocolate heaven," Deborah said.

Sharon laughed. "Deborah thinks chocolate should be its own food group."

Claire smiled in agreement. "It's certainly my favorite antioxidant."

"I understand they normally offer a chocolate peanut butter cheesecake, but several people on the tour have a peanut allergy, including your husband," I said to Deborah. "I haven't seen him yet today."

"He decided to skip this tour," Deborah explained.

"Where did Tom go?" asked Rick. "I could have sworn I saw him with you a little earlier."

"He's hot on the trail of the killer," Gran announced.

Claire's face paled. "The killer followed us to this island?"

"There's nothing for us to worry about," I said, shooting Gran a dirty look. "The captain just needed to chat with him."

"I'm glad your husband is involved," Claire said. "These days, you never know when someone will take a pot shot at you just driving down the freeway. We have all sorts of crazies in Southern California."

"That's why I always wear protective gear," Mabel said. She unbuttoned her madras plaid shirt to reveal a bulletproof vest. "Ya gotta be prepared in case there's a crackpot out there."

As far as I was concerned, there were way too many crackpots capering through *my* life lately.

CHAPTER FORTY-THREE

Our tour group arrived back at the dock forty-five minutes before the ship would set sail. Once we passed through security, Sierra raced off to track down Zac and find out how the rehearsal went. Mother and I returned to our respective staterooms. I walked in and found Tom seated on the sofa, scrolling through his laptop.

I plopped down and waited for a sizzling kiss that never arrived. I waved my hand in front of his preoccupied face.

"Sweetie, your wonderful wife has returned." I placed my hand on his muscular thigh. A surefire way to get his attention.

He looked up, his dark eyes perplexed and concerned.

"What's going on?" I asked him. "Are you researching something?"

"I'm going through some video footage again. We downloaded an extra copy onto my laptop."

I peered at the tiny screen of his compact laptop. "That's convenient although it could prove disruptive to our honeymoon."

He sent me a weak smile. "What we discovered is beyond disruptive. It's damaging evidence about the person who might have killed Sanjay."

I squinted as I tried to identify the person whose fuzzy image had been captured on Tom's laptop.

My eyes opened wide, and I leaned forward, my nose almost touching the computer screen.

"That's not who I think it is, is it?" I asked Tom.

"It's your cousin. In living color."

"Where was this taken?"

"On the staircase leading from the tenth floor deck to the eleventh."

"Sierra's job duties take her all over this ship," I said. "Why do you think her movements are a problem?"

Tom adjusted the magnification on his screen. It didn't help the fuzziness factor, but Sierra's frame increased thirty percent in size. Tom pointed directly at the back of Sierra's head.

"See those two chopsticks stuck in her hair?"

I nodded. "I was with her in her stateroom when she was styling it that way."

"Well, there's additional footage in this same stairwell showing her coming back down about ten minutes later."

"Okay…" I said, waiting for him to get to his point.

"The additional footage shows Sierra walking back downstairs minus one of the chopsticks."

Ouch. I got his point—sharp and clear.

"I'm sure there's an innocent explanation." My mind raced as I tried to come up with some possible scenarios. "It could have fallen out of her hair somewhere along the way. You don't know where the chopstick that killed Sanjay came from. His girlfriend might have taken one from the restaurant."

"The FBI took that particular chopstick into evidence. We could send them a DNA sample from Sierra to see if it matches up to the weapon."

I slumped into the cushions of the sofa. It was bad enough when Mrs. Peabody called Sierra a thief. But to think that my cousin could be a murderer?

No way.

"Even if Sierra's chopstick was the one used to kill Sanjay, it doesn't necessarily make her his murderer."

"True. But I wish she had mentioned she was in the vicinity shortly before Sanjay was killed. The captain and I find that omission highly suspicious. We need to have a chat with her."

"Chat with her or interrogate her?" I said. "I'm coming along."

Tom put his arm around me and finally delivered that long-awaited sizzling kiss. Then he murmured in my ear. "No, you're not."

I placed my palms against his chest and pushed him away. "Sierra is entitled to legal counsel."

"Legal counsel?"

"Hey, I watch *The Good Wife*. I've picked up a few things."

"Laurel, this is a murder investigation. I don't want you interfering with my case."

"Technically, this isn't your case. You're just assisting the captain since he asked for your help."

Tom sighed. "U.S. cruise law mandates that cruise ships handle crimes based on the laws of the country where the ships are registered. Since Sanjay isn't a U.S. citizen, and the boat is registered in Liberia, and the murder took place in international waters, the FBI has assigned the case a very low priority. In fact, no priority. Especially with that recent nightclub shooting in Miami that enlisted most of the agents in the southeast. So the cruise line is begging for my assistance. In exchange, the captain offered us a free cruise anywhere we want."

He reached for my hand. "How does a free cruise sound to you?"

At the rate this vacation was going, I'd rather have someone stick a chopstick in MY ear than take another cruise. But I appreciated Tom's efforts to help the cruise line, as well as our limited travel budget.

If only one of my relatives hadn't become his top murder suspect.

CHAPTER FORTY-FOUR

Tom left to meet with the captain. As soon as the door shut behind him, I called my mother.

"Mother, we have a crisis," I said, my voice breaking.

"Laurel, you always seem to have a crisis lately. Do you need help figuring out what to wear this evening? Why don't you give your cousin a call? She has excellent taste."

I doubted my cousin would be in any position to give fashion advice right now. For all I knew, in a few days, or even hours, Sierra could be wearing the latest in prison chic.

"This is serious and it concerns Sierra. Tom and Bradford discovered some video footage that places her in Sanjay's vicinity around the time of his murder. Tom left to meet with the captain to question her."

"Sierra would never skewer someone with a chopstick," Mother asserted. "She would devise something far more tasteful—like a poisoned margarita."

That was so like my elegant mother. I could just imagine her writing a book titled *The Girls' Guide to Classy Murder*.

"What are you going to do?" she asked.

"Hopefully, what I do best," I replied. "Come up with an alternative list of suspects."

While I waited for Tom to return, I picked up a pen and a sheet of stationery from the packet provided the passengers. My goal was to come up with a top ten list of suspects with a reason for killing the chief security officer. Although given over two thousand passengers plus eight hundred staff on board, I should come up with a top one hundred list.

But I had to start someplace.

1. Sanjay's girlfriend, Mizuki. She was in good shape with easy access to the weapon. She also had a very strong motive. I put an asterisk beside her name.

2. The two crew members Sanjay was blackmailing. Did one of them do it?

3. Were there other blackmail victims? How many more and how could I locate them?

4. The assistant security chief. Did he want his boss's job? Always an excellent motive.

5. The jewel thief. Would he or she kill to avoid discovery?

6. Evelyn Peabody.

Okay, I should probably strike her name off the list. Just because she's an annoying witch wasn't a good enough reason to place her on my suspect list. I flung my pen down on the desk. Searching for a killer on this ship was like hunting for a needle in the Empire State Building.

I wondered whether Tom would disclose the names of the two crew who admitted Sanjay had blackmailed them so I could chat them up.

I didn't need to ask him that question to know the answer.

Which meant I would need to be both discreet and creative.

CHAPTER FORTY-FIVE

Tom had shared very little about the blackmail victims other than one was a female bartender. That substantially narrowed down the list.

I glanced at the clock. If I threw on a sundress and a pair of sandals, I could check out the cocktail lounges before the evening rush began. Tom should be tied up for a while interviewing Sierra.

With the cruise directory in my hand, I set off for a shipboard version of a pub crawl. I decided to start with deck two and work my way up. My first stop would be the Fish Grotto.

The Fish Grotto resembled a cross between Pier One and *Finding Nemo*. Rainbow-colored tropical fish swam in a huge aquarium along one wall, while artsy fish sculptures decorated the walls and dangled from the ceiling. I plopped my soft bottom on a very hard metal bar stool whose lone column resembled a mermaid's tail.

Although the bartender was a guy, I figured he would know the schedule of the other bartenders for tonight's shifts. When he asked for my order, I chose the cocktail special of the day. The Ty-D-Bol blue color initially put me off, but it turned out to be quite refreshing.

Definitely tastier than the toilet bowl cleaner, not that I had any means of comparison.

There were only two other passengers seated at the bar, providing me the opportunity to chat up the young man.

"So, Ivan, it looks like you're from..." I squinted trying to read his name tag.

"Belarus," he replied with a slight accent.

"I haven't traveled there yet," I said, not admitting that the list of places I hadn't traveled was far longer than the places I had visited.

"It's not so popular with Americans."

"Are there other bartenders from your country on board?" I asked, leading my witness into hopefully identifying the female bartender for me.

He nodded. "Yes, Natasha, another bartender is from near there."

"I think she served me the other night. Is she usually in the Queen's Lounge?"

"We rotate around the ship. I think tonight she is up in Trident Lounge. Where the jazz band plays."

"She's very sweet," I said.

His face darkened but he merely replied, "If you say so."

Interesting response. One of the other passengers waved Ivan over, and he zipped off to serve them. I took a few more sips of my drink and left the glass on the counter. If I planned on conducting my investigation at multiple bars, I needed to limit my alcoholic intake.

Not to mention my calories. So far the only exercise I'd gotten on this trip was rolling around the mattress with my husband.

I smiled. Not a bad way to burn off the calories. But probably not sufficient for the fine wine and cuisine I'd been consuming all week.

I checked my watch once more. The Trident Lounge was only two decks up. I could squeeze in a quick visit before I returned to our cabin. I walked up both flights of stairs, eliminating almost twenty of the calories I'd just swallowed.

The Trident Lounge proved to be on the opposite side of the ship. Couples dressed in casual or tropical wear milled around in every direction. I walked past the photo gallery. A number of passengers were scrutinizing their formal photos. One of these days I needed to check out ours. Not that we were lacking in iPhone photos. But these eight by ten pictures seemed more glamorous than our spontaneous shots.

Plus I never seemed to get around to actually printing up any of our photos. Did anyone?

The Trident Lounge was half full, although more people were seated at the small tables than at the bar. I sank onto a tall, but comfortable bar stool. I mentally congratulated the interior designer who chose comfort over faddish designs.

Natasha, the bartender, was very pretty with her round, rosy-cheeked face, soft hazel eyes, and long dark-blond hair done up in a ponytail that brushed her shoulders. She wore the same tailored uniform of black pants and burgundy vest that all the bartenders wore, although her vest looked ready to burst open as it struggled to restrain her generous curves.

When Natasha came to take my order I settled on a diet-cola. She smiled as she set down the glass, a tiny slice of lime neatly attached to the rim.

"*Spasibo,*" I replied. Her eyes widened at my thank you.

"You speak Russian," she said to me.

"*Da*, I mean yes. A tiny bit," I clarified. Technically the only other Russian word I knew was vodka. "I understand you're from Belarus. You're a long way from home."

She nodded.

"Do you enjoy working on the ship?" I realized she probably got asked that question all day long. Cruisers are a curious group.

She reached for a cloth from under the counter and began wiping a spot of condensation from the bar top.

"Yes, it is a good job." Her eyes grew wistful for a split second. Then she straightened and smiled.

"You are liking your cruise?" she asked.

"It's been lovely," I leaned forward and spoke softly. "Except for that horrible murder. Can you believe someone killed the chief security officer?"

"Maybe he not such a good guy," she offered.

"Did you personally have problems with him?" I asked sympathetically, ready to reverse our roles and have the bartender cry on my shoulder.

She lowered her eyes, her thick dark lashes forming shadows on her sculpted cheekbones.

"He preyed on people. On the crew."

"You too?"

Natasha nodded. "A big security guy like that has access to all crew information. Much private stuff, too. It is not good when a bad person know too much."

I gasped. "Did he threaten you?"

Her shoulders drooped. "No, worse. He want to trade information for something more desirable."

"What?"

She pointed to her chest. "Me."

CHAPTER FORTY-SIX

My short conversation with Natasha resulted in an entirely new line of questioning. One that I was more than happy to hand over to an expert. From what I gathered from her, Sanjay maintained files on every crew member. With his elite position, he had access to criminal records from around the world.

Sanjay had threatened to share some information about Natasha's past with the captain. In order to keep him from divulging a previous arrest for shoplifting five years earlier, he'd demanded sex with her.

Fortunately for Natasha, the combination of her long hours along with the increasing number of thefts on board the ship, had kept Sanjay occupied, and she'd been able to delay any assignation with the man.

I couldn't think of a tactful way to ask her if she'd killed Sanjay, so I told her I would keep our conversation to myself. Although I would share it with Tom. Who would, of course, be thrilled with this new information I'd discovered.

Or not.

When I returned to the stateroom, I found my husband waiting for me, arms crossed with a dour expression on his face. I shared Natasha's information with him, hoping that would turn his frown into a smile.

"Honestly, Laurel, how many times do you have to be clobbered before you get some sense into that thick skull of yours? What if Natasha turns out to be the killer? Now she knows who you are and what cabin we're in."

"She doesn't know who I am other than a sympathetic bystander." Wounded by his comment, I added, "And my head isn't that thick."

"When you purchased your soda, did you give her your ship card with your name and cabin number on it?"

Oops. Reminder to self. Never buy drinks from a potential killer. So much for the ease of a cashless payment system.

I plopped down on the bed, my thick skull resting against the even thicker pillow. Tears welled up in my eyes. Tears of frustration combined with fear.

Not the fear of a murderer seeking me out, although if I wasn't so thickheaded maybe I would be concerned about that. No, it was fear that I'd somehow drilled a tiny hole into our relationship by once again ignoring my husband's wise advice. Would I ever learn?

Tom glared at me for a few more seconds before dropping heavily onto the bedspread. His large palm stroked my tear-stained cheek.

"I'm sorry, honey." Tom's voice broke. "You know my only concern is for your safety. I love you so much. I can't bear the thought of losing you."

I sat up and wrapped my arms around his neck. We clung to each other for a few minutes. I finally released him and walked into the bathroom to grab a few tissues to wipe away all signs of my cryfest.

"Are you okay?" he called out.

I hurried out of the bathroom. "I'm fine, or I will be. And I promise to try really hard not to land in any trouble. You know I only want to help Sierra." I stopped and stared at him. "So what is the latest on your conversation with her? Did she satisfy your curiosity about the missing chopstick?"

He shoved his hand through his thick hair. "Not really. If Sierra wasn't your cousin, I would have significant doubts about her explanation."

"What did she say?"

He sighed and tugged on his right ear lobe, always a sign that something was bothering him.

"According to Sierra," he said, "she'd gone up to the Crystal Lounge on the tenth floor to check on the sound system. One of the performers had complained about it not working properly the previous night."

"That sounds innocent enough."

"I agree. Then she remembered we were all meeting at Chopsticks that night. She decided to swing upstairs and talk to the hostess to ensure we would get great seating and service."

"No good deed goes unpunished?"

"Possibly. It depends if her explanation holds up. She supposedly chatted with the hostess and asked her if she'd seen Sanjay around. Sierra told the hostess she'd been trying to track him down all afternoon."

"She told me the same thing when I stopped to visit her."

"That helps somewhat. Sierra stopped in the private cabana area and called out Sanjay's name, but she didn't see him anywhere. She claims she doesn't remember if any of the curtains were drawn across any of the private cabanas."

"That's it?"

"Pretty much," Tom said. "According to Sierra, she didn't even realize she'd lost one of her chopsticks until later. For all she knew, her chopstick was lying at the scene of the crime before it actually became a scene of the crime."

My head hurt trying to follow that last sentence. From my biased nepotistic point of view, my cousin had nothing to worry about.

"So the killer could have picked up the chopstick and murdered Sanjay in a fit of passion."

"Or rage. Or whatever." Tom's face looked drawn, not the image of a man enjoying his honeymoon. I needed to find a way to make it up to him.

I bent over and kissed him. Despite our stress levels, I could feel the same magnetic charge I always did. And based on Tom's expression, he did, too.

"When this honeymoon is over, I promise I'll make it up to you," I said, trying to look as seductive as possible.

"And I will definitely hold you to that promise." He wrapped his arm around me and gave me a comforting squeeze. "Now, let's go eat. I'm looking forward to a crime-free dinner."

Who knew homicide cops were such optimists?

CHAPTER FORTY-SEVEN

Tom and I attempted to find a secluded alcove to dine together. Alone. Without friends, family or murder suspects. And once again, we were unsuccessful. I waved at Danielle dining with her husband. Or, so I assumed, since I could only see Pierre's back seated in his wheelchair. I certainly couldn't begrudge them an intimate evening together. It was nice that although wheelchair bound, her husband could enjoy the cruise, too.

We ended up at a table for eight with some friendly and not so friendly faces. Margaret sat beside an older fellow with a fake orange-glazed tan who looked nothing like her husband, Fred. Evelyn Peabody, bejeweled in a glittering array of emeralds, was seated next to her sister, Vera. Lucille and Glenn smiled and greeted us warmly.

Once seated, the maître d' handed us the menus. I held the large menu in front of my face, hoping to block Mrs. Peabody's view of me. Why I thought that would work was beyond me.

"I've been waiting for you to report in," she said, waving her fork in the air, sprinkling droplets of gravy in its wake. "Do you know who did it?"

"Do I know who killed Sanjay?" I asked.

"Who's Sanjay?" she asked, looking confused.

'The chief security officer," Tom informed her, his voice echoing from behind his menu.

She wrinkled her large nose. "Not my problem. Do you know who took my watch?" When we both shook our heads, she clicked her tongue in reproof. "You two aren't real quick for detectives. Maybe I should hire someone else."

"Excellent idea," I said as the waiter approached our table. Tom ordered a bottle of chardonnay. An even better idea.

"What's the latest on the murder?" asked Margaret's companion.

Tom lowered his menu. "I'm sorry but I'm not at liberty to say. Who are you?"

"Chet Goodman," the man replied. "Dance host."

My ears perked up at his introduction. I so loved to dance. I only wished my almost perfect husband felt the same way. "Do you give lessons?" I asked Chet.

"I teach a group ballroom lesson every afternoon at three o'clock. In the evenings, I'm available to dance with any single woman looking for a partner."

"But Margaret isn't single," I blurted out.

Margaret glared at me. As the saying goes, if looks could kill.

"Chet has been kind enough to give me a few private lessons," she explained, "while Fred is laid up with the flu. It's been such a trial caring for him. The dance lessons are a nice reprieve."

Chet beamed at her and she smiled back.

Mrs. Peabody, not normally the most astute person in the room, added her two cents. "While the cat's away, the mice will cha-cha."

Tom and Chet looked confused, but Margaret and I caught her drift. Margaret blushed and concentrated on eating her dinner.

"Do you sign a long-term commitment like the rest of the crew?" I asked Chet.

He shook his head. "Dance escorts basically get to cruise for free. We provide a service for the ship since there are always more single women than single men on board. The cruise lines like to keep those women happy and turn them into repeat passengers." He and Margaret exchanged glances making me wonder if Chet and the cruise line agreed on the definition of "a happy passenger."

Evelyn snorted. "Swell. So back to my missing jewelry. What's your plan? You're down to thirty-six hours to recover them before the ship docks. I'd hate to return home empty-handed."

Vera jumped in for the first time. "There's always the insurance, Evelyn, in case they can't retrieve the items."

"That's not the point, Vera," Evelyn replied, her face growing redder by the minute.

Tom and I exchanged glances. Very interesting.

"I told Laurel I would help with her detectin'," Lucille chimed in. "And I may have a clue for you." As she leaned forward, her bifocals slipped down her small pug nose. She shoved them back up and continued, "I was talking to Javier, our cabin steward, and he said he heard the cruise director's been stealing all the stuff. Can you believe it? The cruise director."

"I told you so." Mrs. Peabody pounded her fork on the table. She turned to Lucille. "Javier is our cabin steward as well. He knows what's going on."

"So who is investigating the thefts?" Glenn asked Tom. "Are you?"

Tom shrugged. "More or less."

"Seems like less to me," said Mrs. Peabody.

That was the last straw. "There are a few things more important than your stupid watch," I said curtly. "Like a dead security officer and a missing person."

Vera looked startled by my pronouncement. "Who's missing?"

"We're not sure." I stared at Margaret who stared back. Although her face appeared impassive, her right hand clutched the string of pearls around her neck. "But we won't stop investigating until we find out."

The silence at the table would have been deafening were it not for the sound of tiny oyster-white pearls scattering across the marble floor.

CHAPTER FORTY-EIGHT

In the scramble to retrieve the tiny pearls before someone slipped and crash-landed on the glossy surface, we failed to realize that both Margaret and Chet had scattered even faster than the obstreperous pearls.

I dropped the smattering of pearls I'd recovered on my empty bread plate and Tom did the same. "Where the heck did they go," he complained as the tiny gems clanked against the fine china.

I looked around the room. "I don't know. Was it something I said?"

Evelyn Peabody poked at the red snapper on her plate. "Looks like you scared them off. They must be up to no good." She wolfed down her fish and smacked her lips. "Good stuff. So you two going after them?"

"We don't really have cause to chase them," Tom explained. "Perhaps they misinterpreted something my wife said." He patted my thigh and smiled at me. "That happens—frequently."

"Innocent people don't run," I replied.

"That's right," Lucille said in agreement. When Tom stared at her, she amended her statement, "Well, that's what they say on all the crime shows."

Tom and Glenn both rolled their eyes at her remark, but I mouthed a verbal thanks to her.

"There's not much we can do, Laurel. It's not like I'm going to use my list of the passengers to track them down." Tom's face suddenly closed up as he realized he'd made a major oops.

I dropped my fork on the table. "You possess a list of all the passengers? Since when? And why didn't you tell me? That list could help me with my investigation."

"Laurel, I am in the middle of an investigation," Tom said firmly. "*You* are not."

Evelyn replied before I could come up with a smart retort of my own. "Your wife seems to have a mind of her own. And you're wrong. She is involved in an official investigation."

"I am?"

"Yes. My missing watch and jewels. Now stop worrying about that missing body of yours and focus on something really important."

Tom stifled a grin at her remark. I decided to ignore both of them for now and concentrate on my delicious salmon entrée. Afterward, my husband and I were going to have a serious discussion.

After a full day of sightseeing and a considerable amount of detecting by each of us, Tom and I were more than ready to jump into bed together.

And sleep.

We lay parallel to one another. Tom in his black boxers and nothing else. Me in my royal blue satin chemise and shorty bottoms. Tom kissed me goodnight then stretched his arms around me. I leaned back against him. We fit so well together.

"Honey," I began the conversation that had been formulating in my brain since Tom's accidental disclosure at dinner.

He snuggled closer. "Not tonight, sweetheart. I'm bushed."

"Poor baby. Do you have to go back to the captain's quarters early tomorrow to review those passenger lists?" My heart thumped almost as loudly as if we were doing something more vigorous than spooning. "I'd certainly hate for you to miss that kayak trip we booked."

"No, no," Tom murmured into my ear. "The captain emailed them to me in case I needed to cross reference a name with a stateroom. We'll be able to kayak tomorrow and..." His voice dropped simultaneously with his arm falling below my waist. The gentle snores that filled the room were music to my inquisitive ears.

I waited a few minutes before slipping out of our bed. Since we were on our honeymoon, we'd seen no need for each of us to bring a laptop on the cruise. In case of an emergency, we'd decided to play it safe and had exchanged passwords.

An excellent decision as it turned out.

I lifted Tom's laptop out of his backpack. Then I opened the heavy door and crept out on our balcony, making sure his computer was secure under my arm. The seas were calm. The almost full moon lit the night sky as well as our balcony. Perfect detecting weather.

I had no desire to interfere with the murder investigation. My sole goal was to locate Margaret and Fred Johnson's cabin number and determine if the man was okay. I convinced myself that I wasn't prying, merely doing a good deed for a fellow passenger.

I entered Tom's password and the screen lit up. The passenger list proved easy to access since it was the newest document reviewed by Tom. The list contained four columns: name, address, cabin number, and each passenger's individually assigned Nordic American number. I scrolled down the alphabetical list until I arrived at Johnson. There were five Johnson couples listed on board. Not surprising considering the number of passengers on the ship. But only one Fred Johnson in cabin 10046, three decks above us.

Nice. The tenth floor offered the larger suites on the ship. I vaguely remembered Margaret mentioning the first night we met that she and Fred qualified for special status due to them cruising more than ten times on this particular line.

It would be a shame if Fred missed most of the cruise because he was ill.

But it would be even more of a shame if he missed most of the cruise because someone had thrown him overboard!

CHAPTER FORTY-NINE

Tom woke early the next day and left to meet with the captain. I wouldn't have minded a few more hours in the sack, but I also had detecting to do before our scheduled kayak trip at noon. I debated whether to climb up to the tenth floor and knock on the Johnson's cabin or get breakfast. My stomach chimed in, making that an easy decision. I decided to make the Lido Café my first stop. Besides if Fred was still sick in bed, it would be rude of me to wake him too early.

It might be considered rude to disturb the couple at all, but if something had happened to Fred Johnson, I would never forgive myself if I didn't make one attempt to ensure he was alive and well.

Or, at least alive.

I walked into a filled-to-capacity Lido Café. The passengers must be trying to squeeze in an early breakfast before whatever excursion they had arranged for Sunshine Cay, the private island in the Bahamas that the cruise line leased for its passengers.

I maneuvered around dozens of people lined up for the make-your-own omelet station and headed for something healthier. Oatmeal. By the time I finished loading it with brown sugar and sweet golden raisins, it wasn't quite as nutritious, although it was definitely tastier. I added a small bowl of mixed tropical fruit then wandered around looking for a seat somewhere.

Gran's yodel caught my attention. As well as most of the people waiting in line for an omelet. I tried to follow the sound of her voice since it could be difficult to find the small woman. Plus one never knew what color her hair would be on any given day. I finally tracked her down to a large table. Seated at the table were Mabel, Margaret and an unexpected face.

I almost dropped my tray upon seeing Fred Johnson. He was alive.

Fred gave me a weak smile at my greeting. "Nice to see you again, Laurel."

"And it is very nice to see you," I replied. "I was worried about you."

"So Margaret said." Although Fred's skin tone was a grayish milk chocolate in color, his dark eyes twinkled at me. "Margaret told me you were concerned she might have thrown me overboard." He chuckled. "I'm not that easy to get rid of, norovirus notwithstanding."

"We don't know for sure if that's what you had," Margaret chided her husband. She turned to me. "We were trying to stay low key about Fred's situation. Once the ship suspects someone might have norovirus, even if the passenger hasn't been officially diagnosed, they have the right to implement a quarantine."

"And cancel the whole cruise," Mabel added, displaying chunks of pineapple between the gaps in her teeth. "I read about that. Appreciate you keeping mum about it. I wouldn't have wanted to go home early. It's snowing back there."

"Are you feeling better?" I asked him.

He nodded. "I'm on the mend. We're going to plop ourselves down on some lounge chairs on the beach. Take it easy for today." He clutched Margaret's hand. "My poor wife hasn't experienced a very good trip either. She's been a real sport about everything."

Margaret remained silent. As did I, even though I possessed some qualms about what and whom Fred's wife had been doing. I was just pleased to see him up and around for a change.

So that meant I must have imagined someone was thrown overboard that first night on the ship.

Right?

With one mystery solved, that only left two more. Or was it three? I felt like I was juggling more crime-filled plates than usual.

"What's on your schedule today?" Gran asked me. "Playing tourist or detective? Don't forget Mabel and me is here to help. Probably would have solved all these cases by now if the captain woulda' let us assist him."

Mabel nodded. "I was thinking maybe we should follow that Peabody woman. Find out if the jewel thief is stalking her."

I blinked. "That's not a half-bad idea, Mabel." Plus it would keep both women occupied and out of my hair. "Don't do anything dangerous though."

Gran harrumphed. "I'm eighty-eight, Laurel. Just breathing can be dangerous at this age. Let me have fun while I still can."

I threw my arms around her and gave her a hug. I hoped I would have as much energy when I got to be her age.

Actually, I wished I had her energy levels now. I snatched a chocolate chip cookie on my way out of the café. A mid-morning endorphin boost. I bumped into Deborah and Sharon near the entrance to the spa.

"What are you ladies up to today?" I asked them.

"We're just grabbing a bite to eat before our kayak trip," Deborah replied.

"The one at noon? Tom and I are taking that. It's my first time kayaking so I'm a little nervous about it."

"You'll love it," Sharon said. "I'm sure the scenery on the island will be breathtaking."

"Is your husband kayaking?" I asked Deborah. "I haven't seen him since that first evening."

Sharon and Deborah exchanged glances. "Oh, you know how men are."

As far as I was concerned, it would take the rest of my life to understand the male psyche. But Deborah's husband, Darren, had to be one of the worst examples. She was lucky she'd run into her friend on board the ship, and they could hang out together.

I walked away from the two women, reflecting on the absence of Deborah's husband on this cruise. Why would you go on a cruise with your beloved wife and then disappear for seven days?

I stopped suddenly. Not the wisest thing to do when two elderly women in walkers are hot on your flip-flops. One of them almost knocked me over. Instead she scooted around me, cussing me out under her breath.

My brain was spinning and so were my feet as I headed for my room. How could I have been so blind? Deborah's stateroom was two floors above ours. I'd noticed it the other morning when I'd stopped at my mother's cabin. Her friend Sharon was a large, solid woman. The two of them could easily have pushed Darren off the balcony. Never to be seen again.

Except by one person.

Me.

CHAPTER FIFTY

I burst through the door of our stateroom, fueled by the affirmation that I really had seen someone go overboard. I couldn't wait to share my theory with Tom. But as I entered the empty room, I realized I would have to wait. Something I was not particularly good at.

I opened the door and walked onto our balcony overlooking the shoreline of Sunshine Cay. The ship's tenders filled with a constant stream of people. The boats would take the passengers to the island, offload them, and then return to the *Celebration* to collect some more folks. I thrummed my fingers on the railing. Surely there was some way I could entertain myself until Tom returned.

A brilliant thought came to me. Or, so it seemed at that very second. Since Mother and Bradford's stateroom was only two rooms away from the Abernathy's room, maybe I could talk to their cabin steward to see if he had seen Darren recently. If so, I could remove the missing husband from my missing person's list.

Armed with a reasonable plan, I left our cabin and headed for the stairwell. I flew up the two flights of stairs, exhilarated by my new theory. When I arrived at their corridor, no one was around, including any of the cabin stewards. I banged on Mother's door but received no response. They were most likely eating breakfast. Or maybe they'd already set off for Sunshine Cay. They had opted for a more tranquil tour of the island's lagoon—via a motorized boat.

I glanced at my biceps. Or lack thereof. I might need a motorized boat to bring me back to shore if we ended up kayaking out too far. The only time I exercised my upper arms was when I opened up a bottle of wine with my stubborn corkscrew.

I debated what to do next. My indecisiveness was rewarded when Deborah and Darren's stateroom door opened. A room service attendant struggled to hold the door open while she exited, her arms weighted down with a huge tray of dishes.

I held the door open for her, and she smiled her thanks before walking away. With no actual plan in mind, I entered their cabin, the heavy door slamming shut behind me. There was no sound other than my heart thumping louder than a bass player. I called out Darren's name, but there was no reply. A half hour had passed since I'd bumped into Deborah and Sharon so I needed to be quick.

Given the size of the staterooms, it wouldn't take long for me to do a cursory search. I walked onto their balcony, an identical replica of ours. I lifted both cushions and checked for bloodstains or anything out of the ordinary. Although any self-respecting murderer would have covered up the evidence before the steward cleaned the room the next day.

I peeked in the tiny but efficient bathroom. A man's razor rested by a can of shaving cream, but I couldn't tell how recently it had been used. Small sample-size moisturizer bottles were scattered across the narrow counter.

I moved to the closet and slid the door open. Wow. Deborah owned a closetful of glitzy clothes. And Tom thought I was a closet hog. Poor Darren only had...three shirts? I quickly rummaged through the drawers built into the closet. One drawer with two pairs of men's slacks and a pair of shorts.

Deborah's husband certainly traveled light. As opposed to his wife. Who needs six formals for an eight-day cruise? I eyed a full-length red sequin gown. Wasn't Sharon wearing that the other night? Did she and Deborah exchange dresses or...did her friend move into the cabin after they dumped Darren overboard?

I slammed the closet door shut and leaned back against it, my breath coming fast and furious. My heart beat so loudly I almost didn't notice the sound of voices in the hallway outside the cabin door. Deborah and Sharon were back.

I moved to the bed, bent down and lifted the spread. Suitcases completely covered the floor from one end of the bed to the other. What should I do?

The voices grew louder and my hands grew clammier as the truth sank in.

There was nowhere to hide.

CHAPTER FIFTY-ONE

After struggling with the keycard, Deborah and Sharon entered the room. Grateful that the women appeared to be as keycard-challenged as I am, I'd hidden on the balcony behind the folds of the drapes on the other side of the glass pane. If they decided they needed a full view of the island, my hiding place would be discovered in an instant.

The bathroom door slammed shut. Not long after the television blared on. Both women were temporarily occupied. I peered around the partial privacy wall of their balcony to the next stateroom. By my calculations, my mother's room was less than two balconies over.

An easy climb. For Simone Biles.

For Laurel McKay, it was a heart-stopping drop if I made a wrong move.

That could be the title of my biography if I didn't survive this cruise. I peered down into the sea far below. The extra height of this deck made the view down even scarier than from our balcony. I tried to comfort myself with the fact I could swim. And one time I even dove off the high board in high school.

Although now that I reflected back, my ex-husband had pushed me off that high board. Why on earth I ever married that man is beyond me. But, irrelevant now. More relevant was the phone call I was making to the kids, regardless of the expense, once I survived my current challenge.

The sound of the bathroom door banging open startled me. It was now or never.

I quietly dragged the chair over to the wall, climbed on top and lifted my left leg over the barrier. I swung my right foot out, and it collided with the balcony railing. My flip-flop slipped off my foot and tumbled below.

I shivered. Better a rubber shoe than me. I slid down the adjoining wall onto their neighbor's balcony. My landing was less graceful and far noisier than I'd envisioned. A familiar bald head peered around the privacy wall on the opposite side.

"What the hell?" Bradford bellowed.

I placed my finger against my lips and shushed him. I peered through the plate-glass window but didn't see any signs of activity in this particular stateroom. The occupants had obligingly left their balcony door unlocked assuming no one in their right mind would be balcony hopping. I waved goodbye to Bradford, slipped through the glass door, crept across the carpet, and was out the cabin door before you could say—

"Laurel?" My mother and my stepfather stood at the entrance to their stateroom, arms folded, almost identical frowns on their faces.

I shot them a cheery smile. "Hi, guys. How was breakfast?"

Bradford jerked his thumb toward their stateroom. I gulped and entered their room, plopping down on the sofa, one shoe on and one shoe off.

I glanced at my watch. "I only have a few minutes to spare. Tom and I scheduled the noon kayak tour."

"Would you like to tell us why you were invading our neighbor's stateroom?" Mother asked.

"I think the wife in that cabin might have shoved her husband overboard."

"And your reasons for that assumption?" Bradford asked, his expression skeptical.

"You know I still believe I saw someone fall overboard that first night despite no one reporting a missing person. Ever since our second day on board, Deborah in cabin 9066 has been hanging around with a girlfriend. Her husband is nowhere to be found."

"So you felt obligated to search their room?" Bradford asked.

"Well, I sort of fell into that. Literally," I claimed. "I only intended to make a quick search, but the two women returned while I was still in there. Hence my rather unorthodox escape."

"You could have been killed." My mother shuddered. "I swear between yours and Robert's escapades, I'm going to have a heart attack one of these days."

Bradford grinned for the first time since he'd caught me snooping, and I smiled back. "How about I promise to keep a look out for the missing hubby, and you promise to stay out of strange cabins?" he asked me.

I nodded. Absolutely no more balcony gymnastics for me. I was saving those antics for my mattress.

CHAPTER FIFTY-TWO

I bumped into Jimmy Bond on my way back to our stateroom. Dressed in a logo-trimmed white polo shirt and creased tan khakis, the man looked like a GQ cover model—the senior version.

"What are you up to today?" I asked him.

"I'm going to meander around and grab a bite to eat while I watch the other passengers burn themselves to a crisp."

I laughed. "You always have such a great attitude. Do you ever mind traveling alone?"

He spread his arms out wide. "How can one be alone when you're surrounded by the grandeur of the seas?" A family passed by us, the parents' arms loaded with beach bags and towels, as they herded their three noisy children down the stairs. "And an ever-changing slice of humanity," Jimmy added. "And how, may I ask, are you and your husband occupying your day on the island?"

"Kayaking," I said unenthusiastically. "Or, knowing me, falling off the kayak and swimming in the lagoon. I hope no alligators reside on this island."

"Be careful, my dear," he warned me. "I don't know about alligators, but there are nasty critters everywhere." He held up his hand and disappeared into the sea of passengers. As enigmatic as ever.

I was still puzzling over my short conversation with Jimmy when I ran into my cousin. Sierra was dressed in a crisp white short-sleeved Nordic American blouse and navy slacks.

"You look so official," I said. "Are you leading a tour on the island today?"

She grimaced. "The captain asked me to join him for a meeting. I didn't get the impression it was a social occasion."

"Do you think you'll be terminated?"

Her gold braid epaulets moved up and down as she shrugged. "Honestly, I would have no problem having my tenure on this ship shortened. But I can't afford a black mark on my employment record."

"I guess it could be worse. At least they're not threatening to arrest you for Sanjay's murder."

She narrowed her eyes at me. "Gee, thanks for the vote of confidence. I could tell your husband didn't completely buy my explanation of my whereabouts when Sanjay was killed, but I certainly thought you would be on my side."

Her sharp reprimand brought back reminders of my youth when Sierra would make me stand in the corner of the dining room whenever I misbehaved. I might be too old to be punished by my former babysitter, but her words still cut me to the quick.

"I'm sorry. Of course I believe you. You were my role model as a kid. Prom Queen, head cheerleader, female lead in the school musicals. I wanted to be you when I grew up."

"I think you did alright." Sierra smiled at me. "You have a wonderful husband with high integrity, two great kids and an excellent job at the bank. I should be so lucky." She looked at her watch. "Oops. I better get going. There's nothing Captain Andriessen hates more than a lack of punctuality. I'm going to need a dose of good luck if I'm going to stay employed."

She raced off in one direction and so did I. When I arrived at our room, Tom kissed me before pointing to the clock. Since I was one flip-flop short, I slipped on a pair of sandals then packed everything I could possibly need in my super-sized straw tote and handed it to Tom.

"What's this?" he asked.

"Remember our wedding ceremony? You promised to love, cherish and haul my gear all over the place."

Tom rolled his eyes but kept silent. A wise choice on his part.

The corridors and elevators were crowded with passengers, and I began to worry we would be late for our kayaking expedition. Luckily we got the last two seats in the tender and arrived on the island with fifteen minutes to spare. We bumped into Danielle and Jacques in the main square. I asked them about their plans for the day.

"We ride the horses on the beach," she said with a winsome smile, tucking a strand of hair behind her ear. "I have always wanted to gallop through the waves. Pierre sent Jacques to make sure I don't fall off and make big splash."

"That sounds like fun." I turned to Tom. "Doesn't it honey?" He shook his head, evidently not as enthralled with the notion of equine water sports as I was.

"You are doing something fun on the island, too?" Danielle asked us as Mother and Bradford approached.

"Hopefully, not looking for any missing bodies," Bradford said, sending me a stern look.

"Nope, no detecting for us today. Just kayaking."

Jacques looked confused. "What are these missing bodies you look for? Is a Pokemon game, *non*?"

"No, is a, I mean it's not a game," I replied. "It's a crime. A real one."

"Laurel thought she saw someone go overboard the first night of the cruise," Mother explained as Claire and Rick joined our group, having arrived via the second tender.

"*C'est terrible*," Danielle said. "What is the captain doing about this missing person? I do not recall hearing about it."

Not a heck of a lot from my point of view. But I wasn't in charge of the ship.

"Isn't it odd the ship didn't stop?" said Rick. "Wouldn't that be the normal protocol when someone is reported missing?"

"If a specific passenger had been reported missing, the captain definitely would have stopped to search," Tom explained. "But no one appears to be missing."

"So it really is a mystery," Claire said. "You know I like to watch crime shows. Can I help look for clues? Wouldn't it be fun if we discovered something?" Her dark eyes lit up at the thought.

"*Moi aussi*," Danielle said. "I can be the female Hercule Poirot, *non*?"

I looked at the tall, slender young woman whose chestnut hair cascaded below her waist. Definitely, no. But I appreciated both women's offers to help. I guess everyone has a secret urge to play amateur detective.

Mother asked Rick and Claire about their plans. "Rick is joining the jet-ski tour around the island," Claire said, "and I'm going to find one of those hammocks they advertised, get a daiquiri and read my Kindle. How about you?" she asked my mother.

"Robert and I signed up for the glass boat tour, while Laurel and Tom will peacefully kayak around the lagoon."

From Mother's lips to my paddles. I certainly hoped our kayak journey would be without incident and that the serene ambiance wouldn't be rent with my cries for help if I fell overboard.

But I sure wouldn't count on it.

CHAPTER FIFTY-THREE

Ten minutes and one pit-stop later, Tom and I joined the rest of our tour group. Sharon and Deborah waved hello at us. Deborah wore her standard dull beige polo shirt and matching shorts while Sharon sported a black T-shirt featuring an oversized cocktail glass on the front and the words DYING FOR A DAIQUIRI etched in sequins on the back.

I might not concur with her fashion choices, but I wouldn't have minded a daiquiri myself. The liquid kind.

We boarded an open-air shuttle bus that would take us on the short drive to the lagoon. After a few minutes of total silence, an unusual event for his loquacious wife, Tom's knee bumped against mine.

"You're kind of quiet," he said. "Anything wrong?"

"Just reflecting on our trip," I replied with a sigh. "Hard to believe we'll be back home tomorrow night. This cruise has gone by so quickly."

"Want to sign up for another week?"

"Wouldn't that be lovely?" I snuggled against his shoulder. "To have the freedom to go on vacation more than two weeks a year. To be your own boss."

"You mean you're not counting the hours until you can work on Hangtown Bank's next marketing campaign?" Tom teased me.

My uncensored reply was drowned out in a squeal of aged brakes as the shuttle came to an abrupt stop.

The tour director advised us to leave our bags and valuables on board the bus. The driver promised to keep tabs on our belongings while we kayaked.

Tom unfurled his long legs, stood and waited while I slid across the cracked vinyl seat. "Do you think it's safe to leave our stuff here?" I asked him. "What if the jewel thief is on this excursion? Maybe I should stay behind and keep an eye out."

"And miss out on your first kayaking trip?" Tom said. "Not to worry. The bus driver will be here. Everything will be fine." He squeezed my shoulders. "Trust me."

I climbed down the steps wishing I felt as optimistic as Tom. Although I wasn't anywhere near as old as many of the seniors on this excursion, what I lacked in years, I more than made up for in klutziness.

The guide led our group to a long, narrow beach where rainbow-colored kayaks waited for us. A few puffy clouds dotted the sky, but the weather was about as perfect as you could ask for. Sunshine, low humidity and a slight breeze that caused barely a ripple on the calm surface of the lagoon.

My spirits perked up and my shoulders relaxed as I realized kayaking could possibly end up as one of my favorite excursions.

I'd originally thought Tom and I would be sharing a kayak built for two, but they only offered single kayaks on this island. He selected a red kayak and I chose a blue one in the exact shade as my worried eyes. The guide gave us a quick lesson on the art of paddling. It didn't seem that complicated, but I paid careful attention to his instructions. Our group set out to explore the lagoon with my husband in the next boat over, keeping a watchful eye on me.

Eventually our guide led us to a narrow passage lined with green mangrove trees on each side. Our group fell into place with one kayak trailing behind another. I ended up following Sharon who was behind Deborah, while Tom paddled directly behind me. Sharon must have kayaked before. Her strokes were strong and even as opposed to my more erratic paddling that favored my right side. Her posture was excellent, something I tried to mimic. But every time I attempted to sit up straight, my boobs, encased in the bulky life jacket, bumped into my paddle.

I was so busy concentrating on my technique that I failed to notice our guide had stopped to point out a blue heron diving for his dinner. Sharon halted along with everyone else.

Everyone, that is, except me.

Thwack. I crashed into the side of Sharon's boat. As I tried to move my paddle out of the way, the wide end smacked her in the back of her head.

Sharon flipped into the water, her arms flailing in the air.

I leaned forward and my kayak swayed to the left before righting itself. But Sharon's safety was my main concern. I shoved my paddle toward her, hoping she could grab it for support. I don't know whether Sharon was confused about my attempt to help her, or ticked off at me. The next thing I knew, my paddle was yanked out of my hand.

I toppled over and hit the water with a resounding splash.

CHAPTER FIFTY-FOUR

The first word I uttered when I surfaced was "glub." Behind me, someone shouted a string of four-letter words somewhat more specific than mine. I blinked my mascara-gunked eyelashes several times before my contacts settled down. The sight that greeted me was not at all pleasant. A bald stranger treaded water, his descriptive curses aimed in my direction.

Where had he come from and what happened to Sharon? Did she need to be rescued? I couldn't remember if she had chosen to wear a life vest or not, since the decision was up to the individual kayaker.

My own personal rescue team swam up to me. "Are you okay, hon?" Tom asked, droplets of water on his eyelashes. He wrapped his arms around me, holding me tight against him as he treaded water.

"I'm fine." Then I yelped as a furry beast rubbed against the hand I'd been trailing in the lagoon. What the heck?

Tom stretched his arm around me and grabbed hold of the critter. Neither a mammal nor a reptile.

Merely one soggy blond wig.

I glanced at the tall man who remained in the water. His gaze locked on the item in Tom's hand.

How could I have been so dense? Deborah hadn't pushed her husband overboard. Darren was not only her spouse, he was also her best friend—Sharon. You could have fooled me!

Actually, he had fooled me.

Tom swam over to Darren/Sharon. While Tom held on to the kayak, he/she pulled himself or herself into the kayak. At this point, I had no idea which pronoun was the most appropriate. I was just grateful that Darren was alive and well.

No thanks to me. He and Tom conversed briefly while I clung to my upside down kayak trying to figure out the most graceful way to climb back inside.

By now, our guide had paddled up to us. He rolled my kayak back over for me. Then while the guide held my blue kayak steady, Tom eased me back inside. At least he tried to. The first two attempts didn't go that well, and both the boat and I tipped over each time. Tom finally resorted to a move he must have used in his patrol officer days when he had to shove a suspect into the back of a squad car. But it worked.

Even though the guide had recommended leaving our valuables in the bus, it appeared that several intrepid seniors had ignored him. The sound of whirring long distance lenses focusing on me did not improve my mood. I could only hope they were clueless about downloading their videos onto YouTube.

By now, Sharon, I mean, Darren, and Deborah had paddled far away, evidently fearful of being in close proximity to a klutzy kayaker. The rest of the group followed our guide who had once again taken the lead position with Tom and me at the very rear of the pack.

"Hanging in there, hon?" he asked from a few feet away. Even my husband was nervous about being too close to my vicinity.

"Sure, just another wonderful day in paradise," I grumbled, wondering if any squirmy sea critters had lodged in my curls. I didn't dare take my hand off my paddle to find out.

"Look at it this way. You have one less missing husband to worry about." Tom's shoulders shook with laughter. "The expression on Darren's face when we pulled his wig out of the water was priceless."

I began giggling although I kept it in check so as not to jostle my boat. Most detectives attempt to turn over clues.

Only I could manage to turn over my suspect!

CHAPTER FIFTY-FIVE

The rest of our expedition progressed without further incident. Tom and I maintained a respectable distance from everyone else. Despite feeling slimy and bedraggled, I kind of enjoyed it, although I looked forward to docking our kayaks on shore.

Tom climbed out of his kayak then walked over to assist me. He helped me out then pulled me into a sticky hug.

"Ugh." I shifted away from him. "I love you to pieces, but we could both use a hot shower and the sooner the better."

We were the last couple to board the bus. A few passengers sent us baleful looks, but the majority of them inquired if we were okay. One person even thanked me for providing his favorite comic moment of the trip.

Any time.

We slipped into the only two empty seats in the back, located across the aisle from Darren and Sharon.

I motioned to Tom to take the window seat so I could sit on the aisle. I needed to apologize to the other couple for the mishap. I waited until the bus turned onto the main road, figuring the noisy exhaust would muffle our conversation from any eavesdroppers.

I leaned across the aisle and spoke to Deborah. Her husband's eyes were closed, his bald head resting against the window. "I'm so sorry about what happened. Is Darren okay?"

She nodded and spoke softly. "More embarrassed than anything." She snuck a peek at her husband. "He really adored that wig."

I snorted in an attempt to stifle a giggle. "He certainly fooled me."

One of Darren's eyes popped open. I noticed that his mascara had remained on his exceptionally long eyelashes far better than mine had. He leaned across his wife and asked, "We really did manage to sucker you, didn't we? Deborah and I almost wondered if you were going to report her husband as missing."

The three of us burst into laughter. "So, why the get-up?" I asked.

Deborah replied first. "It started with one Halloween party when everyone complimented Darren on his Cher costume. It was so much fun, we tried a few weekend getaways where he assumed the Sharon persona."

"It was a kick fooling folks," Darren added. "This was the first lengthy trip we tried. It's been great fun." He eyed me. "Except for losing my favorite wig."

I colored but the couple both laughed and told me not to worry about it. The bus screeched to a stop, interrupting our conversation. Tom lifted my tote bag for me, and we brought up the rear as everyone piled out of the bus.

"What's next?" Tom asked as we both looked around. "I could really use some food right now." He lifted his head and sniffed like a bloodhound on the trail of his quarry.

"BBQ," he said and pointed to our left. I remembered that the ship provided a luncheon buffet for the cruisers from eleven until two. We passed by some restrooms and I ducked inside. I washed up as best I could, grateful that I'd tucked a ball cap and extra T-shirt in my bag.

Klutzes come prepared.

Feeling somewhat refreshed, I joined my husband, who despite his dunking in the lagoon, still looked as hunky as ever.

As the tangy smell of spicy BBQ drew closer, Tom's strides grew longer. We finally reached the shaded lunch area, our anxious taste buds ready for almost anything. The aroma of grilled meats had attracted half the passengers on the ship. Although there were five different buffet stations, all the lines were long.

I gazed at a sea of picnic tables filled with happy diners. I asked Tom to bring back a plate of food for me while I scoured the area for empty seats. I picked up two glasses of iced tea and began my search.

There were multiple dining areas for the throngs of passengers, although most were completely filled. I kept searching and finally found a seating area a long way from the buffet. Only a few people occupied the redwood tables.

I slid onto a bench seat facing the direction Tom would be coming, although the odds of him finding me were not high. I should have dropped a trail of bread crumbs, or in my case, chocolate chips. I sipped on my tea and fanned myself.

I noticed Claire headed my way and I waved my hand at her. She walked over to our table, a plate in one hand and a drink in the other.

"Can I join you?" she asked.

"Of course." I smiled at her. "Is Rick still out with his tour group?"

"I think so. It was a two-hour wave runner ride. Much too long for me."

"The one and only time I rode on the back of a jet ski in Tahoe, we bounced over the waves so hard I thought my boobs would knock the contacts out of my eyes."

Claire choked on her stir fry, undoubtedly, at my overly visual description. One of these days I needed to add a filter to my conversation.

"Have you enjoyed the cruise so far?" I asked. "You must have been surprised when Rick presented you with the tickets for your anniversary."

She nodded. "Very much so, although I actually came across the reservation when I was hunting for a screwdriver. The one place I know I'll never find the tool I need is in Rick's toolbox. He always chucks his tools wherever he used them last. After going through our kitchen drawers, I switched to his office and found the cruise information under a few papers in his desk drawer. When he came home from work that night, I ended up surprising him."

"Did you ever find the screwdriver?"

"I did. Under our bathroom sink." She and I both swapped smiles. Typical male behavior.

"Twenty-five years of marriage is a success story these days," I said. "What's your secret?"

"Patience, and lots of it." Claire stopped eating and gazed out toward the sea. "I'm lucky that my husband is an excellent provider. It gave me the opportunity to stay home with the kids. But now that my last little chick has flown the coop, I'm trying to figure out who I really am, outside of a supportive wife and mother."

"What kind of work does Rick do? Maybe you two could work together."

She scrunched up her nose. "I couldn't last a minute in that environment." When I sent a questioning look in her direction, she replied. "He's with a large talent agency, TTCA. Stands for Top Talent Creative Agency. He deals with lots of prima donnas."

"It sounds challenging but also interesting. You must have met your fair share of actors through the years."

She sipped her tea. "As Rick says, they all put their underwear on one leg at a time. Most of the actors and singers I've met were quite nice." She grimaced. "With a few exceptions. He has some horror stories he could share."

"Maybe he'll share them right now." I pointed behind her as our husbands approached. Her dark hair whipped around as she turned to greet Rick.

Both men bore plates of food. My stomach growled at the tantalizing scents wafting from Tom's two colorful plates. He'd even managed to add a small plate piled high with tropical desserts.

My husband knew me so well.

I kissed Tom, snatched my loaded plate from him and barely greeted Rick before biting into a char-grilled hot dog. Yum.

"I'm surprised you found us, dear," Claire said to her husband.

"Tom and I started chatting while we waited in that long buffet line. His detective skills led us to the two of you."

I narrowed my eyes at my husband. "Got lucky, didn't you?"

He laughed and saluted me with his fork. "I kept walking and figured eventually we'd come across you. That pink shirt helped." He waggled his eyebrows at me, evidently noticing that my hot pink tee was tighter than when I'd boarded the ship eight days earlier. No doubt due to the fine dining the past week.

"How was your excursion?" Claire asked Rick.

"Fine." He rolled his shoulders and winced. "Although I'm a little stiff. Sometimes my head forgets my body belongs to a fifty-five year old male."

"I'm only forty, and I can empathize with you," I said to Rick. "Claire told me about your job as a talent agent. It sounds so exciting."

"It has its perks. Los Angeles is an expensive place to live, and my career has provided for my wife and kids. But my job demands constant travel away from Claire." He turned to his wife and placed his palm over hers. "This vacation has been an eye-opener for me. It's given me time to reflect on what's important to me. To us. A career is wonderful, but my wife means everything to me."

I was touched to see tears form on Claire's eyelashes. She swiped her palm across her eye. "That sea air sure brings out the romantic in our guys, doesn't it?"

I nodded in blushing agreement. I certainly couldn't complain about any of our nocturnal activities. Or morning activities. If we could continue on this way for the next fifteen years, we could be as happy as this middle-aged couple.

"I'm looking forward to the show tonight," said Claire. "*Grease* is one of my favorite musicals."

"Don't get your hopes too high," I replied. "The girl who originally was supposed to play the Sandy part left the cruise to be with her boyfriend, and then the singer taking her place accidentally clobbered the guy playing Danny Zuko when she was aiming for Rizzo."

Both Rick and Claire looked confused, and I didn't blame them. I just hoped Zac could keep track of his performers tonight.

"Our friend, Stan, will finally have his big night on stage." Tom looked at me. "This has the potential to be a shipboard disaster."

"Or the most comical musical we've ever seen," I said.

Tom and I exchanged smiles. If nothing else, tonight's production of *Grease* should be interesting.

Rick's back was still hurting from his wave runner excursion. He decided a dose of ibuprofen would be a better choice than a second helping of BBQ so he and Claire headed for the ship. Tom and I finished our lunch then took a leisurely stroll back to the tenders.

We stopped for a moment to gaze at the few remaining swimmers and sunbathers dotting the pristine beach. Tall palm trees formed a cinematic backdrop, the bright green fronds swaying in the balmy breeze, almost as if they were waving farewell to us.

I felt pensive. Our honeymoon had been wonderful in most respects. Yet, here we were on the final day of our cruise with a few nagging questions still to be resolved.

More than nagging questions. Crimes had been committed. At least one murder plus multiple thefts. Would we be able to resolve everything in less than twenty-four hours?

What if we didn't?

CHAPTER FIFTY-SIX

Back on the ship, Tom and I bumped into Gran and Mabel in front of the elevators. Gran's smile spread wide across the patchwork of faint wrinkles on her fair complexion.

"You look like you won the lottery," I said to her.

"Close. I'm in the bingo finals this afternoon," she crowed.

I gave her a gentle hug. "Congratulations. What kind of prize are we talking about?"

"Five smackeroos."

"Five dollars?" asked Tom. My husband might be an excellent homicide detective, but he was clueless when it came to bingo.

"Five thousand dollars," she chortled.

Tom and I were both stunned by the large amount. Who knew bingo could be so lucrative?

"Did you discover anything more about Mrs. Peabody and her sister?" I asked Gran.

"Only that she likes to play bingo and is not a happy camper when she loses. When Peabody didn't make it into the finals, she mumbled something about the bingo being rigged and left the lounge." Gran sent me an apologetic look. "Sorry, kiddo. I got so caught up in my winning cards, I fell down on my sleuthing. I shoulda' followed her and her sister."

I patted her arm. "Not to worry. I'm glad you and Mabel had fun."

"How was your kayak trip?" Gran tilted her curly head at us. "You got the look of someone who's been rode hard and put away wet."

Mabel sniffed. "You smell kinda like Eau de Swamp."

"We had an unexpected dunking in the lagoon," Tom explained.

"You gotta expect the unexpected when you're with my granddaughter," Gran cackled.

Truer words were never spoken.

When we returned to our stateroom, Tom picked up a message from the captain requesting both his and my stepfather's presence. I was disappointed, although not surprised to learn my name wasn't included in the invitation. I let Tom shower first with minimal distractions then took my turn. I used half the coconut-scented shower gel in the jumbo dispenser provided by the ship, trying to eliminate any trace of my immersion in the lagoon.

Tom returned to our room as I was finishing putting on my makeup in front of the mirror. I brushed coral blush over my newly tanned and freckled cheekbones and applied fresh lip gloss to my chapped lips.

Tom spun me around and gave me a hearty kiss.

"Yum. You taste like a strawberry daiquiri," he said, licking his lips.

I held up a small gold canister. "New lip gloss, guaranteed to make your honey crave you."

"Or crave a daiquiri, which also sounds good right now. Too bad it will have to wait."

I pushed my strawberry-pink lower lip out in a pout. "What's going on? Why did the captain need you and Bradford?"

"Remember when you asked me to review the video footage for that time period when you thought you saw someone fall overboard?"

"You mean footage for the time when I *did see* someone fall overboard," I emphasized between clenched teeth. "Did you finally find some physical evidence to prove it?"

"What we found is a lack of evidence," he replied. "The footage during that time frame doesn't exist."

"What do you mean it doesn't exist?"

"There are two possibilities. Either multiple cameras were not functioning, which could happen but is fairly unlikely, or someone erased the footage."

I plunked down on the sofa, trying to comprehend the extent of Tom's statement.

"So...," I said slowly while my mind raced furiously, "is there a possibility that Sanjay messed with the videos?"

Tom plopped next to me. "Yep. I think that's the most likely scenario."

"Since we've learned Sanjay had a nasty propensity to blackmail people, what are the odds he decided to blackmail the killer once he looked at the footage?"

"If I were in Vegas right now, I'd take those odds," Tom said.

"This is interesting although it's not going to help us catch a killer."

"But it could mean Sanjay's murder was tied to your missing person as opposed to the jewel thief."

"Or his girlfriend," I added.

"Or the two crew members being blackmailed," Tom said. "Or your cousin who is still a suspect."

I sighed and latched on to Tom's hand.

"Next time we take on a case, I hope it's not so complicated."

"Funny you should mention that." He hesitated when someone pounded on our door. Tom opened the door to be greeted by my cousin. Sierra entered the room, still dressed in her official uniform, her face looking as stormy as the clouds that had been gathering on the horizon since our return to the ship.

"What's wrong?" I asked her. "Are there problems with tonight's show?"

"Or with the captain?" Tom asked.

Sierra shot him a dark look as she flopped onto the sofa. "Do you have insider information, detective?"

"The captain is under a lot of pressure from the home office."

"And I'm under a lot of pressure myself," she said tearfully. "I'm trying to ensure that all the entertainment and tours go on as normal. That the passengers have the time of their life. Yet I'm still being treated as a lowlife suspect by the captain and even some of the crew. Even after Mrs. Peabody's watch was stolen from the spa, and I was nowhere around at the time."

"What happened when you met with Captain Andriessen?" I asked. "He didn't fire you, did he?"

"He came this close." She squeezed her right thumb and index finger together. "Then Zac called with another production crisis. Between the loss of his chief security officer and a temporary stage director producing his first big show, the captain decided to give me one last chance."

I patted her knee. "That's good news."

"There's one provision." She glanced at me and then at Tom. "What's that?"

"Somebody determines for once and for all that I am neither a thief nor a murderer." She sent Tom a beseeching glance. "My future is in your hands."

CHAPTER FIFTY-SEVEN

On that note, Sierra left for the theater to help Zac with his latest emergency. During the dress rehearsal for *Grease,* Elizabeth Axelrod discovered that the black leather costume she would wear in the finale was missing from the wardrobe department. It was too late to make a new outfit for her, but Sierra figured the costume had to be somewhere. She couldn't imagine that Nicole would have taken it with her.

Sierra's parting words hit me right in my heavy heart. Once she left, I turned to Tom.

"We have to help her," I said.

"You're right. Even if Sierra isn't found guilty of either crime, she'll have a suspicious cloud hanging over her head for the rest of her career."

"What should I do?"

Tom walked over to the sofa, sat down and placed a hand on my thigh. "You should enjoy the rest of this cruise while I attempt to solve a hideous crime."

"No, seriously, what should I do? You know I can't just sit around doing nothing."

Tom heaved a deep sigh. "I know. Tell you what, I'll ask the captain if I can talk to the passengers in the cabins located on the decks above ours. Ostensibly, Sanjay already did that, but maybe someone saw or heard something that has yet to be disclosed."

"What if Sanjay learned something important but chose to keep it to himself. Do you want me to help?"

"No, I'll get Bradford to come along with me. I have an idea for you, though. When we interviewed Mizuki, she shared the information about Sanjay and his blackmail schemes, but talking to her was like pulling out wisdom teeth. She might respond better to a woman. Someone who could coax her out of her shell."

"Right. And who's better than me at chit chat?"

"You are indeed the chit chat queen." He kissed my hand and took off, leaving me to wonder if my husband had complimented me or not. I finally shrugged and decided it didn't matter. I had a job to do.

It took longer to track Mizuki down than I originally anticipated. Neither Chopsticks nor the Lido Café were open yet. I finally discovered her clearing tables in the Seaside Café located by the pool.

Only a few people lingered on this deck, including one couple frolicking in the pool and a foursome playing cards. The majority of the passengers might be getting dressed for a last evening at sea, or napping, something I wouldn't mind doing myself. But my detective husband had assigned me a task, and I wanted to prove I could handle it.

I tapped Mizuki on the shoulder and explained that the captain had asked me to speak with her. Indirectly he had, since he'd asked Tom to resolve the murder situation before we docked the next day.

She deposited the tray of empty dishes back on the table. I asked her to sit, and she reluctantly did so, her trepidation obvious.

With her dark almond-shaped eyes focused on me, I explained how Tom and I became involved in the investigation, and in particular, how important it was to me to erase any suspicions the captain might have about my cousin.

"Ah, Sierra, she is your cousin." Mizuki frowned as she looked me up and down.

"No family resemblance as you can tell," I said. "Sierra used to babysit me when I was a little kid."

Mizuki gave a small smile at my comment. "It is good when family take care of one another."

"Yes, it is. And the crew should also be looking out for one another. One big happy family, right?"

Her small hands, previously resting on her lap, clenched together.

"I guess that's not the case on board the *Celebration*, is it?" I asked.

She lowered her eyes but nodded slightly.

"I understand that you were with Sanjay prior to his murder."

She nodded again.

"Did you see anyone before or after you met with him?"

"I saw your cousin," Mizuki said. "She came into Chopsticks looking for Sanjay. But I do not think she would kill him."

"I don't think she would either. That's why I'm asking these questions." We sat in silence while I contemplated what else I could ask her.

"Sanjay was very good to me at first," she said quietly. "Very sweet. But then he started gambling at the casinos when the ship would dock." Mizuki's straight shiny black hair swung back and forth as she shook her head. "I think he owed bad people money. Maybe that is why he turned to blackmail."

"Can you think of anyone else? Not just crew, but possibly passengers?"

"No. I am sorry. I was most upset from talking with Sanjay. I was not paying much attention that afternoon."

"Of course. Nothing worse than getting…" I tried to think of a better word than dumped. "It must have been terrible for you."

Her eyes glittered with tears. "I ran out of there. To the ladies room to cry."

The poor dear. My heart went out to her. She'd gone through so much, and here I was dredging up that terrible day all over again.

"I'm so sorry to have bothered you. Thank you for speaking with me." I reached into my tote and scribbled our room number on a coupon I'd stuffed in my bag. "Please call my room if you think of anything helpful."

She stood, picked up the tray of dishes and went behind the serving bar. I drummed my fingers on the table while I tried to visualize that fateful moment. The killer must have met with Sanjay shortly after Mizuki ran out of the area, possibly while she was crying her eyes out inside the ladies room.

I glanced at my watch. Time to get ready for dinner. As I neared the exit doors, Mizuki placed a hand on my arm to stop me.

"I remembered something. When I was coming out of the ladies room, I bumped into someone."

"A man or a woman?" I asked, suddenly excited. Maybe I'd have a lead after all.

"I'm not sure. The person wore one of those sweatshirts with the hood?" She looked at me for confirmation. "Like the Facebook man wears."

"Right, a hoodie. They are very popular. What color was it?"

"It was gray. And the person wore sunglasses. I remember thinking how odd to wear sunglasses inside, but perhaps they were going to the sunbathing area."

"Was this person short like me, or tall?" I lifted my hand a foot above my head for a reference.

She pursed her lips. "I think tall. Or maybe medium size. This is not so helpful, is it?"

Not so far. But maybe we could narrow it down to gender. "Did you see the restroom the person went into?"

She tapped her finger against her chin. "Yes, into the men's room. Is this helpful?"

Yes. It certainly was.

CHAPTER FIFTY-EIGHT

My knee hurt from my kayak expedition, so I decided to wait for the elevator. It gave me time to process the information Mizuki had shared. If the person in the gray hoodie was the killer, we now knew they were tall or medium, as she put it. That meant anywhere from five foot seven to six foot two.

My cousin was five foot nine. Although I couldn't quite picture Sierra in that outfit, and I was certain my mother would agree.

The hoodie and sunglasses made for a gender neutral disguise. Whomever arranged to meet Sanjay had planned ahead. Was it a crime of passion or not?

The elevator pinged and I stepped inside and pressed the button for our floor. As I headed for our stateroom I kept hoping a burst of brilliance would erupt before I crossed the threshold.

When I opened the door, I was surprised to see Sierra and Tom with their heads together. They looked up when the door slammed shut.

"Did you learn anything from Mizuki?" Tom asked.

"Maybe," I replied then turned to Sierra. "Do you own a gray hoodie?"

She wrinkled her nose. "Good grief, no. It would completely wash me out."

" I have one possible lead. But what are you two up to?"

"I needed Tom's advice," Sierra said. "We couldn't find Nicole's costume anywhere so I figured she'd left it in her room. The cabin attendant said he hadn't been in the room since she put the DO NOT DISTURB sign out the first night. No one told him she'd left the cruise. When Zac saw her email, he assumed she'd flown home just like her message said. So nobody checked to see when she'd left the ship. And where we were docked at the time."

"Sierra asked the attendant to let her in the room," Tom explained. "She discovered Nicole's clothing plus her makeup in the bathroom, and her suitcases stuffed under the bed."

"So everything was still in her room?" I asked.

"Everything but Nicole," Sierra replied.

"It seems odd she would leave that much stuff behind."

"I couldn't tell if any of her purses were missing," Sierra said. "But there was no sign of a cell phone anywhere."

"We're waiting for someone in security to bring a passkey so we can open her safe and see if her wallet and passport are in there."

I flopped down on the bed that our steward had made up for the evening. Marcel had already placed our nightly towel animal on the bedspread. I picked up the unrecognizable animal. Tyrannosaurus Rex?

"So if everything is still in the room except for Nicole then that means…" I clutched the Jurassic Park wannabe towel to my chest as Tom finished my sentence for me.

"That means we may have discovered your 'missing' missing person."

CHAPTER FIFTY-NINE

Sierra left to deliver the *Grease* costume to the wardrobe mistress and then to change into a cocktail dress. Prior to the show, she would be giving a brief speech thanking all of the passengers and providing them with last minute disembarkation instructions. I didn't envy her job and almost felt she would be better off making a career change.

Whoever said cruising is great for your health had never cruised with *me*.

The assistant security officer called, and we arranged to meet him in Nicole's stateroom. Since Sierra and the stateroom attendant had already tromped all over the room, Tom decided I might as well come along provided I didn't touch anything. An extra set of eyes couldn't hurt.

I had assumed performers were assigned staterooms on the lower decks, but Nicole's room was on deck ten. Jared, the assistant security officer, waited for us in the hall.

The men went directly to the closet where the safe was located. Tom pushed aside some beautiful designer outfits while Jared opened the door of the safe with his master key. The door popped open to reveal a passport, wallet and small jewelry case.

"Nicole certainly couldn't have gone far without her passport and wallet," I remarked. "This doesn't look good."

Tom gazed around the room with the critical eye of a detective.

224

Sierra and the cabin attendant had possibly compromised a potential crime scene without knowing it.

The bedspread covered the queen-size bed, yet it didn't seem to be tucked in as neatly as we were used to experiencing in our own cabin. Tom grabbed a tissue and turned the spread over.

My stomach churned when I saw the two dark splotches staining the underside of the bedspread. Tom sniffed then set it back down.

"We'll need to tread carefully from now on. This could be a crime scene."

"Do you want to check the balcony?" I asked him. He nodded and I followed in his carefully placed footsteps. Jared decided to scrutinize the bathroom for anything suspicious while we examined the outside area.

Tom used the tissue to grab hold of the door handle. When he pulled on the handle, the heavy door flew open and banged against the glass. The gray clouds that had gathered earlier had turned into a full-fledged storm. Rain streamed past the balcony, tiny droplets bouncing on and off the mahogany railing.

Tom scrutinized the railing. "If there was any dried blood, it's washed away by now."

I stood close to him and peered over the railing. Our own balcony was directly below and three decks down, but it wasn't visible from way up here.

The brown webbed chairs didn't provide any additional information. The cushions that normally sat on the chairs had blown over to the side of the balcony. While Tom continued to look for clues, I picked up the soggy cushions. No sign of any blood on the first cushion nor the second one. But in the far corner something sparkled. Something that had remained hidden under the cushions.

I tapped Tom on his shoulder and pointed. His eyes lit up and he threw me a big smile. By now, his tissue had disintegrated from the moisture. He went back into the cabin and selected a clean hand towel then returned to the balcony. He bent down to pick up the item.

"That's gorgeous," I said, admiring the diamond tennis bracelet. "How do you think it landed way over there?"

He examined the catch. "It looks like it unlatched and fell off of whomever was wearing it. Nicole might have dropped it. Or..."

"Or the killer might have dropped it," I replied, excited about this potential clue.

"Or whomever has been stealing jewels might have dropped it," Tom said. "Which means..."

"That whomever threw Nicole over the balcony could also be the jewel thief."

Which brought us back to square one.

Too many suspects and not enough time!

CHAPTER SIXTY

Tom and I debated our next move. The probable crime scene needed to be secured. We both had loads of questions about the missing occupant. Other than the fact Nicole was cute, blond, petite, and an excellent singer, we knew nothing.

"Either Zac or Sierra should have some type of resume and contact information for Nicole," I said. "Do you want me to check with them while you," I waved my hand around, "do more official stuff?"

Tom blew out a breath. "I suppose you can't get into trouble talking to those two. Although, knowing you…"

"I might just crack this case, right? Isn't that what you were going to say?"

"Right. But please be careful, especially around the entertainers. Any one of them could have thrown Nicole overboard. Assuming that's what happened here."

"It must be a man, right?" I asked. "Someone strong enough to force her over the railing."

"Most likely, although not necessarily. Someone the size of your cousin could shove someone over. Especially if they were knocked out already." His eyes met my angry ones. "Not that I'm accusing Sierra of anything." He looked at the diamond bracelet sitting on the desk, still wrapped in the clean towel. "If Sierra were the jewel thief, she could have attempted to steal Nicole's bracelet and in the altercation, Nicole flew over the railing."

I glared at him. "Do you seriously think that's a possibility?"

"Anything is possible when it comes to murder. But that scenario would not make my top ten list so you can stop stabbing me with your beautiful blue eyes."

I glanced at the bracelet again. Despite sitting in the corner of the balcony all week, it still sparkled. "What are you going to do with the bracelet?"

"We could attempt to process it for DNA or fingerprints, but given the outside moisture, the odds aren't great. And we certainly wouldn't get the feedback before we docked in Fort Lauderdale tomorrow morning."

"I have an idea."

Tom placed his hand over his heart. "The four words that strike fear in a husband."

"Very funny. Given the limited time we have left, what if I wore the bracelet tonight? I could show it off at dinner and in the theater. Maybe wave it around backstage. Someone might recognize it."

He rubbed his ear lobe. Evidently not a huge fan of my plan. "I'm not crazy about it, but since you'll be surrounded by your family tonight, I suppose it can't hurt. Just don't do anything rash."

Moi?

"And take your cell with you."

Now it was my turn to look shocked. "At five dollars a minute?"

He blew a kiss to me. "See how much I love you."

CHAPTER SIXTY-ONE

Tom told me he intended to search through Nicole's dresser to see if he could learn anything further about her relationships, family, career, etc. Jared brought caution tape from the security office, and the minute I walked out, the door into her stateroom was crisscrossed in yellow strips. It seemed kind of late to turn the cabin into an official crime scene, but I wasn't in charge, as usual.

My mission was to subtly flaunt the diamond tennis bracelet all over the ship. I returned to our room and changed into a full-skirted sleeveless red cotton dress. The diamond bracelet gleamed against the bright scarlet.

I slid my watch on my other wrist, grabbed a clutch large enough to hold my phone, and set off on my mission. My first stop would be backstage at the theater. I'd never gone behind the scenes before so this was an excellent excuse. Plus Stan could probably use a pep talk by now.

I called Sierra's room, hoping she was still there. I wasn't certain how I could gain access to the backstage area without someone's permission.

"On my way out the door, Zac," Sierra muttered into the phone.

"It's Laurel," I blurted out before she could hang up on me. "I need to go backstage for a couple of minutes. Can you arrange it?"

"Are you ready to leave right now?" she asked.

"Yep. Just tell me where to meet you."

Sierra gave me instructions, and the minute we hung up I left our room and headed for the elevator. I couldn't help rotating my wrist back and forth, admiring the way the diamonds sparkled under the ship's gleaming chandeliers. The elevator doors pinged open, and I greeted Danielle and her husband, Pierre.

I walked inside and pressed the button for the second floor.

"Such a lovely bracelet you are wearing," Danielle cooed at me. "Did you buy it on one of the islands?"

Tricky question. "It was a gift," I replied and held my arm out for her to admire the bracelet. She delved into her purse, pulled out a jeweler's loupe and held my wrist right up to the device.

"The stones, they are *tres belle*." Danielle reluctantly relinquished my arm. "Maybe ten carats. From your husband?"

Another trick question. Technically, Tom did pick up the bracelet from Nicole's balcony and hand it over to me.

I simply replied "yes" then pointed to her loupe. "Are you in the jewelry business?"

"I own a share of a diamond mine in Canada," Pierre said. "Our diamonds are very popular with people who boycott the blood diamonds from Africa."

"So this trip is for business?" I asked.

He nodded. "The cruise provided a good opportunity to visit some of the larger diamond store chains that purchase their gems from our mine. And make some acquisitions of our own. We discovered the perfect setting for my wife's diamond."

Danielle displayed an emerald-cut diamond the size of a sugar cube on the fourth finger of her left hand.

I wagered she knew exactly how many carats her own ring contained.

The elevator stopped at the third floor. I held the door open while she pushed Pierre's wheelchair through the opening. "*Au revoir,*" she said with a slight wave, her giant diamond glistening as they walked away.

The doors slammed shut then whooshed open as we landed on the second floor. I stepped out and looked to the left and right, trying to get my bearings. I checked the map and confirmed the theater was at the opposite end of the ship from where I was currently standing by the entrance to the Main Dining Room.

One thing this ship was good for was enforced exercise. I headed for the theater, walking against the crowd moving toward the dining room. I thought about my conversation with Danielle and Pierre. If they owned a diamond mine, they certainly wouldn't need to resort to stealing any of the passengers' jewelry. Unless they made up that story to throw me off their crooked trail. Danielle certainly was quick with that jeweler's loupe. She'd whipped it out of her purse before I could blink.

This trip was making me suspicious of everyone. Even my own family members. I needed to be on my guard for the next few hours if I wanted to catch a thief.

And a murderer.

CHAPTER SIXTY-TWO

Sierra waited for me in front of the closed doors of the theater. She also wore red, although it was more of a cranberry shade in a sheath-style dress that flattered her curves. Dark shadows under her eyes were the only sign of her stress.

We exchanged quick hugs before getting down to business.

"So what's the pressing need to go backstage?" she asked. "I imagine it's a zoo back there."

I brushed my bangs off my forehead and she shrieked. "Where did you find that bracelet?"

I pulled away from her. "Why are you asking me that question?"

"That looks like one of the items Sanjay mentioned was stolen, although I don't remember who reported it. Diamond tennis bracelets are fairly common, but the one you're wearing isn't your everyday garden variety tennis bracelet."

I held it up for her inspection. "Close to ten carats according to one of the passengers who claims to be a jewelry expert."

"I presume Tom didn't purchase it for you."

"Are you kidding? This bracelet would pay Jenna's college tuition for a year. We found it lying on the floor of Nicole's balcony. Hidden in the corner."

Sierra chewed on her lip as she contemplated the bracelet. "It probably belongs to Nicole. I heard that her boyfriend was fairly well off. I still don't understand what could have happened to her."

As we walked down the aisle toward the stage, I told Sierra about the blood stains we'd found on the bedspread in Nicole's stateroom, along with the personal items that had been left in the safe. Sierra's face turned whiter than Casper the Ghost. "That's horrible. It never occurred to me to worry about Nicole. I just thought she was being a diva. There are so many of them in this business. I hope she hasn't come to any harm, but it doesn't sound too positive at this point. What now?"

"My husband doesn't want me to do anything dangerous, but he said I could wander around flaunting this bracelet, hoping to pick up a lead somehow."

"I agree with Tom. One bump on the noggin is sufficient for you on this trip. Does Tom think whoever killed Sanjay also did away with Nicole?"

I shrugged. "That's one possibility. Unfortunately, there are many others."

Sierra warned me to be careful then led me backstage, where the activity could best be described as chaotic.

Elizabeth Axelrod, the singer who had taken Nicole's place, stood next to Seth, the understudy now cast as Danny Zuko. The previous lead had flown back home to get new dental veneers put in. This show had turned out to be a terrific opportunity for both understudies. I studied the woman now playing the role of Sandy. Was she desperate enough to throw Nicole over her balcony railing to get the part?

Or was I so desperate to find the murderer that I was seeing killers at every corner?

While Sierra searched for Zac, I ambled over to the two lead singers. "I'm looking forward to the show tonight." I put my hand out to shake each of theirs, wondering if they would notice my diamond bracelet.

Elizabeth and Seth each shook my hand, mumbled their thanks, ignored my glittering accessory, and went back to their scripts. So much for my subtle sleuthing.

I wandered off hoping to find Stan. I hadn't laid eyes on my friend for almost two days. I finally found him leaning against one of the show's props—a full-scale jalopy. At least, the front half of one.

This cruise line certainly did not stint on its sets.

I walked up behind Stan and tapped him on his leather-jacketed shoulder. He jumped, twirled and landed in a pose that screamed "bad-ass wannabe."

I would have rolled my eyes but Stan needed my support, and I needed his skill set. I was certain that in the short amount of time Stan had been practicing with the dance crew, that he would rival TMZ when it came to cruise gossip.

"You look great," I said. "Just like one of the guys in the gang."

His eyes lit up. "I do?"

Not really, since he would be the first kid at Ryder High with a receding hairline. But from a distance, most passengers wouldn't notice.

"What are you doing backstage?" he asked.

"I wanted to wish you good luck."

"Thanks, I'll need it. This routine is harder than I realized when I was watching rehearsals earlier in the week."

"I have confidence in you." I reached up and rearranged the collar of his jacket. He grabbed my wrist and appraised my new trinket.

"Whoa. Those are some diamonds. Did Tom win a jackpot in the casino?"

"I wish." I placed the tip of my finger on his lips. "This is confidential, but Tom and I found this bracelet in Nicole's cabin. Did you ever see her wearing it?"

Stan examined the bracelet more closely. "I suppose she might have worn it at the opening show. She wore that long red sequin gown for the final number. Maybe her sugar daddy gave it to her. I wonder why she didn't take it with her when she took off."

"I'm about to share something with you, but if you repeat it to anyone," I shook my finger at him, "I will tell Zac about our trip to Hawaii and your time with the Samoan dancers."

Stan's light gray eyes turned a terrified charcoal. He lifted his right hand. "Scouts honor. Tell all."

"There are signs of a struggle in Nicole's room including bloodstains on the bedspread. Plus all her personal items, her wallet and passport are still in the safe."

"So you think someone kidnapped her?"

"Worse. Nicole may be the person I saw go overboard."

CHAPTER SIXTY-THREE

Stan's eyes popped open so wide he looked like an oversized Jiminy Cricket clad in a black leather jacket.

"OMG times ten," he exclaimed. "What are we going to do now?"

"You are doing nothing except sharing any gossip you've heard about Nicole. You mentioned a sugar daddy. Do you know who he is?"

Stan pursed his lips and pondered. "I went to congratulate Zac backstage that first night and walked right past Nicole. Other than telling her that her performance was awesome, we didn't chat. But I remember Elizabeth complaining when Nicole didn't show for rehearsal the next day that the only reason Nicole got the starring role in *Grease* was that she slept her way to the top."

I frowned. "Top of what? The stage? The ship? Zac?"

"Puh-leeze. Honestly, I really don't know. I didn't want to pry."

"Since when?" I asked him. He merely shrugged.

"Let's ask Elizabeth," I said. "She might know the boyfriend's name."

We scooted around a couple of workers and ran into Sierra and Zac in a heated discussion.

"What's the matter?" I asked them.

"I know you told me to keep quiet about Nicole, but I felt Zac needed to know. What if one of the performers killed her?" Sierra asked. "Do you think we should disclose to the cast what happened so they can stay alert?"

The bristles of Zac's blond hair stood straight up like rows of dominoes. "You can't do that before the show. It would be a complete disaster."

I stepped between them. "I agree with Zac. The performance is important to this troupe. In the meantime, maybe you," I nudged Sierra, "and Zac and Stan can keep an eye on everyone. I'll ask Tom if and when he thinks Nicole's situation should be disclosed to the cast. At this point, we don't know exactly what happened to her. It's just highly suspicious."

Sierra heaved an Oscar-worthy sigh. "I suppose that's for the best. I still can't believe what's been going on aboard this cruise."

"Yeah, it makes sailing on the Titanic look almost fun in comparison," Stan said. Zac looked upward, put his hands together and mumbled a quick prayer.

One of the stagehands walked by, and Zac called out to him. I stopped Zac before he could disappear on me.

"Do you know the name of Nicole's boyfriend? Tom would like to contact him to see if he has any information about her disappearance."

"No, although one of the girls might know. He's in show business from what I've gathered." Zac scanned the room and then pointed to the woman playing the part of Rizzo. "Go ask Gina. She has her nose in everyone's business."

Zac and Sierra walked away so Stan and I moseyed up to Gina. As head of the Pink Ladies, Gina was dressed in black capris and a pink satin jacket. When I tapped her on her shoulder, she knocked my hand off and shouted, "Whadaya want?"

I stepped back, wondering if she was staying in character or if she hailed from the Bronx.

"Sorry to bother you. Zac sent us over."

"Well, make it quick. I got a show to do, you know."

"And you are so awesome in it." Stan fawned over her.

She blew him a kiss. "Thanks sweetie. Good thing that loser Nicole flew home, or I'd still be stuck in the chorus."

"Right," I said. "That's what we wanted to talk to you about. Do you know the name of Nicole's boyfriend?"

Gina examined her flamingo pink nails. "Sure do. That bimbo was schtupping her agent."

"Her agent?" I asked, confused at first. "Oh, you mean her talent agent."

"Who else would I mean?"

"There are a lot of agents out there. Do you happen to remember his name?"

She scrunched her face in thought. "Let's see. Ralph? Robert? No, that's not it. Gimme a minute."

"If it comes to you, please tell Stan and he'll get the information to me."

"Yeah. For some reason I got the feeling the guy was a dick."

That was helpful. Not.

Her face suddenly lit up. "Hey, that's it. His name was Richard. But he wasn't a Dick, he was a Rick."

CHAPTER SIXTY-FOUR

What were the odds that the only talent agent I'd ever met was on this cruise ship? And also named Rick.

"Was it Rick Nerwinski from Top Talent Creative Agency?" I asked Gina.

"Yeah, maybe. Not sure how many guys named Rick work at TTCA, but that's her agency. Mine too." Gina rolled her heavily made-up eyes. "Although I don't need to schtupp my agent to get parts. If you talk to Nicole, tell her thanks from me for taking off." Gina let out a brassy laugh and wandered away.

"You look like you've been sucker punched," Stan said. "Do you want to sit down?" He led me to the jalopy we'd stood by earlier and opened the passenger door for me. What do you know? It even came with seats, of a sort.

I plopped down, deep in thought. What if Nicole had threatened to tell Claire about her relationship with Rick? Would he resort to killing her to save his marriage? Was Nicole in love with him and was he in love with her? Or was she just another notch on a very long belt. I imagined that wouldn't be unusual for a high profile Hollywood agent.

Poor Claire.

And poor, poor Nicole. Another starlet whose star was extinguished far too soon.

I shivered as cold air swirled around me. Then I wondered if Nicole's spirit still flitted aboard the ship, hoping someone would solve her murder.

Had I solved the case of the missing singer or was I jumping to conclusions? Then a thunderbolt hit me when I remembered Mizuki's remark that the person in the hoodie went into the men's room. That could be the last nail in Rick's coffin.

It was time for me to track down my husband and tell him what I'd discovered. Even more worrisome, to me, was Claire's safety. If Rick had killed once, he also might have killed Sanjay, assuming the security officer had tried to blackmail the agent.

Did that mean Claire was in danger?

A bell went off, disturbing my reverie.

"You have to go," Stan said, leaping out of his side of the fake fifty-three Chevy. "That's the twenty-minute warning."

I glanced at my watch. Yikes. Where had the time gone? The show was starting in twenty minutes, and I hadn't even eaten dinner. My stomach chose that moment to growl, in case I hadn't noticed my increasing hunger pangs.

Solving murders always trumped stuffing my face. Although wasn't tonight the night they served all you could eat crab legs? Next time I went looking for a killer, I would time it a little better.

Stan showed me a hidden passageway that led from the backstage area to the disco. Since the disco didn't open until ten o'clock, they occasionally brought in performers and props using this passage.

I wound around the hallway that was decorated in noir. Black walls with minimal lighting. At the end was a door. I pushed on it and found myself in the empty disco.

I pulled my cell out of my purse to tell Tom about my discovery. First, I texted him, but my iPhone informed me the text couldn't be sent.

Darn those stupid satellite blockers the cruise ships install so they can rape and pillage their passengers the old-fashioned way. By overcharging us for the internet. Although we'd been able to use our phones at our island stops, it was impossible to get a connection on the ship.

I zipped out of the disco and found myself in a hallway teeming with people intent on getting a good seat for the only performance of *Grease* that evening. The theater would be packed in minutes.

I followed the stream of people and then noticed one of the ship's phones not too far from the ladies room. I picked up the phone and dialed our cabin. No one answered. Tom was likely still processing any evidence he could find in Nicole's cabin.

I left a message for him to meet me at the theater. Sierra had been able to reserve seats for our family in the third row. Since the show would begin shortly, I decided to check if the rest of my relatives were already seated. I might even find Tom with them, although I doubted it.

I stood at the top of the staircase on the left side of the large room, which looked filled to capacity. Thank goodness, Sierra reserved those seats for us. On the opposite side of the theater, I noticed Jimmy Bond escorting the Peabody sisters. That man was a glutton for punishment. I hoped they'd find seats or he would never hear the end of it.

Latecomers crowded the steps, scanning the theater for empty seats. I eased my way past some frustrated passengers and eventually discovered most of my family already seated. I slid into an empty seat between Gran and Mother. Two vacant seats were on her left.

"Isn't Robert coming to the show?" I asked Mother.

"Evidently his former partner stumbled onto a crime scene." She drilled me with an annoyed look. "Would you know anything about that?"

"Sorry," I apologized. "But you wouldn't want a murderer to get away, would you? This is the last night before we dock so it's the last chance to catch him." I leaned closer and murmured, "And I think I know who the killer is. But I can't get in touch with Tom."

"Did you call him?"

I nodded. "I left a message in our stateroom, but my cell is useless on board."

She looked at her watch. "Five minutes until the show starts. The killer can't escape off the ship, so you might as well wait for the men to show up. Robert promised me they would try to make part of the show."

I settled into my seat. Mother was right. I couldn't exactly wander around the ship looking for Rick and Claire. I would enjoy the production until my husband appeared then share my supposition with him.

Sierra walked onto the stage. To the audience, she appeared as professional and enthusiastic as usual. But I detected a few beads of perspiration on her normally placid brow. When she moved to the wings, the curtain opened wide and the stage filled with the *Grease* gang.

Other than one dancer, by the name of Stan, who occasionally moved out of sync with the rest of the dance crew, the first half of the show mesmerized the crowd. A huge round of applause erupted when the curtain went down for the fifteen-minute intermission.

I popped out of my chair, wondering if Tom and my stepfather were waiting for the intermission to join us. The stairways were crowded with folks taking advantage of the short restroom break. I couldn't locate either of the men so I sat back down. Mabel flagged down a waiter and ordered a round of drinks for us.

I checked my cell looking for any form of communication from my husband but nothing appeared. I rose once again and scanned the enormous theater, hoping to find one of the guys. I found one, but not the one I was currently searching for.

Rick Nerwinski stood in the front row of the theater close to the far left aisle, thumbing through the program. The seat next to him was vacant.

What did that mean? Had he done something horrible to his lovely wife?

I breathed a sigh of relief when I saw Claire, dressed in a black sheath, making her way down the crowded stairs. I called out to her, not sure if she would hear me from fifteen seats away.

Claire glanced to her right, her expression confused until I waved to her. She smiled then abruptly stopped on the stairs. She brought her hand up to her throat and stared at me for a few seconds, oblivious to the people now forced to maneuver around her still figure. Then she responded with a small flick of her hand and hurried down the stairs to join her husband.

Omigosh. Claire looked frightened to death. The lights began to dim for Act Two, but I couldn't sit through the entire second half without checking on her first. Perhaps I could talk Claire into sitting with my family. Our seats were higher with a better view of the stage. Anything to get her away from her husband.

"Where you goin'?" Gran asked as I rose from my seat. "The show's about to start."

"I need to check on someone." I stumbled over Gran's shiny pink tote, climbed over Mabel's fleshy knees and trotted down the center aisle. I narrowly missed colliding with the server who was passing out our drinks. He handed my daiquiri to me as I walked past him.

Claire and Rick stood arguing with one another in the front row. She snatched a large black clutch and attempted to leave, but Rick blocked her escape with his arm. I rushed forward to join them before he could harm her.

The curtain rose and the orchestra began playing.

"Stop," I said to Rick. "Don't hurt her."

Rick looked at me like I was crazy, while the people in the rows behind us yelled at our trio to sit down and shut up.

With fifteen hundred people sitting in the audience, I wasn't afraid of Rick, but I didn't want him to lead his wife away, possibly to her doom. He dropped her hand as I moved between them, prepared to douse him with my daiquiri if necessary.

"What the..." Rick stopped as he gazed down at my left wrist. "Laurel, why are you wearing Claire's bracelet. Are you the thief?"

Between the murmurs from the people seated around us, and the noise blasting from the stage as the cast performed the opening number of Act Two, I could barely hear Rick.

"Did you ask if I'm the thief?"

He nodded and pointed to my wrist. "That's Claire's bracelet. It's been missing since the first night."

Uh oh.

CHAPTER SIXTY-FIVE

I turned to see Claire sidling away from us toward the exit.

"Stop," I screamed at her. She pivoted on one foot and raced up the stairs leading to the stage where the dancers were now in the middle of the infamous hand jive dance sequence.

Claire disappeared into a sea of pastel-colored dresses and guys dressed in tight black pants. I dropped my drink on a serving tray and attempted to follow her. The next thing I knew one of the male dancers picked me up and flipped me upside down in a dance move not designed for chubby forty-year-old women. My legs wiggled back and forth until he flipped me right side up. I pointed up with my finger, and he grabbed me around my waist and lifted me straight up in front of him, giving me a better viewing perspective while I searched for my quarry.

Claire had reached a bottleneck in center stage. The dancers surrounded her in a wide circle, their fingers snapping to the beat of the music. It looked like the performers were clueless as to what was going on. Maybe they thought the choreographer was improvising by including audience members in the routine. Anything goes on the last night of the cruise.

My dancer finally put me down as the Deejay sang out "How low can you go?" The cast swiveled their hips lower and lower until eventually Claire and I were the only ones left standing. Hands on hips, we glared at one another.

High noon on the high seas.

I finally spied Stan among the dancers and called out to him.
"Stan, stop her." I pointed to Claire. Stan looked startled but he grabbed her with one arm around her waist while she attempted to pull away. Claire escaped his grasp and smacked him with her purse. Stan tumbled to the floor but managed to take Claire down with him. He started to rise, but the tall, fifty-plus woman recovered faster than my friend. She reached into her clutch and pulled out a gleaming chopstick.

Before you could say Taekwondo, Claire's well-muscled arm wrapped around Stan's throat, the sharp pointed end of the silver chopstick less than an inch from piercing the thin skin of his scrawny neck. I was close enough to see his Adam's apple bobble in fear.

When Danny and two members of his gang attempted to close in on Claire, she brought the chopstick even closer to Stan's carotid artery.

Claire began inching backstage, her captive held tight in her grip. Stan's eyes bulged out as he mouthed the words "Help me."

A familiar baritone called out from the audience. "Claire. Stop." I looked to my right to see Tom standing in the middle of the center aisle, his eyes locked on Claire. His voice rang out. "You don't want to hurt anyone else. Put your weapon down."

I shivered. Claire's eyes were moving frantically from one end of the stage to the other. She looked completely deranged and prepared to do anything at this point. Even if it made no sense in the long run. As far as I could tell, there was nowhere for her to escape.

"I want a helicopter to take us away. You can arrange that. I've seen it on TV."

I remembered that Claire had described herself as a crime show aficionado. How could someone so crazy remain cool and composed for so long? And where was Tom going to get a helicopter?

I could sense the frustration in Tom's voice as he tried to calm her down. He'd been involved in hostage situations before. I shivered again, vividly remembering one of those situations when

I had been the chosen hostage of a crazed killer. That situation had led to a frigid snowmobile chase and me being thrown into Lake Tahoe in the dead of the winter.

I couldn't let my friend Stan suffer. But what could I do?

"Hey, toots," Gran's hoarse voice called out. I looked down and saw my tiny grandmother standing directly below the stage. She reached into her gigantic tote and pulled out the rubber chicken she'd won the other night.

"Heads up," she shouted as she threw the chicken at me. I could hear gasps and muttering from the dance crew and the audience as the sickly yellow item flew through the air, landing safely in my waiting hands. Even Claire seemed distracted by the unusual aerial activity.

Ever grateful for all of those years of softball practice, I flung the fowl directly at the chopstick.

CHAPTER SIXTY-SIX

Out! And game over. My lob completely missed the skinny chopstick I was aiming for. Instead, the plummeting poultry smacked Claire at the bridge of her elegant nose. She dropped her weapon and put both hands on her damaged proboscis.

Tom managed a very impressive leap onto the stage and grabbed hold of Claire. With help from the actress playing the role of Frenchy, the pink-wigged Beauty School Dropout, he secured Claire's hands with a pair of hair ties then marched her up the aisle. The audience applauded with abandon. They would certainly have a story to share with their friends when they returned home.

The cast also clapped, several of them patting me on my back. One male dancer attempted to throw me up in the air in celebration, but we compromised with a hug. Zac and Stan joined me, their arms around each other.

"I will love you forever," Zac said as he kissed me on both cheeks.

Then it was Stan's turn. "You are my hero," he said. I gave him a big hug, grateful he was now safe. Mother, Gran and Mabel joined us on the stage.

"You sure gave her the bird." Mabel slapped me on my back, almost knocking me into my grandmother.

"Thanks for the assist, Gran."

She looked around the stage. "Anytime, kiddo. Now where's my chicken? You never know when you need to bop someone."

Stan went off to recover Gran's bird, while my mother proceeded to lecture me. "Laurel, you need to stop putting yourself in these dangerous situations."

I put my hands up to stop her tirade. "I was never in danger. I just didn't want Claire to hurt anyone else. In her crazed state, anything could have happened."

"Well," she acquiesced, "next time, could you wait until the second half of the show is over. I was looking forward to the finale."

Someone tapped me on the back. Still pent up from the excitement, I swiveled around, almost punching Sierra in the face.

"Nice move, cuz," she said. "You always did have a good arm. Even as a toddler. Remember that time you whacked me with your Cabbage Patch doll?"

"I do remember that stunt. It landed me in the corner for an hour. I expect Claire's punishment will be far more severe."

I looked out into the almost empty theater. The patrons had dispersed to the various bars and other late night activities. One man remained seated in the front row, tears openly running down his face.

I left my family to rehash everything, walked down the steps and sat next to Rick.

He gazed at me, his eyes filled with pain. His face had aged a decade in the past few minutes.

"Did you have any idea what Claire had done?" I asked him.

He shook his head, the tears still rolling down his gaunt cheeks. "No. But this is all my fault."

Yeah, pretty much.

"What do you think happened?" I figured Tom would eventually get the story from Claire, but it would be interesting to get Rick's perspective.

He sighed. "I'm an idiot." I agreed but urged him to elaborate. "Nicole is, I mean, was my client. I was going through a mid-life crisis, and somehow we ended up having an affair. I'd arranged this gig for her. Then I decided to upgrade her suite and spend the week with her. I wanted to find out if it was merely a fling, or if I was really in love with her."

"Claire told me she found the tickets and assumed it was a surprise for her."

"Yep. I talked my way out of it by telling her it was an anniversary present. So then I booked another cabin for us. I couldn't believe it when we ended up on the same deck, only a few doors away from Nicole's stateroom."

"So what went on that first night? How did Claire find out about your affair?"

"You got me. I have to confess something far worse." He covered his eyes for a minute before he continued. "I arranged to meet Nicole when the show was over. I ordered a bottle of champagne for Claire and me to celebrate our anniversary. I filled two glasses then dumped some ground up Ambien into my wife's glass. I knew it wouldn't hurt her. Claire would just have a good night's rest. Or that's what I told myself."

"I remember Claire mentioning she was hungover that second day."

He scrunched his face. "Yeah, that's the weird thing. I ended up crashing on the bed and never made it to Nicole's cabin. I figured I'd mixed the glasses up and drank the wrong one. I felt so guilty about the whole thing—I mean who drugs their wife so they can sleep with their mistress? So I decided to end my affair with Nicole."

"You tried to contact her?"

"I emailed her from Grand Turk but never heard back so I figured she was mad at me. I kept worrying that the two women would bump into each other. Then the next day I got an email from Nicole's phone that said she was breaking it off and heading back home."

"Were you relieved?"

"You can believe it. I spent the rest of the week trying to make it the best week of our marriage. I thought I'd succeeded, but…" his voice trailed off.

Sometimes it's just too late.

CHAPTER SIXTY-SEVEN

Much later that evening, I nestled against Tom as he shared what he'd learned from Claire. He confirmed that Claire killed Nicole. She'd suspected Rick of having an affair for a long time. Once she figured out his cell phone password, she began reading his texts. When she discovered he planned to meet Nicole that first evening of the cruise, she became livid.

Full aware of her husband's plans, she remained vigilant. She caught him drugging her glass of champagne and managed to distract him and switch glasses. Once he fell asleep, she plotted how to best save her marriage.

Claire's first thought was to talk to Nicole, to plead with her to leave Rick alone. She knew they were supposed to meet at midnight, so Claire left her stateroom a few minutes before twelve. She seized one of the large room service trays someone had set in the hallway for a server to pick up. Then she knocked on Nicole's door. When it opened, Claire walked in and smashed the metal tray into Nicole's face, knocking her out and cutting her in the forehead. That was the cause of the blood we found on the bedspread.

At that point, she supposedly lost it. Nicole was petite, almost a foot shorter than Claire. She rolled Nicole onto the bedspread and dragged her across the stateroom. Claire knew there weren't any cameras on the balcony. She hoped if she pushed Nicole overboard, that her disappearance would remain unnoticed.

Forever.

"I assume Sanjay discovered what happened," I said to Tom, wondering about the strangeness of our bedtime conversation. Oh, well. The family that detects together, stays together.

Tom squeezed me tighter. "Yeah, that was actually our fault. Remember, you insisted on him going back through the video tapes to look for your missing person. We'll never know for sure, but according to Claire, he discovered something on the tapes that led him to her."

"That was probably all he needed," I said. "Since Sanjay's hobby was blackmail, he probably decided to up the ante this time around."

Tom nodded. "Supposedly when he learned Rick worked for a well-known entertainment management company, he figured Claire could come up with some big bucks. Enough to pay his gambling losses."

"Was she unwilling to pay?" I asked.

"From what I gather, this was another situation where she reacted unexpectedly. Sanjay made his demands and she came unglued. She noticed the chopstick, which I assume belonged to Sierra, lying on the ground. She plucked it off the floor and slammed it into Sanjay's neck. Then he fell over and Claire shoved it into his ear. She claims he just looked far too pleased with himself, and she couldn't bear it."

"Methinks Claire has some anger management issues."

"She'll have a lot of time in isolation to work on that."

"Has Rick spoken with Claire?" I asked. "I know he feels dreadful about everything."

"He should. It all began with his infidelity. The last I heard he was arranging for a top defense attorney to take on his wife's case."

"She might plead insanity. She certainly behaved like she was crazy. There are easier ways to get even with your spouse. Taking him to the cleaners with a divorce, for instance."

"You would never do that to me, would you?" Tom murmured, in between doing wonderful things to my ear lobe.

I cuddled closer to him. "As long as you keep that up, I'm all yours, sweetheart."

CHAPTER SIXTY-EIGHT

Disembarking is never quite as much fun as boarding a cruise ship. For one thing, you have to place your suitcases outside your cabin door by midnight. And you have to remember not to pack anything you might need in there. Like your toothbrush.

The captain had requested that Tom stay behind to oversee Claire's transfer to local authorities. None of them were quite certain under whose jurisdiction the murders should be handled since one victim was a U.S. citizen and the other, an Indian national. Not to mention the murders occurred in international waters. Claire would remain in custody while the multiple agencies figured it out.

My family agreed to meet for a light breakfast while we waited for our assigned color-coded disembarkation groups to be called. I arrived at the Lido Café a little after seven, groggy but hungry.

A few passengers nodded at me. Others commended me on my performance the previous evening. They must have thought I was one of the actors. If they only knew.

I shared everything I'd learned from Tom with my family, Stan and Zac. Since Zac still had two weeks left on his contract, Stan would spend another week with him before returning home.

"How are you feeling?" Mother asked, in full maternal mode. Usually I'd be annoyed by her question, but sometimes a girl, even a forty-year-old married girl, can use a little tea and sympathy from her mom.

"I'm fine. Just glad we didn't lose another member of the *Grease* cast."

Stan blew me a grateful kiss from across the table. "And thanks, Ginny," he said to Gran.

"I figured if I couldn't pack a pistol in my purse, I'd pack that piece of poultry," Gran said. She scowled at me. "Your hubby took it away, Laurel. Claimed it was evidence."

Mother choked and I giggled. It was more likely Tom kept the bird in order to keep everyone else safe. From Gran.

"Travelin' with your family has been a real hoot," Mabel said to Gran. "You got any other trips coming up?"

A chorus of "no" sounded from all sides of the table. My stepfather added his deep basso encore as he joined us.

"Is Tom almost done?" I asked him.

"Close. He's waiting for someone to assume responsibility for the prisoner."

"What a sad way to end our vacation," I said to no one in particular. "I feel terrible about Claire. If I hadn't been hungover that first night…"

"Then no one would ever know what happened to poor Nicole," Stan reminded me. "Justice must be served."

"You sound like an episode of *Law and Order*," I snapped, still feeling remorseful.

"You and your husband make a great team," Zac said. "Reminded me of those old *Thin Man* movies from the thirties. With William Powell and Myrna Loy." Zac eyed me. "You look a little like her with that curly reddish-brown hair and your lovely blue eyes."

Zac needed new contacts. I could fit two Myrna Loy's into one of my dresses, but since I loved her work, I would gratefully accept his compliment. Tom and I did make a good team. And for a change, we weren't on opposing sides.

A familiar face stopped at our table. "Loved the finale, Laurel," said Jimmy Bond. "That rubber chicken was an unexpected plot twist."

"Couldn't have done it without Gran's arsenal of assorted weaponry," I said. She beamed at me then asked Jimmy what his plans were for the rest of the day. He pulled up a chair and joined our crowded table.

"I booked the optional Everglades tour for this afternoon," he said. "My plane doesn't leave until tomorrow."

"Where's your fan club?" Gran asked.

"Probably pestering the captain about her missing watch and other items," Jimmy replied, his forehead creasing in a deep frown. "I still can't believe I couldn't suss out the thief."

"So you were investigating the jewel thefts," I said accusingly.

He nodded, his eyes a troubled blue-gray. "I occasionally consult for Lloyds. I made a valiant attempt, but I've been most unsuccessful. I shall return to Lloyd's empty-handed."

Gran reached out and clasped his hand in hers. "Not completely empty-handed. You've made new friends. And you're welcome to visit us anytime you're in California."

Jimmy lifted her liver-spotted hand to his lips before he set it back down. "It's a date, luv."

Gran blushed and said nothing. Now that was a first.

Sierra stopped at our table. She was dressed to the nautical nines in her brass-buttoned, perfectly-pressed uniform. The circles under her eyes almost matched her dark blue skirt. But her smile was wide as she greeted us.

"I guess you'll never forget this cruise," she said. "Can you believe that not one but two murders occurred on board?"

Stan pointed his finger at me. "All in a day's work for Laurel and her family. Next time I travel with you, I'm packing my own weapon." He turned to my grandmother. "Got any more of those chickens in stock?"

We all laughed, although our laughter was tinged with melancholy. Death was no laughing matter.

"Do you have time to join us?" I asked Sierra.

She shook her head, her hair curling nicely on her shoulders. Sierra had already informed me that she'd sworn off chopstick accessories for the rest of her life.

"Nope. I need to wave goodbye to the passengers then welcome some new entertainers on board and get them situated in their staterooms. We normally have only a couple hours between the current passengers leaving the ship and the next group boarding."

"Are you still worried they might terminate your employment over those missing jewels?" Mother asked Sierra.

"I don't think so, but you never know. The Captain has been occupied with more tragic matters lately. The assistant security officer showed me the list of items, and it wasn't as extensive as they first thought. Primarily those items that Mrs. Peabody lost, a few wallets and items that disappeared when passengers frequented the spa, plus a couple of purses that were emptied and returned."

"That's good news," I said.

"Good news save for Mrs. Peabody," Jimmy chimed in. "Or, rather, my employer. Perhaps it's time for me to retire once again."

Lucille and Glenn walked up to our table. "It's been an experience meeting you all," Lucille said with a broad grin.

I noticed a streak of chocolate on her chin. She must have indulged in one of the more popular buffet items—chocolate croissants. I handed her a napkin and pointed to the dabs of chocolate on her face.

She took the napkin, rubbed her face and turned to me. "Did I remove all the evidence?"

I nodded, although her sudden movement had distracted me. The chocolate remains from her croissant had completely disappeared from her chin. But when she'd lifted her arm to remove the sugary evidence, the sleeve of her floral top exposed something else.

"What a beautiful watch," I said, staring at the diamond-encrusted platinum watch. "Did you purchase it on this trip?"

Lucille blinked twice before replying with a quick and forceful "Yes."

"Gotta go," said Glenn, wrapping his arm around her waist. They ran down the aisle, narrowly missing crashing into a server with a loaded tray, headed for the elevator.

"Blimey," said Jimmy. "Are my old eyes deceiving me or was that woman wearing a watch that looks exactly like the one Evelyn Peabody lost?"

"I never saw Evelyn's watch, but Lucille has never worn that one in my presence," I replied. "And I'm certain I would have noticed something that magnificent." I snapped my fingers. "Lucille was in the spa the afternoon that Evelyn's watch was stolen. And both she and Glenn look like average seniors. They could blend in anywhere."

Sierra turned to Jimmy. "Perhaps we should have a chat with the Blodgetts. Would you care to join me?"

"I would be most happy to, my dear." Jimmy whispered in Gran's ear. She giggled and batted at his arm. He stood and addressed our group. "It's been a most interesting trip. But Sierra and I have work to do."

"What if they get off the ship before you can catch them?" Stan asked, a worried look on his face.

"Not to worry," said Sierra. "The Blodgetts need to pass through customs like everyone else. I happen to have an in with the customs folks. Not to mention close ties with a member of Homeland Security." She hooked her arm around Jimmy's elbow. "Shall we go?"

He doffed an imaginary hat to our group and replied. "Indeed. It is time for James Bond to catch a thief."

CHAPTER SIXTY-NINE

When you're married to someone in law enforcement, you quickly discover the positives as well as the negatives. On the minus side, the amount of time Tom needed to spend before he officially handed Claire over to the authorities made us miss our flight.

On the plus side, the cruise line paid for new flights the next day and upgraded our seats to first-class. They also provided for a night's lodging. In a Ritz Carlton. On the beach. No wife could complain about that.

After a honeymoon spent among thieves, a murderer and my family, Tom suggested we dine alone in our room tonight.

I walked out of the enormous marble bathroom to discover an elegant linen-covered table set for two, a bottle of champagne resting in a silver bucket, and two empty glasses just begging to be filled with the bubbly nectar.

"This is lovely." I stood on my tiptoes to give Tom a heartfelt kiss that was warmly returned.

Tom poured champagne into the empty goblets. "It's about time we enjoyed a romantic dinner with just the two of us."

I swiveled my head around to survey the room.

"What are you looking for?" Tom asked as he returned the champagne bottle to the ice bucket.

"Just making sure none of my family is hiding in this suite." I pointed toward the bedroom. "You know how they love to surprise us. Gran could easily stuff herself in that cherry armoire."

He chuckled. "Your family certainly is..." he chose to be tactful and finished with, "... entertaining."

Tom raised his glass and I lifted mine. "To us," he said. "If we can survive a homicidal honeymoon, I think we can handle anything."

"As long as we're together." Our glasses clinked in harmonious agreement.

While we delved into our delicious entrees, Tom updated me on the fate of the diamond thieves, Lucille and Glenn Blodgett.

"It's a good thing you noticed Lucille wearing Mrs. Peabody's watch," he said. "Otherwise, they would have gotten off scot-free."

"I assume Lucille thought it safe to wear since they were literally minutes from getting off the ship."

"She probably figured she could sneak through customs by wearing as much jewelry as possible, claiming she'd brought it from home."

"I don't suppose Glenn confessed to bopping me in San Juan?" I asked.

Tom shook his head. "Not yet. But no one beans my sweetie and gets away with it. I'll stay on top of this case."

I chuckled at his protectiveness. "We ran into them at several jewelry stores on Grand Turk and St. Thomas. Did they rob the stores, too?"

"That will be for the official authorities to determine," he said. "I'm sure they'll be taking a closer look at the store's security camera footage on the days we were in those ports. Last I heard, Lucille declared all the jewelry in her suitcases and on her person belonged to her."

"What about Evelyn Peabody's fancy watch?"

"Lucille claimed she already owned the identical watch," he said, "although one officer noticed the inscription on the watch was to 'my dearest Evelyn.'"

My fork clunked on my plate. "That woman has some nerve. And to think she wanted to be my sidekick."

Tom reached across the table and clasped my right hand. "Speaking of sidekicks, have I told you lately how special you are to me?"

"Not in the last twenty-four hours." I smiled and squeezed his hand. "You need to up your game."

"I intend to." His eyes darkened and my heart skipped a beat. I picked up my fork, anxious to finish dinner and maximize my time with my husband. Who knew when we would have an intimate evening together again.

"It will be good to see the kids," I said. "I've missed them a ton. Then it's back to our crazy schedules." My lower lip trembled when I thought of Tom flying to the other side of the world for his next mission. "Did your boss tell you when you have to take off? Will we have some quality time with our kids before you go?"

Tom fiddled with his ear lobe.

Uh, oh, not a good sign at all. What bad news was my spouse about to deliver?

Tom stood and walked into the bedroom. He returned holding a small bag in his hand. He reached in and pulled out his Homeland Security badge and dropped it on the table.

I squinted at it. "Am I under arrest, officer?" I said trying to lighten the tension that had settled over the table like a thundercloud.

"Nope. I don't want any more arrests in my future," he replied. "If you agree, I'm giving my notice."

"What?" I was torn between relief that Tom would no longer be embroiled in such a dangerous career and concern about our finances.

"A few days ago, I mentioned that I was giving serious thought to my future." Tom dragged his chair around the table to sit beside me. "Or, to be more precise, our future."

"I'm mostly relieved," I said. "But what would you do?"

"Actually, the better question is what's next for us?" He picked up my hand and did swirly things across my palm that suddenly raised the room temperature. I pulled away, not wanting to be distracted from this serious conversation.

"Are you planning on becoming a beach bum?"

"Hah. Can you imagine me doing that?"

Actually the thought of Tom strolling along the sand, bare chested and clad only in his swim trunks, presented an appealing picture.

I mentally slapped myself. Back to business.

"So what are your intentions?"

"My intentions are quite honorable," he declared. "In the near future, I'd like to be *your* sidekick."

Huh? I smacked my hand against my right ear, wondering if water from my earlier shower had clogged my hearing.

"Can you repeat that, please?"

"Bradford and I have been discussing this over the past few days. We both miss detecting, and we think it's time to open up our own private investigation agency. We each have a pension, although mine is smaller, plus I'll have the equity from my house once it's sold. So financially, we think we're sound."

I cocked my head. "That's actually a great idea. I'm all for it. What are you going to call it?" I giggled and said, "TWO DUDES DETECTIVE AGENCY?"

"Ha. A better name would be TWO DUDES & ONE DUDETTE. We want you as part of our team."

"Moi?" I squealed. "An official detective? Are you toying with me?"

He shook his head. "Completely serious. You've voiced numerous times how unhappy you are working at Hangtown Bank since Adriana took over the marketing department. You possess excellent deductive abilities. Plus a charming personality."

"All true." I nodded in agreement while chuckling to myself.

"And you're the most tenacious person I know. What do you say?"

"I say it's a deal. Should we seal it with a handshake or a kiss?"

He leaned over and placed a tender kiss on my waiting lips before reaching into his bag once again.

"I think I can do better than that." He pulled out a small square blue velvet box, opened it and set it in front of me. "Why don't we seal it with this?"

I stared at the emerald-cut diamond solitaire sparkling under the hotel's chandelier.

Speechless for a change.

"This belonged to my grandmother. I've been waiting," he paused, "and waiting for the right time to surprise you."

"It's absolutely beautiful," I said. "I'll treasure it just as I treasure every day of my life with you."

Tom placed the ring on my finger. With a husky voice he said, "For richer, for poorer, 'til death do us part. Diamonds are forever and so is my love for you."

My eyes teared at his words as I gazed at the ring that sealed the next act of our life together. I picked up my champagne glass and turned to my husband.

"To happy endings," I toasted him with a broad smile. "And new beginnings."

THE END

AUTHOR'S NOTE

I hope you enjoyed reading this book as much as I enjoyed writing it. If so, please consider leaving a review. Favorable reviews help an author more than you can imagine.

All the Laurel McKay Mysteries are listed below.

Dying for a Date (Vol. 1)
Dying for a Dance (Vol. 2)
Dying for a Daiquiri (Vol. 3)
Dying for a Dude (Vol. 4)
Dying for a Donut (Vol.5)
Dying for a Diamond (Vol. 6)
Dying for a Deal (2018)

To find out about new books, upcoming events and contests, please sign up for my newsletter:
http://cindysamplebooks.com/contact/

ACKNOWLEDGEMENTS

Many thanks and hugs to the awesome friends who willingly read my early drafts: Dee Brice, Jonathan Corbett, and two of my favorite mystery authors, Heather Haven and Linda Lovely. As always, my critique group was there to answer my countless emails and plotting questions: Kathy Asay, Pat Foulk, Rae James, and our dear friend, Terri Judd, who left us far too soon.

Thanks to my next door neighbor, Jana Rossi, who makes sure that I have enough chocolate to keep the words flowing.

A special thanks to the chief security officer of the *Nieuw Amsterdam* cruise ship and the entire crew who kept pointing out excellent hiding places for my victims. Thanks also to three wonderful local travel agents, Carol Buchman, Susan Macaluso and Nancy Porter. You were all so much help.

A huge thanks for the support of the incredible DB club, and its founder, Liz Davies. You folks really know how to have fun!

The support and encouragement I receive from my fellow Sisters in Crime (Sacramento and Northern California) and the authors who belong to Sacramento Valley Rose, California Writer's Club and NCPA keeps me motivated when my spirits flag.

Thanks to my editors, Baird Nuckolls and Kathy Asay, and my amazing cover artist, Karen Phillips. I am extremely grateful for the generosity of Elizabeth Axelrod who contributed to the Folsom Symphony. I hope you enjoy your character.

A special thanks to those fans from around the world whose emails keep me motivated. It's not easy to wake up each morning and create an entirely new world. Your words of encouragement make it the best job in the world!

ABOUT THE AUTHOR

Cindy Sample is a former mortgage banking CEO who decided plotting murder was more entertaining than plodding through paperwork. She retired to follow her lifelong dream of becoming a mystery author.

Her experiences with online dating sites fueled the concept for *Dying for a Date*, the first in her national bestselling Laurel McKay mysteries. The sequel, *Dying for a Dance*, winner of the 2011 NCPA Fiction Award, is based on her adventures in the glamorous world of ballroom dancing. Cindy thought her protagonist, Laurel McKay, needed a vacation in Hawaii, which resulted in *Dying for a Daiquiri*, a finalist for the 2014 Silver Falchion Award for Best Traditional Mystery.

Laurel returned to Placerville for her wildest ride yet in in *Dying for a Dude*. The West will never be the same. Then on to *Dying for a Donut*, a lip-smacking mystery set in the Apple Hill area.

It was time for Laurel (or maybe that was Cindy) to take another vacation. You can't beat a Caribbean cruise as the setting for *Dying for a Diamond*.

Cindy is a four-time finalist for the LEFTY Award for best humorous mystery and a past president of the Sacramento chapter of Sisters in Crime. She has served on the boards of the Sacramento Opera and YWCA. She is a member of Mystery Writers of America and Romance Writers of America. Cindy has two wonderful adult children who live too far away. She loves chatting with readers so feel free to contact her on any forum.

Sign up for Cindy's newsletter to find out about upcoming events, contests and new releases. http://cindysamplebooks. com/contact/

Check out www.cindysamplebooks.com for the latest news and blog posts.

Connect with Cindy on Facebook and Twitter
http://facebook.com/cindysampleauthor
http://twitter.com/cindysample1
Email Cindy at cindy@cindysamplebooks.com